Jimn

The Josephine

Baker Affair

By

Kevin P Holdgate

*** 50% of the proceeds from the sale of this book will be donated to 'Breast Cancer Now' through the all- female Brass Band 'Boobs and Brass'***

Acknowledgements

It is often said that everyone has a book inside them waiting to be written. This was certainly true in my case, but it took a life changing event, and the regular chastisement of a very dear friend to stir me into action

In July 2013 my wife Anita was diagnosed with breast cancer. For the following 12 months our lives were quite literally turned upside down. Six months of chemotherapy, followed by major surgery; followed by a further period of radiotherapy took us through to July 2014. This saw us finally able to go on the holiday we had planned, but had to cancel a year earlier.

As we sat on the beach on holiday in Brittany I began to formalise the idea of a story. A visit to the 2nd World War submarine base at Lorient the day before had sparked ideas in my head which I jotted down and emailed to my good friend Jo Priestley back in England.

I believed she was being very kind and humouring me when she edited what I had written and sent it back to me. A few days later she emailed me again to demand more of the story, I knew better than to refuse. Twelve long months and a considerable number of rewrites later I finally completed the novel.

I am indebted to another good friend of mine, Heather Horsley who is an incredibly talented artist and who has designed the cover for me.

Finally I wish to thank you for purchasing this book, 50% of the proceeds of which will go to the 'Breast Cancer Now' charity. The charity does incredible work in sponsoring the research that will one day eradicate this dreadful disease. I have seen close up the effects that it has on the lives of so many people and sadly, some of the brave ladies who had chemotherapy at the same time as my wife are no longer with us.

My friends, the good ladies of the all-female brass band 'Boobs & Brass' have done a fantastic job raising money for the charity since the band's formation in May 2006. By purchasing this book you are contributing towards helping them continue this work.

Thank You
Kevin P Holdgate

Chapter 1

London, 1927

'Good morning, Sir. How are we today?'

Harry Pratt was accustomed to waking his employer from his slumber. He had repeated the task for a number of years, in many parts of the world.

This morning it was proving all the more difficult as the Honourable James St. John Smyth, 3rd Viscount of Stanley – Jimmy V to his friends, had enjoyed a long night playing jazz trombone with the Fred Elizalde Orchestra at the Savoy Hotel. Harry would have normally been in attendance, but for once he had been otherwise engaged. He knew that his employer would have been the last to leave, most likely as dawn was breaking over the London skyline.

Harry looked down on the sleeping form of his master. His gentle ministering hadn't caused Jimmy V to stir. More drastic action was going to be needed to waken him. Pulling back the curtains and lifting the sash window, Harry allowed the early morning light and sounds of the city to burst into the room. Jimmy V immediately pulled the pillow over his head in an attempt to dampen the explosion of sound around him.

Looking out from the window of The Park Lane Hotel over Green Park, with Buckingham Palace just beyond, Harry's mind drifted back to that final concert there in front of King George V and his first meeting with Jimmy V. Many things had happened since that night. He could reasonably expect, following his meeting the previous evening that if the information conveyed to him was correct, the adventures would continue over the coming weeks.

The everyday life of the city was unfolding below him. A legion of nannies were regimentally pushing their precious loads into the park for early morning air. Each was dressed in the identical grey coat and matching hat that formed the uniform of their high society profession.

A butcher's delivery boy laboured along Park Lane with his employer's wares stacked high in both front and back baskets. The load was clearly too heavy for him, but he struggled on, aware that his cargo must be delivered if he were to avoid the wrath of his master.

Further away Harry could see a young postman lingering outside Portman House, as he did each morning. Here he conducted his daily, but brief conversation with the young maid who willingly volunteered to collect the mail.

The great city was slowly coming to life and so it seemed was Jimmy V

'Good morning, Harry. I tell you what, old thing, that chap Livingston is some player!'

Harry smiled. As always, after a night playing his trombone, Jimmy V's first thoughts were of the previous evening's revelries. The latest great saxophonist to journey across the Atlantic and demonstrate his skills to an ever eager London audience, 'Fud' Livingston had been a guest with Elizalde and his accomplished Savoy orchestra.

'You missed a truly memorable event, Harry. I trust you enjoyed an equally fulfilling time?'

Harry knew that his master was irresistibly curious as to the nature of the 'business' that had seen him request his first night off in six years, but he was not about to enlighten him.

'I've prepared breakfast in the morning room, Sir. Do you want me to prepare tea or coffee this morning?'

Jimmy V levered an eyebrow and said, 'So we are not to learn of your night of nefarious deeds, then, Harry?'

'Tea, Sir?'

'Very well. Duly noted. A fine breakfast whilst scanning the morning papers will be just the thing. And tea, I think, Harry. Definitely tea.'

Appearing with a steaming pot of freshly brewed Darjeeling a few minutes later, Harry set out the agenda for the coming day. He had arranged for a hackney carriage to collect them at 12 noon to transport them to Victoria Station. The Golden Arrow boat train was due to depart for Dover at 2pm.

'I have booked us on the SS Canterbury to Calais. Once we get to France, we will board the 'Flèche D'Or' and proceed onwards to Paris. We are scheduled to arrive at the Gare Du Nord at 10.00pm.'

'10pm?'

'That's allowing for the change in time zone. I have arranged a taxi to be ready in Paris, to transport us to the Hôtel Ritz.'

'Well, you're the details man Harry. I always trust you with all of this, you know.'

'Yes, Sir.' Harry knew he had already conveyed far more information than was actually necessary, and therefore resolved not to continue with details of the onward journey to Berlin.

Harry had arranged for their luggage, with the exception of Jimmy V's beloved trombone, to be transported to Victoria ahead of them, so that when the Hackney carriage arrived the two men were able to travel in relative comfort. Or as much comfort as a 6'5'', former American baseball player could expect in a London taxi clearly designed for someone much shorter in stature than Harry.

As the carriage wound its way through the busy streets of London, they sat in silence as they contemplated what lay ahead.

Occasionally, Harry glanced at the white man beside him. A titled man born to wealth and privilege, and yet one called to jazz music. He'd had his troubles, but his face showed none of it. A contradiction in so many ways. Hell, he'd employed Harry, hadn't he? Many wouldn't. Not in his position. Harry settled to the view of the streets as the cab drove on. He figured that Jimmy V was already hearing the music in his head, the scales and notes, the free-form dances of his slide trombone, all the stuff that he looked forward to performing. Jazz music was still in its infancy on mainland Europe but there was already a plethora of new bands in the major cities. It was seemingly reason enough to travel there, ostensibly at least.

Letting Jimmy V be, safely dreaming of the venues ahead of him, Harry contemplated the likely events that he might expect to encounter over the coming weeks. But his thoughts following his meeting the previous evening went far beyond music.

Chapter 2

Lady Julia Mortimer woke early as usual, despite her exertions of the previous evening. Like so many nights before, she had been at the Savoy Hotel dancing to the wonderful sounds of the Fred Elizalde Orchestra with their special guest artist the American saxophonist Fud Livingston.

She had become a devotee of The Savoy Hotel jazz scene over the past several years particularly, of course, when a certain trombone player was in attendance.

Lady Julia was the youngest daughter of the prominent London banker Sir Charles Mortimer and his wife Lady Caroline Fortescue. Strikingly tall and attractive like her mother, Lady Julia was never short of dance partners nor admirers. Regular socialites knew however, that whilst she loved to dance, and revelled in the attention giving to her by so many young beaus, she had eyes for only one man, and that was Jimmy V.

Just like the young Viscount, Lady Julia had enjoyed a privileged upbringing. Educated at Riggleshide College in Norfolk and Le Alpena Institut, a renowned finishing school high up in the

Swiss Alps, she was fluent in French and German, and was a highly accomplished skier.

The early morning silence was broken with a sharp knock at the door. Mary Smith, her lady's maid entered the room as she always did at precisely 7.30am.

'Good morning, Ma'am. I hope you slept well?'

'Very well indeed, thank you, Mary. Can I assume that our travel arrangements have been satisfactorily concluded?'

'Indeed they have Ma'am. We are booked on the Golden Arrow from Victoria Station at 2pm, as you requested.'

Blinking in the early morning light that streamed through the curtains being pulled back into a perfectly symmetrical position by her maid, Lady Julia smiled.

'Excellent, what would I do without you?'

A passing observer may have noted the barely contained twitch of the maid's lips and concluded that this particular thought had crossed Mary Smith's mind on more than one occasion, but it was clearly not a wise idea for the maid to pass comment on it now. Instead, she settled for saying,

'Your luggage is packed and ready to be transported to Victoria Station. I have arranged for it to be collected at 11.30am. We will then follow on at midday.'

It could be said that the making of travel arrangements was not strictly within the job description of a regular lady's maid, however Mary Smith had shared in the life and adventures of Lady Julia for a number of years and had become far more than that. She was well-versed in making whatever arrangements were required, swiftly and efficiently.

'Your bath is prepared Ma'am. I shall serve breakfast in the salon shortly.'

Mary closed the door and walked the short distance to the small kitchen. It was not her place to question why her mistress had suddenly announced her immediate intention to travel to Berlin the previous afternoon. The sudden impulse to travel was obviously linked in some way to her luncheon engagement in Harrods, where she had dined with an unknown companion in the newly opened Egyptian restaurant the previous day.

Past experience had taught Mary that a hastily arranged luncheon date of this nature would result in a request for her to make urgent travel plans.

In anticipation, she had packed the essential items for European travel. She had also contacted the booking office of Southern Railways at Victoria Station and provisionally booked seats on board the Golden Arrow.

As she prepared breakfast, Mary mused over what might lie ahead in the coming weeks. She was confident that it would feature Jimmy V and smiled to herself as she considered, not for the first time, that this would inevitably include Harry Pratt.

A few hours later, the two women were seated in a hackney carriage making their way through the crowded streets of London towards Victoria Station.

Lady Julia travelled in silence, her mind no doubt occupied with thoughts of the imminent journey, and the potential of the alarming information she had received the previous day. Seated beside her, Mary had no such concerns. She could only concentrate   on   one   thing.

Chapter 3

The Golden Arrow was famous. In the Golden Age of rail travel it was something of a celebrity, and here it sat, gently making steam on the eastern side of Victoria station, patiently awaiting the latest group of passengers wishing to journey to Dover and beyond.

At the front of the train, ten large Pullman carriages, catered exclusively for first-class passengers. Each had an identical interior, extravagantly liveried with deep, exquisite armchairs for the cream of society.

The SS Canterbury awaited them in Dover. Built in 1900 she had been conveying her rich and well-heeled travellers in safety and opulent luxury across the English Channel for over a quarter of a century. The depression that had engulfed the whole of Europe following the Great War had badly hit cross-channel travel. From 1921 onwards however, the number of passengers had steadily increased.

Economic conditions had compelled the Golden Arrow to abandon its exclusivity and in recent years, in order to attract more passengers, the first-class monopoly had been reluctantly relinquished. To the rear of the train, beyond the first-class baggage carriages, three second-class cars with somewhat less regal furnishings had now been added. On board the SS Canterbury a separate seating area, which had originally been part of the cargo hold, had been created. It was equipped with lines of upright wooden benches bolted securely to the deck, specifically to accommodate the 2nd class passengers.

On arrival at Victoria the 3rd Viscount Stanley, as befitted his status as a member of the aristocracy, was personally met by Raymond Jones, the concierge and official representative of the Southern Railway Company, who escorted him to the leading Pullman carriage.

Harry walked behind dutifully carrying their hand luggage, his towering physique cutting a rather different figure to that of the concierge.

Raymond Jones was a proud Welshman. He could best be described perhaps as a rather short, rotund fellow, with a badly fitting uniform that threatened to burst forth at any moment. Harry smiled to himself as he waited for the buttons on the man's waistcoat, which he concluded must have been sown on with industrial strength thread, to give way. He prepared himself to duck the threat of flying buttons every time the chap breathed in.

Jones hated having to suck up to the so called 'upper class' passengers who rode daily on his train; leaving the detritus of their journey where they sat; ordering both him and his staff around as if it were some form of sporting activity at their country retreats. But he rather liked Jimmy V.

'Good to see you again, your Honour. Always a pleasure, not like some others of your ilk I could mention.'

'Still gearing up for the old revolution, Raymond?'

'You know me, Sir. A patriot, I am. Fought in the Great War, the Welsh Guards as you know. There's a reason this country's great, and it's the little man, your everyday man, and not so many shows respect to us. Yourself being one of the few exceptions, Sir.'

'And you wouldn't be saying this because my good man-servant here frightens the life out of you?'

'He's a big un, all right. But I reckon come the day of reckoning and Mister MacDonald comes to power, he'll be on our side. Happen he'll put in a good word for you, Sir.' Jimmy V laughed warmly.

'Is that right, Harry?'

'Couldn't possibly comment on such a thing, Sir. But you may want to compensate Raymond for the fright I put up him.'

"Renowned as a generous tipper, you are, Sir,' the concierge said.

'Then of course I must live up to my reputation. As ever, Raymond, it's been a pleasure.'

'Likewise, your Honour. Mr Pratt.'

Having arrived at the station earlier than anticipated, there was plenty of time available for the two men to relax and settle into their new surroundings before the train departed at 2pm.

Looking out of his carriage onto Victoria Station, Jimmy V could see across to the other platforms and observe the legions of people who occupied them. Recently arrived passengers from who knows where, were being met by who knows whom, embraced warmly, hands clasped and shaken vigorously. Relatives not seen for a number of years perhaps? Friends visiting London for the first time? Ordinary people, with ordinary lives, doing ordinary things. Part of him wished for the simplicity of the life that these people he observed seemed to live. A simplicity that he most likely would never enjoy.

Harry too was looking out over the station, and scanning the myriad of faces milling around the concourse. Jimmy V sensed that for some reason, his thoughts were far more focussed.

*

The hackney carriage transporting Lady Julia and Mary Smith had been delayed by the Royal Navy. HMS Warspite, Commander James Somerville and its crew of 1200 men to be precise, as it passed serenely through Tower Bridge on its way to duty in the Mediterranean. Mary, in her usual efficient way had anticipated that such a delay might be possible and therefore made an appropriate time allowance in their schedule.

She had read in the *Times* that Warspite, having recently completed Royal duties, was due to set sail that day. They would still arrive in good time at Victoria to be met by the awaiting concierge.

Lady Julia was the granddaughter of Earl Fortescue, peer of the realm and member of the House of Lords. Without a specific title of her own she had been allocated a compartment in the 4th Pullman car. This was no less grand then any of its predecessors in the convoy, but there was a strict order to be maintained, and Lady Julia, Raymond Jones, and Southern Railways were all well aware of society conventions. Whilst such things made Lady Julia smile, she would never pass comment on the futility of such outdated trivia in public.

The post Great War period had proved on so many levels that society had changed, and in the view of Lady Julia very much for the better. She was far less radical in her views than the concierge. He had made his feelings well known to her during numerous previous encounters and she had no desire to repeat such conversations today.

'Good day Mr. Jones. I trust you are well?'

'Good to see you again Lady Mortimer. Walter!' he bellowed in the direction of a young porter.

'Bags!' he shouted curtly as Walter visibly jumped at his command.

Lady Julia could never be described as a supporter of Mr MacDonald or of the Labour Party. She had witnessed at first hand, with the death of her beloved cousin Bertie in the Battle of Passchendaele, that war showed no respect for class. But even here she observed, regardless of Mr Jones' views on the revolution which the election of the Labour party might bring about, there was very clearly a pecking order. Walter without question occupied the lowest rung.

Seated comfortably in their compartment, the two ladies prepared themselves for their onward journey to Dover. Lady Julia had decided to use the time available to look at the latest proofs that had been sent to her regarding a new weekly music magazine she had been approached to invest in. Although the title was still to be decided upon, she very much favoured 'The Melody Maker'. Mary sat nonchalantly scanning the faces of the crowds on the platform.

*

With the station clock reading 1.50pm, two men carrying travelling bags emerged from the Circle Line underground exit on the south eastern side of the station. They walked slowly, with a deliberate, unhurried pace behind the long line of first class luggage that was being transferred into the baggage cars. Several sweating porters were scrambling to load everything before the train's departure. They were far too busy to pay the two men any attention as they walked past.

The Golden Arrow was always on time and today would be no exception. As the smallest and most puce of the porters threw the final bag into place, the carriage doors were slammed shut, the locking bolts pulled across, and the station master blew his whistle to signal to the driver that all was ready to proceed.

The two men boarded the last carriage as the door banged shut behind them. They folded themselves into their reserved seats, placed their hands on their knees and stared straight ahead.

Chapter 4

With a sonorous hiss of steam and a stately swagger that hardly stirred the Martinis being prepared in the first class carriages, the Golden Arrow rolled away from the platform.

Jimmy V was completely oblivious to the train's departure, being absorbed in the latest batch of jazz 'charts' as the Americans liked to call their music compositions, that he had brought with him. These had arrived, neatly packaged, the previous day.

He had resisted his normal impulse to rip open the parcel as he normally did in the knowledge that his impending journey would afford him the time to study the new music more thoroughly. Harry likened Jimmy V's reaction to the regular arrival of the parcels to that of an over-excited child on Christmas morning.

As he looked at the neatly laid out piles in front of him, Jimmy V reflected with great sadness that it was wholly down to his friendship with Scott Joplin he could sit here now with the very latest and finest American jazz compositions. Joplin had died in 1917 without knowing the true identity of the mysterious benefactor who had given him his big break; the anonymous figure responsible for setting up a company to publish his music, and that of several other unknown and struggling composers in the jungle that was New York's Tin Pan Alley.

The monotonous 'rata-ta-tat' of the Golden Arrow's wheels as it sped through the outer suburbs of the capital and onwards towards Kent was replaced in Jimmy V's head by the wonderful strains of jazz as he read through the charts and imagined the sounds of the saxophone solo, the trumpet blues and the trombone quartet.

Across the table Harry Pratt shifted position in his armchair. He wasn't entirely sure why he had such a disconcerted feeling in his mind. His careful observations on the platform, and from the carriage window prior to their departure had not revealed anything to be alarmed about, and yet alarmed he was.

The quality of the information that he had been given the previous evening had come from the most reliable of sources. His instructions were clear. As brutal as those instructions were Harry was not in the least bit perturbed by them. He had received, and carried out such orders before, but he still felt an unease about this particular mission. An unease that he couldn't clearly identify. He felt that there was more to this matter than anyone knew. His quiet thoughts were abruptly interrupted.

'Did they board the train?'

As the train slowed approaching Swanley Junction, Jimmy V looked up from his music and across the table at his companion.

'I believe so, Sir,' replied Harry.

'Splendid! What carriage were they assigned?'

'I believe that Lady Julia and her maid have been assigned a cabin in Carriage 4, Sir. I understand that they were delayed in their arrival by Tower Bridge.'

Harry had taken the precaution of, and if truth be known a rather sadistic pleasure in speaking to a distinctly nervous looking Mr. Jones shortly before their departure from Victoria, accurately predicting that he would be asked the question at some point in the journey.

'Splendid! Perhaps you would be good enough to invite Lady Julia to join me for drinks, Pratt?'

'It would be my pleasure, Sir.'

Despite the concerns Harry felt, he was confident that whatever the threats there might be along the journey, they did not emanate from within the 1st class carriages. He was quite happy therefore to leave Jimmy V alone with his music, whilst he made his way through the train to pass on the invitation

As the train gathered speed towards Farningham Harry walked over the junction into carriage 2. Several people were seated in the sumptuously upholstered armchairs that lined the carriage. He recognised various members of the House of Lords carefully scanning the court section of The Times, making sure that their presence at a lavish dinner hosted by the Foreign Office or the Home Office or His Majesty the previous evening had been acknowledged and just as importantly, ensuring that someone had not been credited as being present when they had clearly not been there. He nodded at his fellow manservants as he passed, most of whom ignored him, not that this bothered him in the slightest. Indeed, it gave him a certain satisfaction to see them looking so discomforted by his considerable presence.

As he came to the junction between carriages 2 and 3 he glanced out of the window to note they were now passing Longfield Station. Several children on the platform waved as the famous train sped by, its passengers wholly failing to acknowledge the excited youngsters. Seeing the children waving at trains reminded him of his own childhood, playing with his pal Billy in the old railway carriages in the New York sidings. He stood to one side to allow a waiter to pass with his latest load of carefully prepared Martinis.

Two more well-manicured stations passed by, with their neatly laid out flower troughs before he arrived at the gold lettered sign that announced Carriage 4. The armchairs here were replaced by a narrow corridor with individual compartments set off to the left. Still lavishly upholstered and still 1st class, but a very obvious distinction had been made by the railway company to acknowledge the slightly differing social levels of which that class was comprised. Moving along to Cabin D, Harry gently tapped on the glass.

Looking up from her magazine, Lady Julia spotted Harry as his giant form filled the window into the cabin. She had wondered how long it would be before she was invited to join the Viscount.

Mary raised her eyes and smiled coyly at the impressive sight of the man servant in the window. Her thoughts were somewhat different.

'Lady Julia. Viscount Stanley has requested that I enquire as to whether you would care to join him for drinks?'

Harry had no formal training as a gentleman's gentleman and often got his words rather muddled, however he had very quickly learned the mannerisms of the role if not the polished vocabulary of his colleagues.

'How delightful Pratt. I shall be along presently.' Harry nodded formally and left to return to his employer with the message. Mary was sure that she had seen Harry wink his eye at her as he bowed his head, at least she hoped that he had. A pink tinge appeared on her cheek at the mere thought.

Lady Julia laid down the article that she had been reading in the Melody Maker, as she had started to refer to it. The piece had intrigued her, as it was concerning the latest dance craze to hit the London nightclub circuit. She smiled as she decided it was quite apt at that precise moment in time, being called the 'Black Bottom'.

She was well acquainted with the dance of course through her regular visits to such places. She had also had a number of in depth conversations on the subject with Jimmy V, who had seen the dance performed regularly to the music of the renowned pianist, Jelly Roll Morton in America. If memory served her correctly, Jimmy had a piece of music called the 'Black Bottom Stomp' by Jelly Roll in his set list. She must remember to mention it to him. In fact, she would take her copy of the magazine and ask his opinion of it, and of her preferred name for the new publication.

She rose from her seat and glanced out of the window. The train was slowing down, as it passed through Sole Street railway station. The smartly dressed station master respectfully touched the peak of his cap as he made eye contact with her. In turn she acknowledged his greeting. How pretty the flower beds always looked, a cascade of colours in the station gardens. It always occurred to her when she travelled by train that each station must be competing with the others to be the most beautiful of all. The Sole Street station master, with his statuesque, soldier like poise was quite clearly convinced that his station was the unrivalled winner of the prize.

'Do you wish me to accompany you Ma'am?' interrupted Mary.

'I don't believe that will be necessary Mary, but thank you.'

Lady Julia knew of Mary's relationship with regards to Harry Pratt. She had every intention of helping nurture it in any way that she could but it was not necessary for her to be chaperoned on board the train, after all this was the 1920s.

She smiled inwardly to herself at the image of Mary and Harry together. Mary, a touch over 5' tall, with the delicate, porcelain features of a china doll in the arms of the colossus that was Harry Pratt? Now that would be something to see. There would be plenty of time for her to speak with him on board the SS Canterbury, and she had no doubt that Mary would make good use of all the time available to her.

Chapter 5

The train was speeding up again as Lady Julia left her seat and made her way through to carriage 1. She was casually dressed in her normal travelling outfit but she still had the capacity to turn heads. At almost 6 feet in height, and with a figure that rivalled those of the ancient Greek goddesses depicted in the Elgin marbles on display in the British Museum she couldn't exactly blend into a crowd, even if she wanted to.

Edward Huskinson, editor of *The Tatler* magazine had once commented that 'Lady Julia Mortimer is undoubtedly a woman of outstanding beauty and unquestionable style. Her personality and stature shine out like the beacon from a lighthouse across any room, regardless of its grandeur.' She was never quite sure whether she liked being described as 'a lighthouse' but she had to accept that she was considerably taller than the vast majority of women in high society. In heels, which she rarely wore, she towered above most of her admiring dance partners, many of whom complained jokingly of a sore neck.

As she entered carriage 2 she came across the Earl of Carlisle and Lord Fairfax engaged in what was clearly a heated discussion about an article that they had both read in *The Times*.

'I'm telling you Albert that he wasn't there!' blustered the 11th Earl of Carlisle, clearly appalled by the inclusion of a name on the court list that he was now poking at, using one of his sausage like fingers with the greatest of disdain.

'Charles, the listing clearly states that he was. Perhaps you are mistaken,' replied the 12th Lord Fairfax.

'It's damned preposterous! I shall write to the editor immediately upon my return. Hartington at the Palace after the scandal of that affair with his wife's maid? Unthinkable! His Majesty being exposed to such things is downright scandalous!' blurted the Earl of Carlisle for everyone, and anyone to hear.

'Alleged, dear boy, only alleged affair. The girl was well catered for I am sure. Not the first to be caught with his fingers in the pantry,' commented Lord Fairfax, much to the disgust of Lady Julia.

Although she had come to expect such things, she was still appalled by the continuing archaic attitudes of the upper classes. She marvelled that so many of them failed to recognise that servants were not as subservient as they had been before the war. They were now very different people, with ideas and aspirations way beyond those of their forebears.

Why couldn't the so called 'elite' of society recognise that incredible changes were taking place under their noses? The post war generation had the vote and with the groundswell of opinion now changing, they would be using it to destroy the aristocracy-led world unless it was prepared to reform and change its ways. Women over the age of 30 had been given the vote in 1918, and increasingly voices were being raised to call for that age restriction to be further lowered to 21.

'Come on old boy, let's have another drink and deal with the matter on our return. Perhaps a game of cards?' Lord Fairfax placed a consoling hand on the shoulder of his friend and they moved off to the card table with its immaculate green baize top and unopened pack of complimentary Southern Railway playing cards.

Lady Julia watched as the two men lit cigars and motioned nonchalantly at the immaculately attired young waiter behind the bar, indicating that they wished for more drinks. She also noted that neither man appeared to have his wife with him for the journey to Paris.

Making her way through the increasing fog of cigar smoke she made her way to Jimmy V and the sanctuary she knew awaited her.

Passing over the crossing into the first carriage, she paused to look out of the window as once again the train was slowing. New Brompton railway station was equally festooned in colour. The station gardens and hanging baskets seemed to ooze with flowers in every conceivable colour. From each of the ornate iron purlins holding the canopy of the station roof in place, there were wonderfully symmetrical baskets full of trailing lobelia, verbena, and petunia in full bloom. The station sign was almost totally obscured by the profusion of flowering shrubs clambering out of the stone troughs that stood guard around it.

As she entered carriage 1 she was smiling contentedly. Sensing her presence Jimmy V looked up from his music and believed that he was witnessing an apparition of near biblical significance. Lady Julia bathed in the sunlight streaming through the window, her hair surrounded by a halo of light was indeed a vision of loveliness that would surely stir the soul of any man.

'Good afternoon Ladybee',

A pet name that Jimmy V had used for many years to describe Lady Julia.

'How good of you to join me.'

'Good afternoon James. How are you?'

Although Lady Julia was happy to refer to Jimmy V by his 'jazz' name in conversation with friends, the conventions of her upbringing dictated that she could not do so in public.

Jimmy V rose from his seat and led her to the vacant chair at his now overladen table. Glancing around she noted that there were several members of royalty present in the carriage. Seated a little distance away at the front of the carriage was a man that she instantly recognised as the famous racehorse owner the Maharaja of Rajpipla. Seated across from him was his wife the Maharani. They were surrounded by several richly dressed attendants. She imagined that they might be en route to the famous bloodstock sales in Deauville, judging from what appeared to be a sales catalogue being perused by the Maharaja.

Glancing at the contents of the table between them she instantly recognised that he had received his latest batch of music from America.

'Has anything good arrived?' she inquired, indicating with her left hand the neatly arranged piles of music that now surrounded the table. She knew that this would instantly trigger the start of a long conversation on the relative merits and stylistic tendencies that each of the composers in Jimmy V's stable possessed

Five minutes into his explanation of the distinctive features of west coast jazz versus the New Orleans style of composition their conversation was cut short as the train slowed to an almost stop. Past experience told them both that the train had reached the station of Rainham, where the locomotive would take on more water to supply the boiler, and where the passengers could leave the train and stretch their legs if they so wished.

Harry Pratt looked on anxiously as they came to a stop immediately opposite the station master's office. Once again he questioned his own rationality, knowing that this was not an overtly dangerous leg of the journey, however given his past experiences in these types of operation he knew that only a fool would choose to ignore the unexpected. And he was nobody's fool.

Jimmy V proffered his hand to enable Lady Julia to step onto the platform, although he knew that the offer was more out of society correctness than necessity. In turn, Lady Julia accepted his assistance, as to reject it would have been the height of rudeness.

Walking side by side along the platform towards the station name sign with its obligatory troughs of climbing shrubs she glanced up to the footbridge that had been erected between the North and Southbound platforms. Attached to the footbridge was a neat iron sign with gilded letters that stated 44 miles 1260 yards from London. She wasn't sure why but at that moment she couldn't help wondering who on earth had measured the distance so precisely.

Only 1st class passengers were permitted to leave the train at Rainham station, and as if to emphasise the point, the platform extended only long enough to enable the engine and the leading three carriages access.

Harry maintained a discreet, but alert distance behind the couple as they stretched their legs on the platform, his senses alert to any sound that could have been regarded as out of the ordinary. His eyes scanned each and every one of the passengers who now joined them in the late afternoon sun. He was satisfied that there was no threat here, but he remained unnaturally uncomfortable, and it rankled with him that he didn't fully understand why.

Having received the signal from the fireman and driver that the water tender was fully replenished, the station master blew his whistle to notify passengers that the Golden Arrow was ready to continue its journey to Dover. Lady Julia and the Viscount paid compliments to the station master on the beauty of his floral display. Beaming like a child on his birthday he took this as affirmation that his station was the supreme prize winner of the non-existent competition. Lady Julia was convinced that she saw a tear in his eye as he stood proudly to attention as the train left his station.

'I am so pleased that you agreed to join me on this tour Ladybee,' started Jimmy V, when they were once again seated comfortably on the great locomotive.

'I am sure that you will have a splendid time in Berlin. Of course we shall have a wonderful evening in Paris too. I am told that Louis Armstrong and Jack Teagarden are in town at the moment. I so hope that I can arrange to meet up with them both again,' he continued, as if he were talking about his great aunt Florence, and not two of the greatest jazz stars of the 1920s.

Lady Julia was fully aware of course that Jimmy V had a wide range of famous friends across the world, and in particular the United States. She had listened intently to some of the often colourful tales of his early encounters within the jazz fraternity that invariably came about through his friendship with Kid Ory. Louis Armstrong had started his career as the trumpet player with Kid Ory's Riverboat band, steaming up and down the Mississippi.

Lady Julia loved being in the company of Jimmy V. His boyish, uncomplicated enthusiasm was infectious.

As the train sped on towards Dover, passing through the floral wonderlands of Sittingbourne, Teynham, Faversham, Selling, Canterbury and more, with their station master sentries standing proudly to attention, vying for her recognition, Lady Julia sat and listened as Jimmy V regaled her with details of each of the charts in front of him.

The train sped on through the newly developed Kent Coalfield where she could see dozens of fully-laden wagons queuing in sidings, waiting to be collected and transported to replenish the ever greedy ovens of London, but her attention remained focused on Jimmy V and his tales about each of the composers.

With the train slowing down once more for an upcoming station Harry Pratt, who had been sitting silently opposite the couple, coughed gently. Immediately Jimmy V's attention was drawn to him.

'Sir, I believe we are approaching Shepherd's Well Station. Perhaps it is time that I escort Lady Julia back to her cabin so that she can prepare for our arrival in Dover?'

'Of course, Pratt,' replied Jimmy V, aware that he too would need time to collect together his papers that were now scattered around him like large flakes of confetti at a giant's wedding.

'That won't be necessary Harry,' interrupted Lady Julia, 'I am sure that even I can't get lost on a train.'

Looking directly into Harry's eyes she continued,

'Mary and I shall look forward to meeting up with you both on board the Canterbury.'

Although she saw no glimmer of emotion, she was convinced that she had seen the corner of Harry's mouth twitch slightly at the mention of her maid's name.

'Splendid Ladybee. I have a new collection of records that I would very much like to share with you.'

'I am sure that will be delightful way to spend the voyage, James,' remarked Lady Julia as she left the carriage.

Chapter 6

After watching the figure of Lady Julia leave the carriage, Jimmy V set about tidying up the music that lay scattered at his feet and on the table. He methodically ensured that every sheet was collected and put back into sets before replacing them in the carrying case that he had brought along with him.

'Pratt, would you be so kind as to ensure that this case is placed in my travelling trunk? I shall not be requiring it before we arrive in Paris.'

'Certainly Sir,' replied Pratt with a gentle nod of his head.

The train slowed down for Dover Priory Station and instinctively Jimmy V glanced out of the window. The sun was low in the sky now as dusk began to settle over the channel port. Pratt was busying himself making sure that all items of their carry-on luggage had been accounted for and that nothing had been left behind.

There was only a short travelling distance to their destination at Dover Marine Station and the train rolled on at a leisurely pace enabling Jimmy V to note that several of His Majesty's war ships were moored in their final resting place, the Stanlee Shipbreaking and Salvage Co. Ltd area of the eastern docks. With some sadness he noticed the unmistakable, but sadly now broken shape of HMS Superb.

Seeing the ship again brought back memories of his adventure in Istanbul and the daring of their escape in the depths of night through the treacherous waters of the Dardanelles.

He looked across at Harry, still busying himself with their hand luggage, remembering the part that he had played in their escape. Jimmy V had often pondered where Harry had learned to speak Arabic with sufficient fluency to fool the border guards that night.

He smiled as he recalled the joy on his brother, Charles' face when he returned safely to Portsmouth aboard her, bringing with him Charles' darling Princess Sophia. Charles had been convinced that she had suffered the same ghastly fate as so many of her fellow Russian aristocrats at the hands of the communist revolution of 1917. Jimmy V had been his brother's best man, and Lady Julia a guest of honour at their wedding in 1920.

After playing such an heroic part in his family history, Jimmy V was angry that HMS Superb, now a sad and lonely shadow of her former glory, lay in the Stanlee graveyard awaiting her turn to be broken up and sold off for scrap metal. Another innocent and hapless victim of the flaws in the Treaty of Versailles, which restricted the size of armed forces permissible to all sides in the conflict. It angered him that the brave men who had fought and died to win the war had been so badly let down by the politicians who fashioned the peace. A peace that was now going to see HMS Superb doomed to the sacrificial altar.

'Sir, on our arrival I shall proceed to the baggage cars and ensure that all is in order,' remarked Harry, bringing Jimmy V back to the reality of the present.

'If you would kindly remain here, I will return and deal with our hand luggage.'

'Splendid, Pratt,' replied Jimmy V, confident as always that Harry had matters firmly under control.

Looking out of the window as they approached Dover Marine Station at the end of their journey, Jimmy V could see that SS Canterbury was already by the side of the western docks and making steam ready to greet them. There was something quite aristocratic about the whiteness of the smoke rising from her twin funnels into the early evening sky.

In 2nd class, passengers were getting ready to leave the train. Seats couldn't be reserved aboard SS Canterbury within 2nd class, therefore seasoned travellers knew that it was customary for there to be a mad dash as soon as the train wheels had stopped turning.

As the train slowed on its final approach, two men calmly took down their bags from the overhead luggage racks and took their place in the throng of people waiting to throw open the doors.

Mary had used the time that she had been left on her own by Lady Julia to ensure everything was ready for their arrival. She listened as Lady Julia recounted the discussion she had witnessed between the two distinguished members of the House of Lords. Marjorie Jackson, the maid at the centre of the Lord Harrington affair was well known to her.

Marjorie was an attractive, but rather naïve young woman with long blond hair, and startlingly big blue eyes, as Mary recalled. She had met her when Lady Julia had visited Lady Harrington to offer her support following the elopement of her youngest daughter with the Original Dixieland Jazz Band. It had crossed Mary's mind at the time that she appeared unseemly close to his Lordship. On several occasions she believed that she had seen them make overt contact, however, there was nothing that would have alerted her to the consequences that ultimately ensued.

Marjorie was now the doting mother of a baby boy, and as Lord Fairfax had suggested, she had indeed been well provided for. Despite this, Mary still found the nature of the two gentlemen's conversation utterly abhorrent. As she pondered the situation she looked out of the window as the imposing Art Deco façade of the station buildings came into sight.

With a heavy sigh, and an all-enveloping plume of steam, the Golden Arrow settled alongside the platform. As always, despite the length of the journey she was precisely on time. Gone was the striking colour of the rural stations, Dover Marine was a grey, workmanlike edifice designed for functionality rather than beauty. The platform had no seating areas, nor any designated waiting rooms. The station almost screamed at people that it did not approve of them lingering on its platforms.

As soon as the train came to a stop, the doors of the 2nd class carriages were flung back and the massed ranks of passengers poured out on to the platform. Carried within the moving mass of humanity, two men moved innocently towards the seating area in the former cargo hold of the SS Canterbury. They had no doubt that whether they managed to secure a seat or not, the journey ahead would not be a comfortable one. They were well accustomed to such conditions.

Harry waited for the train to come to a complete stop before he collected the precious package of music and made his way to the door of the carriage. The station master was waiting to welcome him.

In direct contrast to his counterpart at Victoria, the station master of Dover Marine could in no way be called rotund. His uniform appeared to have been made for someone several sizes larger. His hands were not visible at the end of his jacket sleeves. His Chaplinesque baggy trousers were so large that there were several pleats around his waist line, held in place by both a large leather belt and a pair of braces. He wore a Southern Railways tie, but the collar of his shirt hung down so low that only the knot was visible above his waistcoat. The weight of the watch chain and time piece that swung like a golden rope in front of him appeared to be causing him to stoop forwards at an unnatural angle. At any moment it threatened to become too much for him, causing him to topple forwards onto the platform.

Harry looked along the length of the platform at the swiftly departing backs of the 2nd Class passengers as they scurried towards the exits. Many were falling behind as they struggled to carry heavy bags and cases. By the time he reached the 1st class baggage cars in the centre of the train, the 2nd class carriages stood empty, their doors hanging open like gaping mouths after being thrown wide by their eager occupants.

A number of out of breath porters were unpacking the first class luggage onto handcarts ready to be transported to the SS Canterbury. Harry quickly identified Jimmy V's travelling trunk and after presenting the appropriate paperwork to the head porter, he was able to access the trunk and pack away the precious case of music. It fitted comfortably next to several other similar packages that he had assembled at Jimmy V's behest a few days earlier. Having closed and secured the lid of the trunk, he looked up in time to see Lady Julia and her maid Mary stepping onto the platform.

Mary, as if by some sixth sense, looked up at the same time and saw the unmistakeable figure of Harry Pratt talking to the porters. Her heart missed a beat as he turned and walked towards them.

'Lady Julia,' started Harry upon reaching them,

'I have arranged for Viscount Stanley and yourself to have dinner in his suite this evening. '

Mary had always loved Harry's American accent. He had all the refinements of a fine English gentleman's gentleman, however when he spoke she imagined that she was watching one of her beloved movies. Harry's voice was how she imagined the legendary Rudolph Valentino might sound.

'Thank you Pratt, that is very good of you. Turbot I presume?' Harry nodded his affirmation with a knowing look.

'Perhaps you would be so kind, whilst we are having dinner, to talk to Mary?' Lady Julia added without any hint of mirth in her voice.

'I believe that she has never travelled to Paris, or indeed Berlin before. I would be most grateful if you could pass on your experience of the cities we shall be visiting on our travels.'

Mary could feel the heat rising from her neck as she blushed uncontrollably with her mouth gaping wide open following Lady Julia's completely unexpected request.

'That would be my pleasure Ma'am,' replied Harry, completely unflustered by the suggestion.

Harry nodded politely to both ladies and took his leave heading back to meet Jimmy V. Mary could only stare still open mouthed at his departing figure.

'Now that was remarkably easy to arrange,' remarked Lady Julia casually.

'Shall we proceed to the Canterbury Mary?'

After first closing her mouth, Mary couldn't suppress a smile that lit up the whole of Dover.

Chapter 7

The SS Canterbury belched bleached white smoke from her twin funnels, as she waited patiently for her latest batch of passengers to push and shove their way into the former cargo hold that now constituted her 2nd Class accommodation. Uniform rows of upright wooden benches were neatly bolted to the steel floor with a single unisex toilet hidden in a shed-like construction in the furthest corner away from the single entrance, the acrid odour of previous voyages giving away its location.

It was perhaps stretching the imagination somewhat to describe this area as accommodation. It could more accurately be described as a holding pen for the ordinary citizen. The two men were fortunate to find seats near to the door which would afford them some relief from the stench that they knew would only get worse during the voyage. They sat in silence with their travel bags positioned between their feet, patiently waiting for the 1st class passengers to board, which would allow for their departure.

As soon as the passengers were safely secured inside the hold, the doors were slammed shut by the ship's crew. A message was then conveyed via one of the porters to the 1st class lounge located in the terminal building that it was now safe for them to make their way to the ship. Viscount Stanley was staring out of the lounge window over to the ship breakers' yard. He noted that the sister ship of HMS Superb, HMS Bellerophon was also awaiting her fate. What a sad end he considered awaited the two mighty Dreadnoughts that had fought so valiantly in the battle of Jutland.

'We are ready to board, Sir.'

'Have you seen HMS Superb, Pratt?'

'A magnificent ship, Sir. Sadly about to become another victim of the war.'

'Victims of a dreadfully flawed peace I fear, Pratt.' Jimmy V shook his head as he turned away from the window.

'Superb and her sister will not be the only victims of Versailles. Mr Wilson and his new League of Nations seem hell bent on disarmament. With such a fragile peace across Europe…' his voice tailed off with more than a hint of despair.

'Lady Julia will be joining you for dinner, Sir,' continued Pratt. 'I have ordered the turbot as you suggested.'

'Splendid Pratt, let's board!'

The 1st class décor aboard SS Canterbury would have graced any of the finest London hotels. Harry had reserved Jimmy V's usual suite, the Prince Albert, located on the upper deck. The décor here was if anything even more opulent.

Rich red velvet drapes hung at the large picture windows in a swags and tails configuration. The vast expanse of glass gave an unrestricted view of the sea on both sides of the ship. The dining area had a large oak table and four Chippendale style chairs upholstered in the same rich material as the curtains. A large crystal candelabra formed a magnificent centre piece on the table which was laid out with Southern Railway's monogrammed crockery and glassware.

The glorious aroma emanating from the galley that adjoined the grand suite was enough to indicate that dinner was well on the way to being prepared. The head chef on board the SS Canterbury had trained at the Savoy Hotel under the guidance of the famous French chef Auguste Escoffier. Jimmy V had enjoyed his signature fish dish of turbot au beurre blanc on many occasions. His mouth watered uncontrollably as the smell penetrated his nostrils.

Jimmy V took up a seat in one of the deep armchairs positioned to look out of the forward window, as the Canterbury slipped her moorings and expertly manoeuvred through the narrow port entrance and out into the still waters of the English Channel.

He looked over towards HMS Superb for one last time. Was it likely that she would be there when he returned? He feared not. He smiled ruefully as he wished her one last farewell.

'Cognac, Sir?'

'Thank you Pratt. A splendid choice of aperitif. Martell I presume?'

'Cordon Bleu, Sir.'

'What else. Thank you Pratt. Do you have plans for this evening?'

'Lady Julia has requested that I speak with her maid concerning Paris and Berlin. I shall accompany her to the dining hall as soon as you are dressed for dinner, Sir'.

Jimmy V suspected that Lady Julia was trying once again to act as matchmaker. He smiled knowingly as Pratt delivered his drink.

'Splendid idea Pratt. I am sure that you will have a pleasant evening.'

The SS Canterbury left the shelter of the white cliffs and headed out into the tidal flow of the channel. The giant ship shook as the first wave gently caressed her bow. On cue, there was a sharp knock at the cabin door.

Pratt was greeted with a salute from a neatly dressed attendant. He wore the same uniform as Raymond Jones and the concierge in Dover, but that was as far as the comparison could be made. The attendant was as smart as a new button with an immaculately pressed suit, starched shirt, and a company tie held in place by the neatest Windsor knot that Harry could remember seeing.

'Sir!' he barked, standing to attention.

'I am instructed by Chef Roberts that dinner will be served in 30 minutes. Sir!'

Without waiting for an acknowledgement he once again saluted and left. Pratt closed the door as the attendant marched smartly away from him.

'It would appear that dinner will be ready in 30 minutes, Pratt.'

'So it would seem, Sir.'

'Splendid. Time enough to finish this most excellent Cognac and dress, I think.'

***

The cool white light from the candelabra, and the finest silver and crystal from Mr Claridge's London store were a stark contrast to the conditions in 2nd class. Here the ambiance was far less salubrious.

In the gloom illuminated by four under powered bulbs hanging limply from black, soot soiled flex, the two men enjoyed a heady cacophony of smells. A unique mixture of engine oil, coal dust, cigarette smoke, numerous body odours and the growing smell emanating from the now overflowing toilet invaded their nostrils.

Several passengers were already exhibiting signs of sea sickness as the Canterbury began to roll in the gentle swell of the English Channel. The two men looked at each other with a growing sense of dread.

Their fears were soon realised as a young girl swayed uncontrollably in their direction, heading towards the toilet. Unable to hold back any longer, she leaned forward and promptly deposited her semi-digested lunch on the floor. The two men in anticipation of what was about to happen quickly raised their feet in unison.

The large male passenger seated next to them showed no such forethought. He was reading some form of journal and had clearly failed to see the young girl's staggering approach. He jumped up in alarm as he received the bulk of the girl's deposit across his shoes and into the hem of his trousers. Her mortified mother was in the midst of a profuse apology as the girl ejected what remained of her lunch down the back of his overcoat.

The two men sighed as they considered the now festering aroma. This would certainly add nothing to the ambiance of the voyage.

Chapter 8

The sun set slowly over the horizon as the SS Canterbury steadily steamed towards France. There was a gentle, almost soothing swell, which complimented the fact that Jimmy V and Lady Julia were planning to enjoy dinner together and would appreciate a calm sea to facilitate their digestive systems.

Lady Julia arrived in good time. She was elegantly dressed as always, in a blue flapper style dress from the house of one of her favourite designers, Jeanne Lanvin. Her tall, slim frame was complimented by a matching pair of Salvatore Ferragamo shoes. The shoes were chosen from a number of pairs she had purchased during her extended visit to Venice alongside Jimmy V a few years before. They had decided to stay in the city for several weeks to help them recuperate from their adventures in Egypt.

Jimmy V, was dressed for dinner in a starched white shirt and collar, black tie and tailcoat. Together they made the perfect society couple.

Dinner started with Chef Roberts' watercress and Irish cream soup, served with wholemeal bread rolls from the ship's own bakery. The couple had enjoyed the exquisite starter, served in SS Canterbury monogrammed Royal Crown Derby bowls on many previous occasions.

Jimmy V sat listening attentively to Lady Julia as she passed on the latest society news. He had never been one to become involved, or remotely interested in London society tittle tattle, but he knew better than to show his lack of interest in the presence of Lady Julia.

'Do you not find it odd? With all the trombone players in Europe to choose from, why would the famous Mr. Paul Whiteman invite you to perform with his band in Berlin, James?' remarked Lady Julia in the middle of a story describing the sordid affair of Lord somebody and the wife of his gamekeeper.

'I believe that Jack Teagarden recommended he ask me to play in his absence. I know most of the music he will be using and I have a new collection of charts to hand over to him that have just arrived.'

'The invitation arrived so late and so near to the tour dates though James. I find that rather intriguing?'

It appeared to Jimmy V that she looked for something intriguing in almost everything. Perhaps she had read a few too many of Miss Christie's novels? Given their propensity for adventures over the last few years, she could have a point though, he conceded to himself.

'I received a telegram from Jack saying that he was unwell, and felt unable to make the voyage to Europe. I am not committed to a band, and touring Europe can be an expensive business for the ordinary musician.'

The arrival of the attendant pushing a trolley bearing its precious load of turbot au beurre blanc brought this line of conversation to a close. Four silver tureens surrounded in perfect symmetry a large central roll-top Bain Marie containing their evening meal.

***

Harry Pratt sat opposite Mary Smith in the central dining room. They had both ordered the roast mutton dinner, preceded by the standard fare of chicken soup, with Victoria sponge and custard for pudding. Harry had chosen a table on the starboard side of the ship so they could look out over the setting sun as it dipped below the horizon.

It had been a long time since Harry had been alone with a woman. Mary had been Lady Julia's travelling companion on many occasions over the years, however he had never really had the opportunity to spend a great deal of time alone with her. The nature of his assignment meant that it would be inappropriate to start any form of serious relationship, but he was comfortable that could enjoy her company this evening in what he knew was the relative security of the SS Canterbury.

The conversation was confined to details regarding Paris and Berlin and he found Mary to be an attentive and intuitive listener. As the dinner drew to a close he felt deeply attracted to the prospect of spending more time in her company. Mary had needed no such stimulus and was pleased to have been the subject of her mistress' manipulations.

***

Jimmy V and Lady Julia completed their meal with a particular favourite of theirs, peche Melba. A simple dish created by the celebrated Auguste Escoffier during his tenure at the Savoy, in honour of the great Australian operatic soprano Nellie Melba. He greatly admired her voice, and had been able to show his appreciation by cooking for her when she stayed at the hotel.

The sun had set, allowing the lights of the port and town of Calais to shine like beacons through the gloom. The couple retired to the comfort of the armchairs to enjoy coffee and the delicious after dinner chocolate mints that had arrived. They sat in silence as the lights of Calais grew ever brighter.

Jimmy V was deep in thought as he recalled the first time he had arrived in a port. That had also been at night time, but on this occasion it was the lights of New York that had played on the horizon. He remembered his mother telling him that most of the lights on Manhattan Island were shining through windows owned by his grandfather.

'What a large house he must have, Mama,' he remembered commenting in his naivety.

Lady Penelope, his mother, had smiled at the small boy looking through the guard rail of the SS Olympia. Lady Penelope, formerly Penelope Fitzherbert, was the eldest daughter of James Fitzherbert of New York. He had been one of the original '49ers', making his fortune in the Californian Gold rush of 1849.

In 1878 he moved to New York, and used his acquired wealth to build a number of hotels on Manhattan Island. These were completed just in time for the opening of the Brooklyn Bridge in 1883, at which point his wealth skyrocketed. Fitzherbert, like many wealthy Americans at the turn of the 20th century, was determined that his daughters should become 'real' Ladies and undertook to ensure that they married into British aristocracy.

General Sir William St. John Smyth, the 2nd Viscount Stanley appeared to fit the bill nicely. Not only did he possess the requisite title, he was also a dashing war hero.

Unbeknown to Fitzherbert and the future Lady Penelope, the dashing Viscount, whilst certainly possessing the title, and a long, proud family pedigree, was also something of a gambler and unfortunately a very poor one. He was always a welcome figure in the gambling clubs of pre-war London, where he had all but gambled away his family's wealth. The proposed liaison with Penelope Fitzherbert was therefore not so much a match made in heaven as a marriage of convenience, born of necessity. James Fitzherbert ensured that his daughter became a fully-fledged Lady, whilst his money allowed the Viscount to avoid the ignominy of bankruptcy.

Whilst the marriage could not in any conventional sense be described as loving, it did result in the birth of a number of children. The arrival of James, the eldest child, had ensured that the succession of the family title was secured.

The young James spent his early childhood mostly with his mother, whilst his father continued his gambling in London. James would also enjoy a number of trips to see his grandparents in the USA, his dual nationality allowing him to move freely between continents. It was on this debut trip that the young James had first encountered the wonderful sounds of Jazz.

Whilst out walking one day with his grandfather in the streets of Manhattan, he heard the faint playing of a piano, joined by one of the most wonderful sounds that he could ever remember hearing. Issuing from a first floor window were the sounds of jazz, a ragtime to be precise, being performed by two black musicians. James was transfixed and resolved to go back without his grandfather as soon as possible and make further enquiries about the music, and the instrument playing it.

The following day, James was standing in the street outside the building. The streets were full of city noise, but there was no trace of the piano playing. As he stood deciding whether to leave, or to risk remaining in an unfamiliar area of town, the pianist walked past him and went to enter the building. The ever confident young James approached him without hesitation and struck up a conversation. The musician's name turned out to be Scott Joplin, and he had moved to New York the year before to seek fame and fortune publishing his compositions in Tin Pan Alley.

James had never heard of the place. Joplin informed him that this was the term used to describe the area on West 28th Street, between Fifth and Sixth Avenues in Manhattan. This was apparently where all the best music publishers were located. James, despite his tender years thought that it was perhaps prudent not to reveal that the buildings along that part of town all belonged to his grandfather, nor did he mention that as the first born grandson, he would eventually inherit them all.

But what of his companion from the previous day? What was the instrument that he had heard?

'That was the slide trombone,' replied Joplin, 'and the guy playing it was a friend of mine from the old town, Edward 'The Kid' Ory,' he continued. 'He's the finest jazz trombonist in the entire United States and he's visiting a while.'

James immediately decided that he would learn to play the slide trombone, and that he would employ Kid Ory to teach him.

Like most musicians, Ory certainly needed the money and it seemed to him that the young Englishman, with the unpronounceable name had access to plenty of it. Whilst his initial motivation for teaching the willing young man was wholly financial, he quickly grew to really like the confident 10 year old. He proved to be a wonderful and inspiring teacher and James a very attentive and willing pupil.

When it was time for James to return to England he did so with a heavy heart, and a nickname given to him by his teacher by which he would become known from that day on, 'Jimmy V'.

'That's a real jazz name, man,' concluded Ory.

He returned to England with a newly manufactured King trombone made for him by the celebrated H N White and company, a present from his grandfather, and several hand written pieces of music from his new friends. As he thought about that first trip to New York, he reflected again how he had kept the secret from his friends that it was he who had arranged for their music to be published.

Lady Julia looked across at Jimmy V as he sat gazing through the window. He was so absorbed in his music. Was he aware of anything else, she mused? She smiled as she thought about the great adventures that they had shared over recent years, and wondered what the future held for them on this trip.

***

Harry and Mary sat quietly drinking tea from slightly chipped cups, as the outer buoys of the port, like sentinels in the darkness warning of impending doom slipped silently past the side of SS Canterbury.

Harry had been a little concerned as to the provenance of the mutton that was served, and could not say that he really enjoyed the somewhat overcooked vegetables, several of which he would be at a loss to satisfactorily identify. Despite its many shortcomings, however, it was a meal that he was grateful for after their journey and the company of Mary had more than made up for its deficiencies.

In the cargo hold, the two men detected the change in pitch of the massive engines as the ship slowed to enter the narrow channel leading to the dock at Calais. They collectively heaved a sigh of relief that their journey had finally come to an end.

The young girl who had created such mayhem earlier was now asleep in her mother's arms, her pallor a particularly unattractive shade of green. The passenger who had borne the brunt of her indiscretion was still chuntering to himself as he sat with his soiled overcoat folded into his travel bag. In the hem of his trousers there was more than a hint of carrot.

The two men sat in silence. Foremost in their minds, surpassing any dangers they might face, was the tantalising prospect of being able to taste fresh air, uncontaminated by human detritus for the first time in several hours.

Chapter 9

The street lamps of Calais stood to attention, their bright white lights shining like beacons in the early evening sky welcoming the SS Canterbury as she steamed her way serenely into port, bearing her latest collection of passengers safely to France.

Mary thought the lights looked remarkably like a string of pearls as they moved from side to side in the gentle English Channel breeze. What a wonderful name for a song that would be...

The glowing colours of the port cafés were a startling contrast to the stark white of the street lights. Mary smiled to herself as she imagined how wonderful it would be to sit in one of those cafés listening to the many street musicians, enjoying the delights of pâté de fois gras with Harry, rather than eating stale Victoria sponge and lumpy custard in the communal confines of the Canterbury's dining room.

In the Prince Albert Suite, Jimmy V looked out at the numerous coloured lights as they danced gently on the horizon. He also was imagining the delights of listening to the street musicians as they moved from café to café, playing their delightful variations of gypsy jazz and folk tunes.

After passing through the outer buoys on her approach to the Port of Calais, SS Canterbury slowed down to take on board M. Leduc, the harbour pilot.

A large and jovial character with a ruddy complexion, borne of an over generous appetite for vin rouge, M. Alphonse Leduc had gained his seafaring knowledge whilst serving in the French navy during the Great War. He had served with distinction as a ship's gunnery officer aboard the giant battleship Bretagne.

The Bretagne, like the entire French navy had been stationed in the Mediterranean throughout the war, and had therefore not seen battle action of any nature. In fact, she had not fired a single shell in anger at an enemy vessel throughout the entire conflict. Despite this, M. Leduc was happy to recount numerous stories of his wartime experiences to anyone willing to buy him a carafe or two at his favourite haunt, Le Café Dubois. His bulbous red nose paid ample tribute to the number of those consumed over the years.

After taking control at the helm of the Canterbury under the watchful, and ever scrutinous eye of Captain Smith and his first officer Lieutenant

Meredith, he gently eased her into port and safely onto her mooring on the eastern quayside.

The crew threw the mooring lines to secure her to the dock and without waiting for so much as a blink of acknowledgement, he handed the vessel safely back to her captain and crew.

Captain Smith had always marvelled at the ease with which this unremarkable Frenchman was able to manoeuvre such a large vessel whilst he was so obviously, from the smell of his breath, under the influence of alcohol.

In the cargo hold, the passengers prepared to escape their confines. The seasoned travellers amongst them knew that although the Golden Arrow had three carriages for 2nd class passengers, the French equivalent, La Flèche D'Or had only two. It was therefore vitally important as the ship approached port to be strategically positioned for the arrival. Paris was 4 hours away, without a single stop. The prospect of spending the journey standing up was not one that any of the 2nd class passengers wished to contemplate. Harold Abrahams, who stunned the world by becoming the Olympic 100 metres champion in Paris a few years earlier would have been impressed by the determination shown on their faces as they waited for the doors to be opened.

The two men remained seated as the passengers gathered their various belongings together and moved towards the exit. They had plans to stay in Calais overnight and proceed onwards to Paris the following day, so they had no desire to become part of the melee that was about to ensue. They anticipated that the train they intended to travel on would be far less crowded. Whilst this arrangement would have been frowned upon under the strict rules of covert operations, it could be justified by the fact that in the unlikely event that they had been seen and identified on their journey from London, they would be able to break the sequence of that observation.

The train they expected to use to continue their journey did not leave Calais until the following afternoon. This would afford them ample time to complete a task they both wished to undertake.

The sound of the engines faded away into silence as the SS Canterbury arrived at the dock side. The 2nd class compartment doors were opened and immediately a stampede of passengers rushed past the startled figure of the attendant in an effort to leave the ship. The gang-plank allowing access to shore had hardly been locked into position, before the first of the passengers was hurtling along it on his way to the waiting train.

The two men left the hold and followed their former fellow inmates ashore, thanking the still startled attendant as they left. After making their way to the now quiet arrivals lounge, they presented their passports to the customs officer and then quietly melted into the night.

Jimmy V and Lady Julia finished their coffee and waited for Harry and Mary to return so that they could prepare for disembarkation. From the windows of the Prince Albert suite it was not possible to see the other passengers leaving the ship, not that this was of any concern to Jimmy V. The Flèche D'Or would wait for as long as necessary for the first class passengers to board, and their luggage to be loaded, before setting out on her journey to Paris.

There was a sharp tap at the door of the cabin and after a dignified pause, Harry appeared in the doorway.

'Sir, I believe we are ready to leave the ship.'

'Splendid Harry. I do hope that you have had a pleasant journey with Mary?'

'Most pleasant.'

'Splendid. Would you be so kind as to accompany Lady Julia to her cabin?'

'Certainly, Sir. It would be my pleasure.'

'Will you be joining me for drinks later Ladybee?'

'Of course James. I am sure that you have several more records for me to listen too.'

'Indeed I have. How splendid!'

Chapter 10

The Flèche D'Or stood spouting white plumes of steam gently into the early evening sky, patiently waiting for her latest load of first class passengers to disembark from the SS Canterbury and settle themselves into the opulence of her ten Pullman carriages. The two men walked on past and smiled as they overheard the increasingly heated arguments taking place in the cramped 2nd class carriages.

There appeared to be a dispute underway about the lack of seating. As they passed, they heard the exasperated voice of the young girl's mother pleading that her daughter was still unwell and needed to lie down on one of the bench seats. Several equally exasperated people who were being prevented from occupying the seat were greeting this with much derision.

The men grimaced as a shout of dismay indicated that the young girl in question had once again chosen to deposit the contents of her stomach on the floor of the carriage. They were thankful that their forethought ensured they were not involved. Without breaking step they quietly passed the end of the train and without a backward glance, marched out of the station and slipped into the gathering darkness of the town.

Crossing the Boulevard du Grande Port, they headed for their hotel on the Rue de Notre Dame in the centre of Calais. As they walked they were surprised by how much the town had changed since their last visit; by 1918 much of the town had been totally destroyed. The austerity of the war years was now replaced by an energy that seemed to spill out on to the streets and clearly the popularity of the cross channel tourist trade had brought renewed prosperity to the town. Everywhere they looked there was colour; innumerable cafés filled with happy, smiling people enjoying fine food and jolly music. Very different from the drab grey weariness that was so prevalent when they were here before.

The two men had served in the Great War and had both been stationed in the Nord Pas de Calais region. They had known Calais well and were pleased that the town had recovered from her ordeal and was so clearly filled with a new vibrancy.

They had arranged rooms at the Hotel Meurice, a hotel with which they were well acquainted. It was one of the oldest establishments in

Calais and could trace its origins all the way back to 1771. It was originally owned by Charles Augustin Meurice, hence its name, and provided welcome accommodation to weary English travellers. During the Great War it had been commandeered as a field hospital and on several occasions during the battles of the Somme it had become the general headquarters for a number of British and Canadian battalions.

As the men crossed over the Place de Rheims the bells of the Eglise de Notre Dame signalled that it was 7 o'clock. Instinctively the two men checked and adjusted their pocket watches to allow for the change in time.

Leaving the square, they heard a high pitched whistle from the dock area, and a returning blast from the engine driver on board the Flèche D'Or signalling that she was pulling her carriages out of the station and starting her journey to Paris.

The men turned and entered their hotel.

***

Jimmy V had a distinct feeling of déjà vu as he sat in an identical armchair, in the same position in the leading Pullman carriage, as that which he had vacated some hours earlier in Dover. The décor, upholstery and furniture were intentionally identical on both trains.

Harry had settled himself down in the armchair opposite and started once again to look through his aviation magazine. He had retrieved from their luggage Jimmy V's latest gadget from America; the very newest model of portable gramophone player produced by the Thomas Edison Company. This now sat on a small table in the centre of the carriage next to a substantial pile of records still in their sleeves. Jimmy V and Harry were the only passengers now occupying carriage No.1. The Maharaja and his entourage, as predicted by Lady Julia earlier, had no intention of journeying to Paris immediately, planning instead to remain in Calais for the evening and travel to the bloodstock sales in Deauville the following day.

'Will you be requiring my services this evening, Sir?' enquired Harry as the train began to move slowly through the outskirts of Calais.

'I don't think so. Not this evening Harry. Perhaps you could continue your chat with Mary? I am sure she would be glad of the company,' offered Jimmy V rather mischievously.

'I believe she has duties she needs to complete this evening, Sir,'

'That's a pity. Perhaps you would be good enough to collect Lady Julia for me?'

'Certainly, Sir'.

On entering carriage No.2, Harry was struck by how contrastingly quiet it was compared to the last time he had visited. The sleeping forms of the 11th Earl of Carlisle and the 12th Lord Fairfax slumped in their armchairs explained the lack of conversation. Perhaps an excessive consumption of wine and cognac over their evening meal aboard the SS Canterbury had ensured that both men would have a restful journey to Paris thought Harry, and smiled to himself as he considered that perhaps their planned excursions amidst the night life of Paris might be best served by a good night's sleep.

Reaching carriage No.4, the manservant found Lady Julia ready and waiting for him.

Harry's giant frame filled the cabin doorway blocking out most of the light from the corridor as he waited for Lady Julia to rise from her seat, causing Mary to glance up momentarily before continuing to re-sew a number of missing sequins onto one of Lady

Julia's dresses. What a powerful figure of a man he was, she thought with a smile.

Harry nodded a polite acknowledgement to Mary and stepped to one side to allow Lady Julia to make her way past him and on towards the front of the train. Mary was sure she saw a twinkle in his eye as he closed the door behind her.

When they passed through carriage No.2 Lady Julia couldn't help feeling that she much preferred to see the good Lords asleep rather than awake. Both men were snoring raucously, much to the amusement of the waiter who stood polishing glasses at the bar. She decided to ensure that the connecting door between the carriages was very firmly closed. She knew that Jimmy V would insist on playing his latest records very loudly, and she had no wish to disturb the gentlemen in their slumbers.

She made her entrance into carriage No.1 as the train slowed down on its approach to the town of Ardres, the first of many stations that it would pass through on its journey to Paris. In the darkness Lady Julia was not able to see the station master, nor was she able to verify whether the French railway stations had entered her imaginary flower competition. She was very familiar with the pretty medieval town of

Ardres and firmly resolved to visit its excellent market again in the near future.

'Good evening Ladybee! Come and sit with me, I have lots of new recordings to share with you. Harry, would you be so kind as to get Lady Julia her usual tipple please.' Jimmy V motioned her to the armchair previously occupied by Harry.

'Certainly, Sir.'

The rest of the journey would pass in the rather pleasant company of Jack Teagarden, Jelly Roll Morton, George Gershwin, and the wonderful voices of blues singers Bessie Smith and Sippie Wallace. So many stars of the jazz world performed perfectly as usual for their exclusive audience.

Harry moved quietly to a table at the rear of the carriage where he could carefully study the latest innovations in aviation.

***

In the Hotel Meurice the two men had a basic but pleasant meal of mutton stew and potatoes, accompanied by a rather sharp tasting bottle of the house wine. They had an early start planned for the morning and therefore decided to refrain from further exploration of the changes to the town, intending to retire immediately after the meal. Their train for

Arras was due to depart at 5.30am the following morning.

Before the darkness and peace of sleep could welcome them into its embrace, both men lay awake and remembered the last time they had been guests at the Hotel. Neither man wished to dwell too long with those thoughts.

Chapter 11

Harry sat looking out into the darkness of the French countryside, his magazine now neatly folded on the small table in front of him. The Flèche D'Or had passed the lights of numerous tiny hamlets and the occasional sleepy station, but for the most part the journey had passed in darkness.

He was barely conscious of the music being played in the background and the chatter between Jimmy V and Lady Julia, his thoughts firmly fixed on events ahead. The meeting he attended before their departure from London had given him some background information relating to the nature of his assignment, but the finer details remained hidden. The intelligence had been verified as being genuine, but he knew that it would be down to him and his instincts to ensure that matters played out satisfactorily.

He was accustomed to this kind of assignment, which was one of the reasons that he could be entrusted with it. He was the most experienced and successful field agent in Europe, with a long established and credible network of contacts in every major city. Despite this, he was very aware that there was a changing mood on the continent. The war that had altered so much already, had now produced a fractured peace. The hated austerity that it brought had created further unrest within virtually every nation.

Harry glanced across the carriage at Jimmy V as the music stopped and he stood up to place yet another record on the turntable of the gramophone. Austerity was not a word that he could in any way understand. His wealth lay in America, a country that had entered the war very late in proceedings and which had been largely unaffected by it. He smiled to himself as he caught sight of Lady Julia gently suppressing a yawn.

'Harry, would you mind refreshing our drinks. There's a good chap.'

Jimmy V's voice quickly brought Harry back from his thoughts.

'Certainly, Sir. Sir, we shall be arriving in Paris in approximately one hour. Shall I prepare a snack prior to our arrival?'

'Excellent thought, Harry. We will certainly need some sustenance before we venture out this evening.'

Harry feigned surprise that they would be sampling the Parisian nightlife immediately upon their arrival in the city. In reality, he had already made provision for a taxi to collect them from the Hotel Ritz and transport them to the Théâtre des Champs-Élysées.

'Come Harry. I assume that you have made some arrangements for our evening's entertainment?' enquired Jimmy V, knowing the answer would be in the affirmative.

'I had considered that Lady Julia would be tired after such a long journey, Sir,' answered Harry, still playing the game

'Nonsense Harry. Ladybee is a woman of outstanding stamina, aren't you my dear?' Jimmy V made a casual hand movement towards Lady Julia without checking or expecting a response.

'I am sure that she will be desperate to sample one of the latest shows, just as I am, Harry.'

'I have reserved a box at the Théâtre des Champs-Élysées, Sir. Miss Josephine Baker is performing.'

'Absolutely splendid Harry. Couldn't be finer.'

'Thank you Harry. I had hoped to be able to see her show whilst we were in Paris. How thoughtful of you,' added Lady Julia.

Harry acknowledged her approval and made his way towards the restaurant car in order to obtain snacks for the couple. As he left, Kid Ory and Louis Armstrong began to play Ory's classic Muskrat Ramble from his latest recording with the 'Hot Five'.

The 'Good Lords' were still sleeping soundly and as he passed through, Harry wondered if they perhaps had an early night planned when they arrived in Paris.

Harry ordered an assiette de charcuterie and a basket of bread in impeccable French from the restaurant car menu. He also requested that a similar order be taken to carriage No.4 which he knew Mary would appreciate as she would not have eaten since their arrival in France.

Darkness enveloped the windows as the Flèche D'Or continued her journey through the French countryside. Harry could see lights from the small farms and communes twinkling as the train inexorably neared her final destination.

Lady Julia looked up at Harry as he returned. Kid Ory struck up the opening chorus of Richard Marigny Jones' song, Big Fat Ma and Skinny Pa, as if to welcome him back. She had always admired Harry's loyalty and devotion to Jimmy V and was very pleased following her own meeting in Harrods that he was once again by his side on this trip.

As the song neared its conclusion, a young waiter pushed open the doors and entered pushing a trolley containing their evening meal.

The waiter was alarmingly handsome with jet black hair, slicked back in the latest fashion and a matching moustache groomed to perfection. His uniform was immaculate

He flashed a smile at Lady Julia as he opened the lid of the trolley, his sparkling white teeth seemed to gleam as they reflected in the gold braid of his waistcoat. The trolley contained a generous dish of prepared continental meats and a basket of freshly baked bread neatly laid out on a silver platter.

'Splendid stuff, Harry,' remarked Jimmy V as he turned to the waiter.

'Thank you my good man.' He pressed a 10 Franc note into the young man's hand and gestured towards the doorway before he could flirt any more with Lady Julia.

Behind the waiter Lady Julia could clearly hear the sounds of two rather annoyed 'Good Lords' who had been abruptly awoken from their slumber by the sound of the trolley rattling through their repose.

Their mood was not lightened by Louis Armstrong rattling through a brilliant cornet chorus as he joined Kid Ory, Jonny Dodds (Clarinet), Jonny St.Cyr (Banjo), and Lil Hardin Armstrong (Piano) in a full bore version of Lil Armstrong's King of the Zulus.

'I love this song James,' remarked Lady Julia,

'it always reminds me of the wonderful time we had in Egypt'.

'No Zulus in Egypt, Ladybee!' remarked Jimmy V jokingly.

'I am fully aware of that James, thank you,' replied Lady Julia rolling her eyes in mock incredulity.

As the waiter opened the carriage door to leave, Lady Julia heard one of the Good Lords shouting out to his companion.

'No chance of sleeping now old boy. Someone's singing something about bloody Zulus…'

Chapter 12

Harry noticed that there were many more lights now emerging from the gloom, which signalled they were approaching the outer suburbs of Paris. Glancing at his time piece he estimated that the Flèche D'Or would be arriving at the Gard Du Nord within the next 20 minutes, precisely on time as expected. It was necessary to start packing away the gramophone and prepare for their imminent arrival.

Harry knew better however than to interrupt the final chorus of Louis Armstrong's Irish Black Bottom. He waited for the final chord to fade away and the gramophone arm to lift off the revolving disc before he began to collect together the various albums that now littered the floor of the carriage like discarded confetti at a wedding.

'Sir, we shall be arriving in approximately 20 minutes. I shall accompany Lady Julia back to her carriage?'

'I can manage perfectly well Harry, thank you. Please remain with James and help him put things in order. You know how untidy he is.'

'Now then Ladybee. That's not strictly true,' Jimmy V replied with mock indignation.

'I was the tidiest child in my nursery.'

'James, you were the only child in your nursery.' replied Lady Julia with a smile.

'True. But I was still the tidiest.'

'Sir, I have arranged for a taxi to meet us at the Gare Du Nord and transport us to the Hotel Ritz. In view of the volume of our luggage, Lady Mortimer and Mary will follow us in a separate taxi.'

'Thank you Harry. That is very thoughtful of you. I shall return to Mary, and we shall see you at the Hotel later, James.'

Lady Julia rose from her chair and took her leave of the two men as they continued packing away the records into their respective sleeves.

She moved swiftly through carriage No.2 without acknowledging the presence of the two Good Lords, with whom she had no desire to speak and onwards down the train. The Flèche D'Or was moving noticeably slower as she cut through the suburbs of northern Paris. Mary was already packed and ready when Lady Julia appeared once more at the door.

'I hope you have had a pleasant journey, Ma'am?'

'Indeed I have. James seems to have so many new records every time we journey together. I hope that your journey has not been too tiresome Mary?'

'I have replaced the missing sequins on both the silver and red gowns. Which will you be requiring this evening?'

'I think red this evening, Mary. We shall be seeing Josephine Baker at the theatre later. I think red is most appropriate for such an occasion.'

'I agree Ma'am. I hear that Miss Baker gives a rather risqué performance involving some kind of fruit?'

'Bananas I believe Mary,' replied Lady Julia, knowing that Mary, like the rest of the population of Europe was fully aware of Josephine Baker and her famous Banana Dance routine.

'Very few sequins to hide her modesty…'

'So I understand Ma'am.'

Mary could see the gothic splendour of the Gare Du Nord coming in to view as the train made its final, snaking approach to the station. The bright lights illuminated the carriage as the train slowed to a stop beside platform No.9.

Almost before the train had come to a complete halt, Mary saw 2nd class passengers stream past their window. Most of them seemed to be dragging huge amounts of luggage and a number of tired looking children behind them, as they rushed towards the station exits. One woman looked particularly bedraggled as she pulled along a very reluctant young girl. The other passengers seemed to be giving her a wide berth for some reason.

She was struck by how dishevelled, and tired all the passengers looked after their journey. She had never travelled in the 2nd class carriages on board a train, but she thought how frightful it must have been judging by the appearance of the people as they streamed past the window.

Harry had finished putting away the records and was dismantling the gramophone into its carrying case as the train eased into the station.

'Sir, I took the liberty of packing your dinner jacket with the hand luggage. Do you wish to change before we depart for the Hotel?'

'What a splendid idea, Harry.'

'It is hanging in the bedroom compartment ready for you, Sir.'

'Splendid.'

How many 'Splendid's was that for today? thought Harry. He had played the game of counting how many times Jimmy V used his favourite word for a number of years. Was that 34 or 35? Not to worry, it was not even close to the all time record as yet.

Twenty minutes later, they were seated in the back of a Unic L26 taxi as it made its way through the streets of Paris towards the Hotel Ritz. Following behind them in a similar taxi were Lady Julia and Mary.

Lady Julia had also decided to change her attire in preparation for the evening ahead. She was now resplendent in a red creation by another of her favourite dress designers, Mme. Coco Chanel. A pearl choker complimented her outfit and matching armlet embellished with an Egyptian themed motif, a design inspired, like much fashion jewellery of the time, by Lord Caernarvon and Mr Howard Carter's discovery of the treasures of Tutankhamen. To complete the outfit she wore another matching pair of Salvatore Ferragamo red shoes from her collection.

As always, she wore the platinum and jade Gruen Guild bracelet watch her father had bought for her when she graduated from La Alpena finishing school.

The streets of Paris were busy with elegantly dressed people moving between the numerous cafés that lined her boulevards. Each seemed to have an army of identically clad waiters dressed in white shirts, black bow tie, with long white aprons. They moved elegantly between tables, balancing impossibly over-loaded trays expertly on the fingers of one hand as they dispensed drinks to their waiting customers.

The sounds of music performed by various accordions, violins and the occasional piano drifted one into another. Jimmy V had lowered his window and was eagerly drinking in the atmosphere of the night as the taxi moved slowly through the brightly lit streets towards the hotel.

Jimmy V and Lady Julia had stayed at the Hotel Ritz on a number of previous occasions. As their taxis arrived at the grand façade, the ever present figure of Georges Lepidus, the concierge appeared to open the doors.

As soon as Georges saw the occupants of the taxis, his spirits lifted and a broad smile appeared on his face.

'Monsieur Viscount,' he effused.

'How pleasant it is to welcome you back to Paris, and the Lady Mortimer too.'

Georges couldn't hide how pleased he was to welcome them back to the hotel. An army of porters was quickly assembled to collect their luggage as he showed his new guests into the lobby of the hotel. He enquired as to pleasantries of their journey and their health as he escorted them to the check in desk. He knew that both of his new guests were very generous with their gratuities and smiled to himself as he decided there would be a few very good days to look forward to.

'If I can be of any assistance during your stay, please do not hesitate to contact me, Sir.'

Georges Lepidus spoke in strongly accented, but more than passable English as a result of his work as a message runner for the British army during the war. He had been injured by shrapnel in the battle of Loos, which had left him with a slight limp in his left leg, which always seemed to become more obvious upon their arrival.

'Thank you Georges. How very kind,' Jimmy V replied, handing him a 10 franc note.

'A pleasure, Sir. Enjoy your stay.' Georges saluted and returned to his duties outside the hotel with a renewed spring in his step. Harry, watching the retreating figure, smiled as he noted that there was now much less sign of his limp.

'Shall we say 15 minutes in the lobby, my dear?'

Lady Julia nodded in affirmation as she completed signing the hotel register.

'Splendid!'

Chapter 13

The Versailles Suite was the largest suite in the Ritz Hotel. It had several rooms, and had provided accommodation for a number of high profile guests, including several presidents of the United States. The room earned its name from being lavishly decorated and furnished in the style of Louis IV. Its crowning feature was without question a magnificent crystal chandelier that overhung the dining table, which was large enough to seat twelve guests comfortably. The suite also boasted adjoining quarters that could easily accommodate a number of servants.

Jimmy V had stayed in the Versailles Suite on a number of occasions when visiting Paris and he loved the views it afforded across the Place Vendome. Its unrivalled opulence made it a truly magnificent place to stay.

Lady Julia was to occupy the Lafayette Suite. This was also located on the 3rd floor, but faced the rear of the hotel, where it offered an excellent view over the terrace and into the rose garden.

The Lafayette Suite comprised of a salon with a balcony and a large bedroom with an adjoining bathroom. There was also a connecting door from the salon leading to a small bedroom for Mary. The accommodation was more than adequate for both of their needs.

Furnished in a slightly less opulent manner, the Lafayette Suite was nevertheless extremely comfortable and was strikingly more feminine in its décor than the Versailles. Its walls were wallpapered with a pattern made up of a variety of flowers in pastel shades of yellow, sky blue and pink. Lady Julia particularly liked the views out over the rose garden in the summer months.

That would have to wait for morning though, as she accepted a night coat from Mary and made her way to the lift to descend to the lobby area where she would meet Jimmy V and Harry.

She knew that she would find them in the Ritz Bar where Jimmy V would no doubt be enjoying one of the legendary cocktails created by the famous barman, Frank Meier.

'Ladybee, how simply splendid you look this evening. You must try Monsieur Meier's latest cocktail my dear.'

'Thank you James'.

Looking around, she recognised a number of people. Seated in one of the private booths was the writer Ernest Hemingway and his latest companion.

Pauline Pfeiffer was a young and very glamorous journalist with The Vogue magazine in Paris. Society gossip had it that it would not be long before she became the new Mrs Hemingway. Lady Julia thought they made a handsome couple.

'Sir, if we are to see Miss Baker's performance we must depart for the theatre as soon as possible.' remarked Harry, consulting his time piece.

'Thank you Harry. Please ask Georges to summon a taxi.'

Harry turned and went to consult the ever willing concierge.

A few minutes later the party were once again passing through the bright lights of Paris on their way to the Théâtre des Champs-Élysées.

Neither Jimmy V nor Lady Julia was familiar with the theatre. Its normal bill of fare was principally made up of ballet and opera productions, neither of which held much of an appeal for them, although Lady Julia had frequently attended Covent Garden when she was younger, where her father maintained a box in order to entertain visiting guests of the bank.

The Théâtre des Champs-Élysées was one of Paris's newer theatres. It had opened for the first time in 1913 with a season by the celebrated Ballet Russe, but then closed again at the start of the war. The theatre's first season was certainly one not to forget. It had included a near riotous premiere of Igor Stravinsky's ballet the Rite of Spring during which the audience boos had drowned out the music.

On their arrival Jimmy V and Lady Julia were surprised by the austere concrete façade that faced them. It could certainly not be described as a place of architectural beauty in the mould of the Palais Garnier or the Théâtre du Châtelet.

They waited outside the unwelcoming grey building whilst Harry went ahead to speak to the theatre manager. A little time later, he emerged with the keys to the box that he had reserved in the dress circle. He was assured that this would afford them the very best view of the stage.

Josephine Baker had quickly become one of the most celebrated and most powerful solo performers in Europe. She attracted a huge following with her uninhibited style of dancing, not to mention her almost complete absence of clothing.

When performing her famous banana dance her costume comprised of nothing more than a string of 16 bananas attached to her waist. In the few short years that she had been in Paris she had acquired a reputation for having thrilled and scandalised audiences in equal measure.

Lady Julia admired her greatly and considered it marvellous that a black woman dancer could command such recognition.

The box would have comfortably seated eight people but for this evening's performance, only Jimmy V and Lady Julia were in attendance. Harry remained standing at the back of the box, although he also had an excellent view of the stage.

The new electric theatre lights dimmed and the orchestra struck up with a tune very familiar to them. The orchestra was playing 'Ain't She Sweet', a tune that Jimmy V had played on many occasions at The Savoy.

After the first 16 bars of the song, the first of the dancers appeared to the raucous cheers of the audience. Eight female dancers 'dressed', if that word is appropriate, in little more than feathers, marched on to the stage singing the opening lines of the song.

Jimmy V thought that the orchestra was excellent and was sure that he must know some of the musicians involved. He would enquire later who was playing.

As the song neared its ending, the fans held by the dancers twirled around to the beat sending a large collection of stray feathers into the orchestra pit. The final chord was met and all sixteen dancers raised their fans into the air to reveal that all were topless.

'What a splendid sound from the orchestra my dear.' remarked Jimmy V as the dancers left the stage to a generous round of applause and more cheers from the audience.

'Yes James, marvellous.'

38 thought Harry without comment.

The orchestra struck up once more with James. P. Johnson's Charleston. The lights from the orchestra pit were too dim to allow for Jimmy V to see the faces of the musicians, but they could certainly play.

As he contemplated who was in Europe that might be playing there was an audible gasp from the audience as Josephine Baker appeared. She was wearing what appeared to be a dress made entirely out of strands of string, interspersed with a number of rather inadequate seashells attached in strategic positions.

Lady Julia glanced over at Jimmy V and smiled to herself. She couldn't be completely certain, but she was sure that she saw his over-starched aristocratic eyebrows twitch.

Harry looked on without flinching. He couldn't help thinking how much Josephine had changed since he last saw her. Then, she had been a scruffily dressed kid dancing for nickels and dimes on St. Louis street corners. He had been so taken with her natural style of dancing that he had encouraged his great friend Joe Alex from the St. Louis vaudeville company to go and see her. The rest, as they say, was history. He couldn't possibly have imagined on that cold winter's day in 1915 that he would be seeing her again all these years later, performing a solo routine in a Parisian theatre.

The song ended and once again the audience burst into applause. Dozens of roses were thrown on to the stage and were duly collected by the theatre staff.

The show continued with a number of dances featuring the supporting performers. Jimmy V listened intently as the musicians showed repeatedly that they were very familiar with the very latest American jazz charts. The style in which they played and their precision was flawless. He particularly admired the trumpet playing in the songs 'Cornet Chop Suey' and 'He likes it slow'.

The gyrating nature of the choreography in this last number had sent the audience into a frenzy, with one theatre-goer trying to climb through the orchestra in order to approach the lead dancer. She was clearly quite unnerved by the experience. Thankfully, the intervention of the 2nd viola player had ensured that the gentleman got no further.

'Always knew there was a far more satisfactory use for the viola than scratching it, my dear.' remarked Jimmy V with a chuckle, as the fellow was laid low by a glancing blow to his temple from the instrument. A number of stage hands waited to remove his semi-conscious figure from the orchestra pit as the song ended.

The lights dimmed once more for the finale and the drummer struck up with an African rhythm. The curtains drew back to reveal a jungle scene complete with ropes wrapped in what looked like ivy leaves representing hanging vines. Seated on a large fallen tree amongst the hanging vines were a number of the dancers. Each one appeared to be completely naked, although a small drum was placed fortuitously in front of each of them to hide their modesty.

'Those girls have a splendid sense of rhythm my dear.'

Lady Julia smiled and nodded in agreement.

39 thought Harry from the back of the box without a change of expression.

The orchestra gradually joined in the song as Josephine Baker appeared from the wings dressed in her famous banana costume. As she danced wildly around the stage, the fruit threatened to give way at any moment.

Josephine was joined for the 2nd verse of the song by the now fully recovered lead dancer, who was similarly dressed. The music rose to a tumultuous climax as all of the dancers joined for the final sixteen bars. Thankfully, when they stood up it became obvious that they too had strings of bananas around their waists. The finale elicited by far the loudest applause of the evening.

Jimmy V and Lady Julia rose to their feet with the rest of the audience as the company took their bows at the end of the show.

'What a splendid show my dear. Certainly not something that you see in London. I thought the music was absolutely top drawer. I must try and speak to the chaps in the Orchestra.'

'Harry, do you think that could be arranged? Perhaps invite them all to the Ritz for a drink? What do you think, Ladybee?'

'That sounds like a marvellous idea James. Perhaps you could extend the invitation to Miss Baker and her colleagues, Harry?'

'I will see what can be done Sir, Ma'am.' replied Harry as he left the back of the box and descended the stairs in an attempt to find the stage manager.

'What did you think to the dancers, James?'

'Splendid. Clearly very accomplished young ladies indeed.'

'I believe that the lead dancer is actually an acquaintance of mine from school.' added Lady Julia.

'Really!' remarked Jimmy V in a shocked tone, several octaves higher than he had intended.

'A Riggleshide girl in naked theatre? Are you sure?'

'No James. Not Riggleshide! Good Lord no! I meant from 'La Alpina'. I believe her mother was a dancer in the Paris theatres. Her father was a French Count, with something of a reputation. He funded her education rather than suffer the scandal of admitting to the affair from which she was the product.'

'I see. Well clearly the girl has inherited her mother's dancing skills.'

'At school her name was Philomena Dutoit, but I understand she now goes by the stage name of Fufu Lamore. After school she returned to Paris, but her father refused to provide any further funds for her. I am afraid that she had little choice but to work alongside her mother as a Gigolette.'

'What a rotter!'

Jimmy V was quite appalled at the behaviour of the man. Clearly he was no gentleman, whether he was a French Count or not thought Jimmy V. For some reason at that moment his thoughts turned to the Good Lords.

'Sir, I have made arrangements for you to meet the orchestra, together with Miss Baker and a number of her colleagues on our return to the Ritz bar.'

'That's absolutely splendid Harry. I really don't know how you manage to achieve such things. I do hope that they will dress appropriately.' he added, with a wink to Lady Julia.

Glancing at his time piece Harry noted that the time was now 12.15pm. The 'Splendid' record would remain for another day.

Chapter 14

The Unic taxi picked its way slowly through the still busy streets of Paris on the return journey to the Hotel Ritz. In the back Jimmy V and Lady Julia were deep in conversation about the music, the scenery, the singing and the minimalist clothing involved in the show they had witnessed earlier. Lady Julia smiled as Jimmy V looked increasingly uncomfortable talking about this latter aspect of the performance. She thought it a very quaint and attractive feature in the man.

Georges, as always it seemed, was at his post outside the hotel and welcomed them back with a happy smile.

'I hope you have had an enjoyable evening, Sir?'

'A splendid evening indeed, Georges. A fabulous show in every respect. Have you seen Miss Baker?'

'No, Sir, but I believe she is the talk of Paris. I hope to see her in the near future.'

'Splendid. You should indeed. We are expecting several guests shortly. Please refer the drivers to Pratt, for payment. Direct my guests to the Ritz bar, there's a good chap.'

Jimmy V pressed another 10 franc note into the hand of the ever smiling concierge as he turned and made his way with Lady Julia into the hotel. Harry remained behind with the concierge, having extracted himself from the seat of the taxi.

Lady Julia was surprised to see that the author Ernest Hemingway and his lady companion were still seated in their booth, although by their demeanour it was apparent that both had clearly enjoyed several more of M. Meier's cocktails since they left.

As Lady Julia continued her sweep of the late night occupants of the Ritz bar, a familiar voice rose high above the general hubbub of conversation.

'Julia! What a marvellous surprise, c'est incroyable!'

From the booth next to the entrance, Lady Julia saw the unmistakeable figure of Mme. Valette Simone accompanied by three neatly attired young men, rise from her seat and walk towards her. The Countess De St. Augustin, as she now was, flung her arms out wide in welcome.

Valette Simone was of a similar age to Lady Julia, although considerably smaller in height. It had been the talk of Parisian society when she married the twice divorced Count de St. Augustin the year before. He was after all senile, and in his late seventies. There was some unkind speculation in the press at the time, because of the vast age difference, as to whether he fully understood in his confused state, that he was marrying Valette and not one of his beloved horses.

Lady Julia had first met Valette Simone near to the Col de Fresse on the ski slopes above Les Tignes, whilst on a holiday break during her final year at La Alpina.

'Bonjour Countess, how nice to see you again. Congratulations on your marriage. How is the Count?' enquired Lady Julia, looking past the approaching figure towards the three young men who remained seated in the booth.

'Thank you, but please I am still Valette. The Count is very happy, I believe. He is in Provence with his horses, and I am not,' the countess laughed, as she kissed Lady Julia on both cheeks.

'May I introduce you to my dear friend, Viscount Stanley?'

'Countess. How charming to meet you,' Jimmy V announced as he politely took hold of the outstretched gloved hand and kissed it.

'Would you and your guests care to join us? We are expecting several guests from the theatre, but you would be most welcome.'

Lady Julia was surprised by the invitation, but was far too courteous to show it. She had spent a pleasant few days with Valette Simone in Les Tignes when they had first met. They had also encountered each other by chance in Harrods on one occasion and had lunched, but she was not what she would call a close friend, more a casual acquaintance.

James is far too polite for his own good on occasions she thought, as Valette accepted the invitation and motioned for the three young men to join her. Lady Julia smiled as she considered the ages of the Countess's companions. Mischievously, she calculated that the three of them together might equal that of the Count.

The first of the taxis had just arrived at the hotel foyer and Harry was on hand to ensure that the drivers were paid and their occupants directed towards the Bar. Several more taxis arrived soon after in a steady procession with Harry repeating the process, welcoming Jimmy V's guests, directing them into the hotel, and settling the bill.

After a full 15 minutes the final taxi appeared. Harry opened the door.

'Harry!' enthused Josephine Baker, as she threw her arms around his neck and planted a bright red lipstick kiss on his startled cheek. Georges Lepidus was visibly shocked to see the brightest new star of Parisian theatre arriving at his hotel and planting a kiss on a servant.

'I didn't know the invitation was from you! They said it was from some English Lord! How great to see you Harry!'

In his mind all Harry could see was the poor little malnourished girl he had first encountered dancing for dimes on the street corner in St. Louis, but so many years had passed since then. Here was a beautiful, vivacious young woman in the prime of her life.

'Miss Baker. It is good to see you again.'

'Harry, you swallowed a brick?' feigning a stern look, Josephine laughed. Harry smiled at the thought that his accent could have changed so much during his self-imposed exile from America.

'Call me Josephine! Without you I doubt I would be called anything except dead!' Josephine continued.

Harry nodded and paid the driver who stood waiting patiently by the door of his taxi as the scene on the pavement had unfolded. Looking at the size of Harry, he had quickly decided that waiting, rather than interrupting was his safest option.

'Miss Baker, my name is Georges Lepidus, it is a pleasure to meet you. I hope to see your show next week,' remarked the concierge as he appeared at the side of Harry, grooming his moustache.

'Too late next week I am afraid. Me and the company are off to Berlin,' continued Josephine.

Harry looked on with hidden delight as the concierge looked visibly deflated by this news. It had been Georges' intention to use the money from his anticipated 'additional' gratuities to purchase a ticket for the hottest show in town. Madame Lepidus would not have been any the wiser. He would give her the same money as he usually did, and use the extra to have a gratuitous night out at the theatre. There would be no harm done in that. After all he had earned the money. What would he do to conceal the spare cash now?

'If you would care to follow me, Miss Baker, I will escort you to the bar and introduce you to Viscount Stanley.'

'I would care Harry. I would care very much indeed. Is he single?' she enquired with a wink.

Harry didn't pass comment and directed Josephine past the deflated concierge and into the hotel lobby. As they entered the bar, the assembled crowd burst into a spontaneous round of applause. Harry was beside her wondering whether he was acting as a proud pseudo father figure, or an equally proud chaperone.

'Miss Baker. How splendid to meet you.'

Josephine looked at the young English aristocrat with a smile. Possibilities here, she thought, as she began to list his qualities in her mind.

1.   Athletic; but not in the Harry mould.
2.   Good looking; not in the Rudolf Valentino mould. Indeed not, she thought, with fond recollection of a night not easily forgotten.
3.   Rich; undoubtedly, given he was picking up the bill for the taxis and the whole party by the looks of things
4.   Available; possibly?

'May I present Lady Julia Mortimer,' continued Jimmy V.

'It's a pleasure to meet you Miss Baker,' began Lady Julia.

'We really enjoyed your performance this evening. Didn't we James?' turning to Jimmy V and hooking her arm through his. Josephine tried not to look too disappointed. Although points 1 to 3 were neatly ticked, clearly point 4 had already been covered. The charming, but tigress demeanour of Lady Julia was making that very clear to her as she guarded her man.

Looking up from 5' 3'' in heels, to the near 6' tall frame of Lady Julia, Josephine Baker realised that the position was very much non-negotiable. 'Why is it that the best ones are always taken?' she thought.

'Harry, would you be kind enough to ensure that our guests have drinks. Miss Baker would you care to join us?'

Jimmy V, always the quintessential Englishman, was not oblivious to Lady Julia marking out her territory. In truth, he was actually quite flattered. As he followed the two women towards the rest of his guests he smiled contentedly.

The atmosphere was now alive with a hubbub of noise, not only from Jimmy V's guests, but also the crowd of onlookers that gathered as the news of Josephine Baker's presence spread around the other bars in the hotel.

No longer the main attraction, Ernest Hemingway had left with his companion and on rather wobbly legs had decided to retire for the night.

Lady Julia smiled as she saw Jimmy V in his natural habitat; surrounded by fellow musicians, talking about the latest trends in jazz.

She recognised the trumpet players Buddy Bolden and Red Nichols from their visit to London the previous summer. They were talking to Fud Livingston and Jimmy Noone. How had Fud managed to arrive in Paris ahead of them? Could he have taken the new early morning flight into Paris? How exciting it would be to be able to simply pop on to an aeroplane and fly around Europe. What could be possible in the future? Breakfast in London, lunch in Paris, and dinner in Rome? What a wonderful thought.

The sound of a thunderous voice emanating from the entrance to the bar interrupted her thoughts.

'I was told I would find you boys here!'

A large, red faced man in a camel coloured Chesterfield coat stood in the doorway, his giant frame silhouetted against the light from the crystal chandeliers of the hotel lobby.

Paul Whiteman, the 'King of Jazz' opened his arms wide as he beamed a smile at the assembled throng of musicians.

'Whiteman's here! Let the party begin!' he bellowed, as he approached the group.

'Jimmy! My man, how good to see you,' slapping a huge bear like fist on his shoulder.

'Lady J! Of course!'

Jimmy V and Lady Julia moved between the various groups of musicians and dancers as they talked about the upcoming tour of Berlin. It seemed to Lady Julia that everyone seemed to be joining them on the journey. In the corner of the room she caught sight of Fufu Lamore. She was with two of her fellow dancers talking to the bass player Wellman Breaux and the drummer Warren 'Baby' Dodds.

Jimmy V was in deep conversation with Paul Whiteman concerning his recent much publicised commissioning of a revolutionary new, full length, jazz concerto from George Gershwin. She decided to politely excuse herself from the conversation and made her way across the room.

'Philomena!'

'Nobody has called me by that name for some time,' replied Fufu Lamore, as she turned around in surprise to see the approaching Lady Julia.

The two embraced warmly. The two ladies left the two dancers and retired to the booth vacated by Ernest Hemingway in order to continue with their conversation. With the numbers now evened up nicely, the two musicians took the opportunity to invite the dancers to join them for dinner, which they readily accepted.

As the two women talked, the rest of the assembly was starting to disperse. Outside, the night sky gave way to daylight and the hotel lobby outside the bar began to come back to life. Jimmy V was still deep in conversation of course. Where did that man get his energy from?

Turning to look through the window, she saw the back of the Countess de St.Augustin as she got into a taxi alongside her three companions. Perhaps Jimmy V was not the only one with far too much energy for his own good.

Fufu confirmed that the entire dance company had been booked to accompany the Paul Whiteman Orchestra in Berlin. Lady Julia had been led to believe that Josephine Baker would be there, but hadn't realised that all eight of her dancers would accompany her. This information changed the dynamics of her mission entirely. Was London aware of this? she wondered.

As she continued to listen to Fufu talking about the ups and downs of her life since they both left La Alpina, principally downs it appeared, she considered the implications of such a large group travelling to Berlin, and the complications this could bring in the event that the intelligence reports were accurate.

By the time Fufu left a short while later at 4.00am, she had decided that her next course of action must be to inform the department in London as soon as possible and seek their direction on the changing situation. She must make contact with the embassy immediately.

Chapter 15

The two men woke early. The sun was barely up as they left the Hotel Meurice and walked the short distance to the train station.

The first train to Arras departed at 04.30. It was essential, if the two men were to conclude their business and return to Calais before the train for Paris left at 14.00, that they were on time; but this was a discipline that was ingrained in both of them.

They marched in silence through the near deserted streets of Calais, each deep in his own thoughts. The clanking of churns on an early morning milk cart startled them as they rounded the corner of Rue Napoleon and they instinctively ducked inside a roadside café.

The Gare de Fontinette was only a short distance from the hotel and as they turned the corner on to the Rue du Gare, they were grateful to see the steam rising above the station buildings. The engine of the Chemins de Fer-Nord railway company was waiting patiently to welcome them.

They purchased their tickets from a sleepy ticket master and boarded the train at 04.20 as planned.

The train was all but deserted and they were able to secure seats in a 2nd class carriage by themselves for the short journey.

The station master blew his whistle and the carriages shuddered as the brake was released and the ancient train jerked forward. The wheels spun and there was an alarming rusty squeal from the bogies below the carriage containing the two men as it lurched on its poorly maintained suspension out of the station.

'Some things never change, Sir,' one of the men said.

'1917,' replied his companion.

'Without shells, Sir!'

'Be thankful for that sergeant, but for how long?'

'We may confirm that in a few weeks, Sir.'

'We shall see Sergeant. We shall see.'

As the train moved through the outskirts of Calais and on into the French countryside, both men fell silent as they looked out of the window at the changed landscape.

The scars of war were barely visible now in the fields and roads around Calais. The train began to pick up a little speed, but nothing to rival the Flèche

D'Or, as the two men began to contemplate their agenda for the days ahead. Whilst the scars on the French countryside had been repaired, the scars in their minds could not be so easily erased.

The train to Arras was direct and the journey passed quickly. After only 30 minutes, the two men saw the town of Arras appear on the horizon before them. The sun was now above the tree line making them blink and shield their eyes as they observed the scaffolding still surrounding many of the buildings.

The famous XIII century bell tower had been almost completely destroyed by German cannon fire in the war. Thanks in no small part to the reparations payments that were crippling the German government the tower was now being restored. The XVIII century Cathédrale Notre-Dame-et-Saint-Vaast d'Arras, which had also been destroyed during the fighting, was also surrounded by scaffolding as it underwent a substantial rebuilding programme.

The train lurched alarmingly as the brakes were applied to bring it to a stop beside the crumbling façade of the Gare D'Arras. The station would also benefit from some restoration work, although whether the crumbling station buildings, pitted as they were by bullet holes, were truly the victims of war or of simple neglect was hard to determine.

They showed their return tickets to a disinterested station master as they passed through the station building and onto the Boulevard Vauban. Waiting by the side of the road was an ancient looking Renault taxi.

Looking at the age, and condition of the vehicle there was every chance that it could have been one of the original Parisian taxis requisitioned by the French government to transport their troops to the Battle of Marne in September 1914.

Their suspicions were heightened when the driver appeared from the station café. He was unaccustomed to collecting passengers at this time of day and had just ordered his morning coffee as the two men appeared from the station.

He was a little happier when the men requested transportation to Faubourg D'Amiens. Only 2 km; he could be there and back before his coffee went cold.

The suspension of the Renault was not much better than that of the train journey, and the two men felt quite nauseous as the vehicle swayed alarmingly from side to side as it bounced along the cobbled streets.

They bounced their way through the first of Arras's two squares, Le Grand Place. All the buildings here were covered in scaffolding it seemed. It was difficult as the taxi continued to weave its way through the square to distinguish whether any of the buildings were actually occupied.

In Le Petit Place the market stalls were being erected as they had been each week since the XII century. The bright colours of the new season's vegetables and the bright blooms of flowers were in stark contrast to the scaffolding that once again adorned nearly all the surrounding structures.

Arras was a town that knew the scars of war. A city of XI century origin being completely rebuilt in the 20th century.

The two men heaved a huge sigh of relief as the white marble entrance of the Faubourg D'Amiens Cemetery wobbled into view. The driver fought to keep control of the taxi as its tyres struggled to maintain its grip on the early morning cobbled streets.

After paying the driver, the two men stood in silence at the entrance to the cemetery whilst they recovered their sense of balance. There were no people on the street at this time of day to see them slip solemnly into the citadel or to observe the tears that both had in their eyes.

They had not visited the cemetery before. But perhaps it should have been very familiar to them. After all, both of them had graves here.

Captain Charles Smith M.C, D.S.O, D.F.O, formerly of the Kings Own Royal Fusiliers and latterly the Royal Flying Corps looked down at the pure white of the Portland marble headstone that bore his name. He was taken by the bright colours of the alternate winter pansies and marigolds that filled the border in front of the grave marker which stood out against the white of the marble.

The early morning sun had now risen high enough to illuminate the inscription that bore his name.

The inscription confirmed that he had been killed near Arras 7th April 1917.

A few rows away Sergeant Perkins, formerly of the Lancashire Regiment was also looking down at an inscription.

It read Sergeant John W Perkins M.M, D.C.M, 11th South Lancashire Regiment. Killed near Arras 17th May 1917.

They both knew that the grave markers were here, but to actually see them in the flesh was an experience that aroused a mixture of emotions.

They knew that the graves were devoid of bodies. When they had been recruited they had known that it would be necessary to go through the charade of a funeral; to make their loved ones, and the rest of the world believe that they had succumbed to their wounds from the battlefield.

The documents presented by the war office to their next of kin had shown that although both men had been recovered from the battlefield with gunshot wounds. They had in fact died from their injuries in a field hospital in Calais. Both had been taken to the hospital set up in the Hotel Meurice, which is where they had first met.

The men had served with distinction and had been recognised and suitably decorated for outstanding gallantry on a number of occasions.

Their identities and distinguished records had been brought to the attention of Lieutenant General Sir Charles Carruthers who was recruiting for a special force that would form the basis of post-war covert operations around Europe. Smith and Perkins would make excellent recruits. Not only were both men outstandingly brave and efficient soldiers, they were also proficient in French and German.

Sombrely the two men made their way quietly back to the entry gate.

'The French keep the place looking smart for us Sir' said Perkins as he opened the gate for his commanding officer to pass through.

'Indeed they do Sergeant. I believe that we can be proud of our last resting place.'

They closed the gate and turned to march smartly back towards the Gare D'Arras where they expected the train would be waiting to take them back to Calais. They had no wish to risk another taxi ride, not that there were any taxis on hand to be hailed. 15 minutes later after a brisk walk in the early morning sunshine they nodded to the driver as they passed once more through the portal of the train station.

The taxi driver sat contentedly, a yellow Gitanes Mais hanging precariously from the corner of his mouth. He was enjoying his third cup of tar black coffee and ignored his earlier passengers as they passed him. His Renault taxi was innocently waiting at the curb side for its next victims.

The train engine had been turned around and was waiting stoically for them to return. As they resumed their seats, the station master blew his whistle and the train groaned its way noisily and reluctantly away from the platform.

In the quiet peace of the cemetery two graves had acquired new adornments. The cap badges of two regiments had been placed carefully and respectfully on top of the grave markers.

Chapter 16

'Good Morning Sir. Breakfast has been ordered for 9.30am and Lady Julia will join you, as requested, Sir.'

The party in the Ritz bar had finished a little after 4.00 am and dutifully, Harry had remained by Jimmy V's side to the very end. He had earlier ensured that breakfast would be served at a time most appropriate for what he knew would be the late finish to the previous evening.

He often marvelled at the stamina of the young Viscount, for whom four hours' sleep was sufficient on most occasions. He was sure that at some point in the future Jimmy V would slow his hectic pace, but for now there was no sign of that. From Harry's point of view he sometimes struggled to manage with so little sleep, however, he knew that on this occasion he needed to remain alert.

'Splendid Harry. I will shower.'

'Very good, Sir'

The Versailles Suite was one of the first in Paris to be fitted with an en-suite shower cubicle within its bathroom. Jimmy V had very little experience of using such a facility and it was several minutes before he could work out the intricacies required to ensure a steady flow of water. As for regulating the temperature? That was proving to be more troublesome.

Harry smiled to himself at the activities going on in the bathroom, as he imagined his employer wrestling with the new technology. Several minutes passed before he heard the door of the shower cubicle open and then a high pitched yelp, as the near freezing water cascaded down on top of him.

Harry's amusement was cut short by a gentle knock on the door.

'Good morning, Ma'am. Breakfast is prepared in the salon. Viscount James will join you presently.' Harry nodded his head to Lady Julia and smiled at Mary as they entered the room.

'Is James wrestling with the new shower contraption Harry?'

'I am afraid that he is Ma'am.'

'In that case could you pour me a cup of coffee please Harry. We may be waiting a while.'

'Indeed Ma'am,' Harry smiled.

'I have arranged a breakfast tray for Mary and myself on the balcony Ma'am. With your permission.'

Harry had placed a silver tray with a light breakfast on a small table on the hotel balcony overlooking the Place de Vendome. The vista from the balcony was magnificent. The Tower of Vendome stood in the centre of the square topped with its statue of Napoleon looking out sternly over Paris. Beyond the tower and along the Rue de Castiglione were the entrance gates to the splendour of the Jardin des Tullleries. Even from this distance, the vibrant colours of the plants sparkled like giant gemstones reflecting the early morning sunlight and Harry considered how pleasant it might be to walk through the gardens with Mary.

He turned as he heard the door of the bathroom open behind him and watched the trembling figure of Jimmy V, draped in a large hotel towel, walk quickly to his bedroom.

'Ma'am if you would excuse me. I will inform Viscount James that you have arrived.' Harry handed Lady Julia her coffee and left the room.

As Harry closed the door, Lady Julia turned to Mary.

'Mary, it is essential that I visit Rue du Faubourg Saint-Honoré as soon as possible. Could you make the necessary arrangements please?

Perhaps you could arrange for a convenient dress fitting with Mme Chanel?'

'Certainly Ma'am, I will telephone immediately.'

'Excellent Mary. What would I do without you?'

Mary nodded and left to make the required telephone calls.

A few moments later Harry opened the salon door and allowed Jimmy V to enter.

'Harry, I am afraid that I had completely forgotten that I had plans for a dress fitting with Mme Chanel this morning. I have asked Mary to confirm the arrangements, she will return presently.'

'Very good, Ma'am'.

Jimmy V was dressed in a vibrant royal blue dressing gown, monogrammed on the breast pocket with the Stanley family crest.

'Ladybee, how splendid you look this morning,' said a beaming Jimmy V.

'How was the shower James?'

'Splendid, my dear. Simply splendid. I intend to get one fitted at Stanley House as soon as possible,' he replied a little too ebulliently.

Lady Julia and Harry looked at each other as they observed that Jimmy V had something of a ruddy glow this morning. Surely not as a result of overly heated water?

'I thought we might take a stroll in the Tuilleries this morning, what do you think?'

'That sounds lovely James. Unfortunately I think that my dress fitting with Mme Chanel will take up much of the morning.'

'I could accompany you if you wish?'

'James! I know how much you detest shopping. Fittings can be so tiresome and I would hate to see you simply sitting around waiting for me. I am sure that you have far more important things to do. We shall meet for lunch. Perhaps in the Café Renard? Now, shall we breakfast?'

'Splendid idea.'

Harry poured the coffee and verified his count at 6, and the time had not yet reached 10 o'clock.

Chapter 17

Paris was sparkling with early morning life. Legions of people were scurrying along in the hazy sunshine, some returning from the previous evening's revelries, whilst others were appropriately dressed in preparation for a day's work.

The pavement cafés emitted a heady aroma of cigarette smoke and coffee, the mixture seeming to saturate the atmosphere like an all pervading mist.

The calm of the morning was punctuated by the cacophony of car horns angrily sounding off in every conceivable pitch, as commuters fought with the taxi drivers seeking their early morning fares.

The taxis seemed to hover like a swarm of bees circling a flowering bush. As soon as a driver caught sight of what he thought might be an outstretched hand, or a hotel concierge approaching the pavement, he would swoop down with little regard for however many lanes of traffic he had to navigate through, or however many cars he had to cut in front of.

Lady Julia and Mary descended in the hotel lift, dressed ready for a day's shopping in the Parisian boutiques. Behind the charade, Lady Julia was deep in thought. She needed to fully order the events of the previous evening before her hastily arranged meeting.

In the Versailles suite, Jimmy V was happy to listen to his records and peruse the early morning edition of Le Figaro. Lady Julia had left him with a copy of her new magazine, The Melody Maker. She was now convinced that should be its title and had decided to ask Jimmy V for his opinion. He was looking forward to reading it, particularly after Lady Julia had informed him that he was in it.

Harry was busy tidying away the breakfast dishes ready for their collection by the hotel maid. He looked at the untouched tray he had prepared for himself and Mary and sighed heavily. There would be other occasions he knew, but he couldn't hide his disappointment that Mary had not had time to return after making her telephone calls.

As the two ladies passed through the foyer, Lady Julia was struck by how busy it was so early in the morning. Every table seemed to be covered in coffee cups and surrounded by groups of men deep in conversation. For once, they seemed to largely ignore the striking figure of Lady Julia as she passed through and out into the early morning sunshine. Out of sight in a corner of the room, however, her departure did not go unnoticed.

'Lady Mortimer, how pleasant to see you this morning.' A beaming Georges Lepidus greeted her as she appeared outside the hotel.

It seemed M. Lepidus was constantly on duty. She smiled as she considered the disappointment he must have felt, after Josephine Baker informed him he would miss her show. Perhaps he would use the additional money she now placed in his hand to buy his wife a new hat?

A melee of shouts from irate drivers suddenly erupted, with a myriad of gestures and a collection of car horns as Georges lifted his right arm to summon a cab.

'Do you require a taxi, Madame?' enquired Georges politely, as several cars drew up by the pavement outside the hotel.

'Yes please, Georges. We wish to go to the boutique of Madame Chanel.'

'La Rue Cambon!' Georges barked out, as the driver of the first taxi opened the door for Lady Julia to enter.

Behind him, two men left the hotel and walked nonchalantly towards the Place de Vendome.

Georges smiled as he waved the taxi on its way and carefully added another 10 franc note to his growing bundle. He was bitterly disappointed not to be able to see Josephine Baker. He wondered whether he might spend his gratuity windfall on a new coat for Mme Lepidus, perhaps that would make her more amenable? After careful thought, he decided that his money would be far better spent on an evening's entertainment at the Folie Bergere instead.

Lady Julia and Mary sat in silence as the taxi weaved its way manically through the streets of Paris. Periodically, their thoughts were interrupted by the driver's horn as he vented his anger at one or more of his colleagues, when they swarmed across in front of him to answer a hail from the pavement.

There were several narrow escapes on the relatively short journey but eventually, and thankfully in one piece, the taxi pulled into the Rue de Faubourg. As soon as the taxi had pulled away from the hotel, Lady Julia had informed the driver of their new destination. Although she had no reason to doubt the discretion of Georges Lepidus, she was far too cautious and experienced to take any chances.

The taxi came to a stop outside No.39 and the driver opened the door to allow his passengers to alight. Lady Julia climbed the three small steps and entered the building. Mary followed her after a brief pause to pay the driver. The fare for the short journey was only 2 francs, but Mary handed the driver a 10 franc note in return for an assurance that should anyone ask, he had delivered them safely to the Rue Cambon.

As the taxi buzzed away from the pavement to the usual accompaniment of several horns, Mary turned and prepared to walk the short distance to Mme Chanel's boutique, where she had arranged to collect a number of new outfits that had been ordered some weeks previously.

Lady Julia looked up at the splendour of the entrance hall to the British Embassy. She marvelled at how grand the building looked with its ornate plaster work and sweeping staircase. So in keeping with its purpose.

On the wall to her left was a full length portrait of King George V in his military splendour, looking down with an all seeing eye. Following the contours of the wall she saw a familiar portrait of the Duke of Wellington astride his horse, Copenhagen.

Formally the Hotel de Charost, the magnificent building that now stood as the British

Embassy had been the residency of the Duke of Wellington, who had acquired the house and gardens from Pauline Borghese, the sister of Napoleon, as a result of his appointment as the British Ambassador to France in 1814.

Lady Julia had been here several times in the past and strode purposefully towards an oak panelled door to the left of the grand staircase. Without breaking stride or knocking, she opened the door and disappeared inside.

A small man in an ill-fitting suit rose as Lady Julia entered the room. Acknowledging her arrival from behind the large oak and red leather inlaid desk, the man nodded his head politely. Lady Julia smiled as she thought how odd he looked behind such a large desk, almost Lilliputian.

'Lady Mortimer, I will inform Sir Charles that you have arrived. Please take a seat.'

As she looked around, she studied the collection of paintings and drawings that adorned the walls of the small waiting room. Although she had been in the room on a number of occasions before, she hadn't noticed what an eclectic mix of subjects decorated the small space. She recognised a fine landscape painting which she believed could be by

Charles Howard Hodges. Her father had a number of his works in the drawing room of his country house.

There was a fine portrait of a soldier in full battle uniform, which looked to her to be in the style of Thomas Gainsborough. Bizarrely, next to this was an engraving from Punch magazine by Archibald Henning, depicting a number of men arguing over a map of some sort.

As she was contemplating what the map could be, the official returned.

'Sir Charles will see you now, Lady Mortimer.' He stepped aside to allow Lady Julia to pass through into a long corridor leading to a single open door.

The walls of the corridor were covered with yet more paintings depicting sea battles and 18th century warships in full sail.

'Lady Julia, how pleasant it is to see you. Please take a seat.'

General Sir Charles Carruthers was a very tall former Grenadier Guardsman. Standing at over 6' 6'' he was one of the few men, other than Harry Pratt, to tower over Lady Julia. He stood proudly to attention in the centre of the room as Lady Julia entered. He was a man who commanded respect with his sheer physical presence.

'Sir Charles, thank you for seeing me.'

Lady Julia took a seat and began to recount her conversation and her concerns from the previous evening. It was clear that Sir Charles had been unaware of the change of arrangements relating to Berlin. He listened intently as Lady Julia listed the number of people that were now making up the party, tapping his fingers together in a pyramid in front of his face.

'I share your concerns.'

A few seconds passed in silence as he considered his next statement.

'You were quite right to bring this to my attention. I will need to communicate the changed dynamics of the operation to our men in the field.

At this stage I don't believe that we can cancel arrangements without needlessly exposing ourselves,' continued Sir Charles,

'But we will certainly need to ensure that our assets on the ground are made fully aware.'

Lady Julia nodded.

'I will make arrangements to contact Smith and Perkins immediately upon their arrival in Paris. Would you care for tea, my dear?'

Lady Julia smiled as she considered that no matter what the crisis, the British always assumed a cup of Darjeeling would help in its solution.

***

Mary collected a number of new outfits from Mme Chanel and settled the account with the boutique. As she looked out of the large first floor window, she noticed two men casually leaning against the wall of a café. The taller of the men had what appeared to be a crescent shaped duelling scar on his right cheek, just below his right eye. His companion was shorter and far less athletic in build. Mary was struck by the fact that both men wore large overcoats and had hats pulled down over their eyes. Given the current weather conditions in Paris, their dress seemed to be wholly inappropriate.

The demeanour of the men as they tried to look inconspicuous made her deeply suspicious. She looked through the net curtains at them for several minutes whilst waiting for the shop assistant to return. Neither man was carrying bags of any nature. They didn't fit in to the category of either curious tourist, or interested window shopper. The Rue Cambon was home to a number of ladies' boutiques, but they didn't give the impression they were waiting for the return of any female companions.

Mary decided that as a precaution she would leave the apartment by the rear exit. She knew from having studied the street plan of Paris this led onto Rue Duphot, the exit being by the side of the Hotel Burgundy. After settling the account, Mary looked out of the window once more. The two men had disappeared. Perhaps her suspicions were unfounded? She looked along the street for any sign they could have moved. Protruding from under a pavement café canopy some distance away, she saw what she thought was the trouser leg of the taller man.

Perhaps it was all in her imagination? Perhaps the two men were tourists after all? Perhaps they were window shopping for gifts for their wives, or mistresses? Whatever, she would leave by the rear exit regardless.

In the Café de Cambon, the two men ordered coffee and continued their surveillance, hoping that their presence had gone unnoticed.

Chapter 18

The return journey from Arras to Calais had passed without incident and in near silence, as Smith and Perkins peered out of the carriage window alone with their own thoughts.

They now sat aboard the Flèche D'Or as it made its way to Paris. With no need for secrecy, they had decided to upgrade their tickets to first class and were enjoying the comfort afforded by the luxurious armchairs in the Pullman carriages.

On arriving back at Calais, they had been surprised to find the station master greeting them with an important telegram he had received from Paris.

According to the telegram, the uncle of Charles Smith had been taken seriously ill and he should proceed with all haste on his arrival in Paris to visit him. The station master had been most concerned that he sought out the correct passenger in order to convey the message, and was pleased with himself when through using his initiative, he had identified the two Englishmen. The fact that they were the only Englishmen travelling in First Class on the train that day didn't concern him. Charles Smith had shown suitable concern for the welfare of his uncle.

'What do you think the old man wants, Sir?' enquired Perkins.

'Our orders were quite clear when we left London.'

'I have no idea Sergeant. Clearly there must be a change of arrangements of some significance to warrant Sir Charles not only breaking with protocol, but also being in Paris.'

'Perhaps the mission has been compromised, Sir? I have taken the liberty of placing my service revolver in my hand luggage.'

'Great minds think alike, Perkins. When we arrive in Paris, we will proceed to the embassy immediately before checking into the hotel.'

'Tea, Sir?'

'Certainly, Perkins. I think I will have a cup of Earl Grey? With lemon of course.'

Chapter 19

Mary arrived at the Café Renard in good time to meet Lady Julia. Anticipating the imminent arrival of Harry and Jimmy V, she quickly relayed her suspicions regarding the two men she believed had been watching out for her on the Rue Cambon. Lady Julia acknowledged her quick thinking and shared her anxiety regarding the purpose of their presence outside Mme Chanel's apartment.

'I feel certain they were waiting for the two of us to appear, Ma'am.'

'I suspect you may be right, Mary'

'Right about what, my dear?'

Jimmy V had appeared from nowhere as the two ladies discussed the morning's events.

'The colour of one of my new outfits, James. It is simply divine. I feel that I should wear it this evening to dinner. Mary, however, thinks it is best kept until we reach Berlin.'

'Splendid, my dear. I am sure that you will come to the right decision. Do they serve Blue Mountain at this café?'

Jimmy V was quite content with Lady Julia's response to his question and the conversation quickly moved on to how pleasant a morning he had spent, listening to his records. Lady Julia in the meantime was still thinking about Mary's experience. Were the men simply tourists or eager to please husbands? Her instincts told her that both scenarios were unlikely. She was gratified with the quick thinking and observation skills of her maid. Clearly the training that she had been giving had paid off. She hoped this had ensured her absence from the dress fitting had gone unnoticed.

'Julia! What a pleasant surprise to see you here.' Turning towards the direction from which the voice emanated, Lady Julia was surprised to see Fufu Lamore walking towards her on the arm of a rather tall and distinguished looking French cavalry officer.

'Charles, may I introduce you to an old school friend of mine, Lady Julia Mortimer, and her companion from London, Viscount James Stanley.'

'The pleasure is indeed mine, Mademoiselle Mortimer; Viscount Stanley.' The officer came to attention and politely bowed his head, before shaking hands with the couple in turn.

'Would you care to join us for some refreshments?' suggested Jimmy V, indicating a number of chairs that were free in the café.

'I am afraid that will not be possible,' began Fufu. 'Unfortunately, the Commandant has received an urgent call to re-join his regiment. They are departing within the hour. Lord knows when I shall see him again.'

'Such is the life of a soldier,' replied the Commandant.

'I was so hoping that we would be able to spend some time together today before I have to leave for Berlin. Particularly with Madame De Gaulle visiting her mother,' continued Fufu.

Lady Julia smiled. How refreshingly honest and Bohemian Fufu had become.

'Seemed like a pleasant enough chap?' Jimmy V announced, as the couple took their leave and headed off towards the Gare de l'Est.

'He had the most extraordinary nose! Reminded me of one of those statues we saw when we visited Rome. Very Julius Caesar. Don't you think Ladybee?'

Lady Julia smiled as she watched the couple walking arm in arm along the path leading from the gardens. She thought they seemed remarkably comfortable in one another's company. She looked across the table at Jimmy V and sighed fondly as she saw him trying to decipher the hand-written menu.

Harry stood silently behind them, watching proceedings. Rather than listening to Jimmy V's endless array of jazz records, he had spent the morning more productively, by ensuring that all the travel arrangements were in order for their departure to Berlin later in the day.

He had confirmed by telephone the first class sleeping compartment for Jimmy V, with a separate compartment next door for himself. The Compagnie Internationale des Wagons-lits train was scheduled to depart from the Gare de l'Est at 7.30pm. It would then travel through the night, taking a little over 12 hours to complete the journey to Berlin.

Harry had made similar arrangements for Lady Julia and Mary.

'Lady Julia, would you permit me to escort Mary back to the Hotel with your parcels?'

'What an excellent suggestion Harry. I am sure that Mary would be very glad of the assistance.'

'Sir, if you would excuse me?'

'Splendid suggestion Harry. Ladybee and I will be perfectly happy to wander back later. It's a splendid day for having a stroll around the gardens. I can't seem to find Blue Mountain on the menu my dear. Will Café de Jamaique Bleu suffice?'

'That will do nicely, James.'

Chapter 20

The birds were singing lustily as Harry and Mary wandered along the avenues of the Jardin des Tuileries. The street artistes were busy plying their trade with a succession of acrobats and tumblers vying unsuccessfully for the couple's attention, as they walked along oblivious to their presence.

Harry found it very easy to talk to Mary and he was greatly enjoying their time together. As they passed the Arc du Carrousel, he suddenly sensed a tension creeping into her responses.

'Are you all right Mary?' enquired Harry, concerned that he had offended her in some way.

'I am fine, thank you Harry. Just a little tired perhaps. It has been a long morning, after a rather late night.'

'I quite understand,' replied Harry, although his senses told him that there was far more to it.

Standing quietly in the shadows of the central archway of the Arc de Carrousel, two men looked on.

Mary couldn't be certain. It was only a fleeting glimpse out of the corner of her eye as she approached from le Grand Allee, but she was convinced she had seen two figures lurking in the shadow of the Napoleon monument as they had passed by. Were they the same men she had seen on the Rue Cambon? She had sensed that she was being watched as she approached, but perhaps it was her imagination?

It was possible that the figures were staring at Harry, after all he was such a striking figure. There weren't too many 6'5'' black men wandering around the streets of Paris accompanying a petite ladies' maid, carrying parcels from a ladies' boutique.

Harry knew that Mary was troubled by something, but didn't believe they were in any immediate danger in such a public place. He was more than capable, and quite happy to deal with any danger, should it arise.

They left the park by the west gate. On passing the statue of Mercury riding the winged horse Pegasus, Mary chanced a look back. She was relieved to see that there was no sign of them being followed.

Harry hailed a taxi, which immediately screamed to a halt beside them amid the customary volley of horns. Mary quickly sought sanctuary in the rear seat, as Harry handed her the various packages he had been carrying.

As the taxi pulled back into the flow of traffic on the Place du Carrousel, eliciting yet another chorus of derision, Mary once again looked anxiously out of the window. There was a sea of faces coming and going from the park, but she was confident that none of them were familiar to her.

Mary relaxed into her seat as the taxi moved onto the Rue de Rivoli. Although if she were being honest, the available space left for her after Harry had folded himself into the back of the Unic taxi left little room for comfort. With the various parcels that were stacked inside, she was thankful that the journey back to the hotel was a short one.

***

In Café Renard, Lady Julia had ensured that Jimmy V had received a large pot of Blue Mountain coffee and they were now sitting looking out over the magnificent gardens with its array of beautiful colours shining brightly in the early afternoon sunshine. She observed fondly the contentment on his face, as he sampled his favourite brew.

'Remember James. You promised to accompany me to Le Louvre. I think it is time that we made our way there.'

'Splendid, Ladybee. It's a pity we must leave this evening. I was reading about a terrific new show at the Folies Bergère by Paul Derval. According to the paper, the orchestra is quite marvellous. Perhaps we can catch it on our way back?'

'Perhaps we can James,' replied Lady Julia with a smile. She considered the proposal with an inward grin. After seeing Jimmy V's discomfort the previous evening at the lack of clothing in Josephine Baker's performance, what would he make of the total nudity on show at the Folies Bergère?

'I believe that Le Louvre has some new exhibits from Egypt on show.'

'Splendid. I do hope they don't carry the same curse that saw off Caernarvon? We did warn him that he was playing a dangerous game. Didn't we?'

'You did James. But I believe these exhibits have arrived from a different site in Egypt. I feel certain that we will be safe.'

Jimmy V paid a very appreciative waiter, who gratefully acknowledged the sizeable gratuity given to him.

The walk to Le Louvre took them along the same path trodden by Harry and Mary earlier. The acrobats and street entertainers were still in abundance, although somewhat more weary. Jimmy V was intrigued by the knife juggler. He spent several minutes observing the various bandages on his hands and wrists which seemed to indicate the level of his competence. He couldn't help thinking that perhaps the chap should consider an alternative career.

Jimmy V threw a generous number of coins onto the collection mat to give the man a start. This clearly took the hapless performer by surprise as he miscalculated his next throw and narrowly escaped severing several toes. Lady Julia decided that it was advisable they left quickly, before he could cause any more damage.

They passed through the central arch of the Arc du Carousel and looked out onto the Louvre Palace. Lady Julia always marvelled at the magnificence of the building with its renaissance architecture which almost screamed of the treasures that it contained. Jimmy V was not enamoured at the prospect of staring endlessly at a succession of paintings, and yet more Egyptian artefacts. He had acquired several valuable pieces of his own of course, on their trip there. They all seemed to blend into one after a while, but he had made the promise, and he knew his place.

For Lady Julia, he would spend an afternoon in the company of great works of art, and make the appropriate noises of appreciation when required.

As the couple made their way over the cobbles of the Place du Louvre there was a cacophony of sound from the Rue du Carrousel behind them. Yet another Unic taxi had pulled across several lanes of traffic to answer a hail from the pavement.

Chapter 21

'I trust that you had a pleasant afternoon, Sir?'

'Splendid Harry. All of the paintings appear to be precisely where they were on my last visit. All is in perfect order. The Mona Lisa is still moaning, the Virgin remains by the Rocks. The Sphinx still guards room 1 of the Egyptian collection. The mummies, I am pleased to say, are still safely wrapped in room 30. The new exhibits appear to be remarkably similar to the old exhibits. All inspected and confirmed.'

'I have dispatched our luggage to the station, Sir. Your trombone, of course, and travelling clothes are laid out in your room. Shall I prepare tea?' Harry struggled to contain his amusement at the thought of Jimmy V being dragged around the Louvre by Lady Julia.

He knew that she would have ensured they visited every corner of the museum. She was greatly interested in art, of course. Her private collection of paintings and that of her father contained dozens of important and valuable works by many artists. However, having had to endure several hours of jazz records on their journey to Paris, he knew she would have taken the opportunity to fully exact her revenge on her companion. Jimmy V was far too much of a gentleman to have complained even the slightest during the ordeal.

'Tea would be splendid. I shall change and shower immediately. ' Jimmy V trudged to his room.

Harry decided that it was perhaps wisest to wait a while before deciding to prepare the tea. An audible cry of surprise shortly afterwards confirmed the correctness of his decision. Whether the water was too hot or too cold was difficult to decide, but the noises emanating from the direction of the bathroom confirmed that battle was once again being waged with the new apparatus.

Mary had decided in anticipation of her mistress' return to prepare a bath for her. She heard the sound of the door handle shake and the room door begin to open behind her. Despite the fact that she was expecting her mistress back at any moment, she was nonetheless quite relieved when she appeared.

'I have dispatched our luggage to the Gare de L'Est, Ma'am. Did you have a pleasant afternoon?'

'Most enjoyable Mary, thank you. I believe that Viscount James will be far too weary to delay our slumber on the train this evening.' With a grin of deep satisfaction Lady Julia removed her hat and gloves and handed them to her maid.

'Shall I prepare tea or do you wish to bathe first, Ma'am?'

'I will bathe first of all, thank you. So much dust in the Egyptian exhibits.' Lady Julia made her way to her bedroom where Mary had neatly laid out her travelling clothes.

'An interesting day to say the least, Mary. I am still most concerned about your encounter this morning. I do believe that the two gentlemen in question may also have followed myself and Viscount James to the Louvre. I couldn't be certain, but from the descriptions that you gave me it would appear quite plausible.'

'Did they follow you into the museum, Ma'am?' enquired Mary, with some unease in her voice.

'I don't believe they did. I think that they hailed a taxi and departed once they had confirmed our final destination.'

After a short pause whilst she removed her attire, Lady Julia spoke again.

'I am most concerned that we take all appropriate precautions on our journey to Berlin. Please ensure that word is sent to the embassy with regard to today's events. You know how.'

'Yes Ma'am. I shall prepare a message immediately.'

***

Smith and Perkins arrived in Paris shortly after 2pm and as planned, travelled to meet General Carruthers at the embassy. They sat in the General's office with a sense of unease as he briefed them in detail on the information conveyed to him earlier in the day. There was a knock at the door which caused the General to pause.

'Sir, my apologies for the intrusion but I have an urgent message for you from our man at the Ritz.'

A tall, immaculately dressed young man had appeared at the door to the office and clicked to attention, before handing a sealed envelope to the General.

The young man was wearing the shiniest pair of shoes that Charles Smith had ever seen. They had the appearance of a pair he recalled seeing on a recent visit to Harrods of Knightsbridge. With a price tag of several hundred pounds, he'd decided that he would resist the temptation to purchase them. Even from across the room, he could see the contours of his own face reflecting back. Quite extraordinary he thought to himself. Perhaps the salaries at the embassy were far greater than he had imagined, or more likely, the young man had independent means.

'Thank you Quentin.' The young man nodded and left without making eye contact with either Smith or Perkins. Quentin? Thought Smith. Another Cambridge type.

General Carruthers carefully read the coded message. Judging from his expression, it was not good news.

Looking up from the page he broke the silence.

'It would appear that the activities of our people have been drawing some unwanted attention, gentlemen. Nevertheless, we shall go ahead as planned.'

Both men nodded in agreement. They knew there was no point asking the General about the contents of the new message. He alone would decide what they needed to know and as soldiers they must accept and trust his judgement.

'Gentlemen, your train departs at 7pm from the Gare de L'Est. Your travel arrangements remain unaltered.'

It was clear the meeting was now at an end and the two agents prepared to take their leave.

'Gentlemen, the continued security and peace in Europe may rest in your hands. I have every confidence that you will act accordingly, regardless of the complications, and ensure a fully successful conclusion to your mission.'

'Thank you, Sir,' responded both men, as they nodded a salute and left the room.

General Carruthers reread the note he had received. He carefully tore the message into small strips and placed the pieces in the bronze ashtray on his desk. He lit the corner of the last piece and watched the flame slowly consume the pile of paper in front of him. His men knew the risks the life they led entailed. There was no need to over burden them with the new information that he had just received. He had every confidence they would deal with matters as they saw fit.

Chapter 22

Jimmy V and Harry waited patiently in the lobby of the Ritz. Harry had arranged with Mary that the party would travel together to the Gare de l'Est. After Mary's experiences earlier in the day, the suggestion had met with instant approval.

As the hotel clock moved to 5.45, Jimmy V consulted his father's Girard-Perregaux wrist watch. The watch had been one of the few things recovered from the ruins of the Chateau Rosendal, following his father's untimely death.

It had been returned to him by the war office along with several of his father's IOU's, and the charred remains of his final poker hand. Ironically, he had held a pair of black eights and aces, the so called 'dead man's hand'.

Looking around the lobby he caught sight of Ernest Hemingway once more making his way towards the hotel bar. He was arm in arm with his companion, the journalist Pauline Pfeiffer. From behind, he heard familiar footsteps approaching across the marble floor.

'James, I hope we haven't delayed you too long?'

'Certainly not, my dear. Fashionably late as always. Shall we?'

Jimmy V held out his arm, which Lady Julia gladly accepted.

'Harry, I think that Ladybee and I shall travel together. Perhaps you would be kind enough to accompany Mary?'

'Certainly, Sir.'

'Splendid!'

'23,' whispered Lady Julia as she passed Harry, who nodded knowingly in response.

Georges Lepidus tried to hide his clear disappointment at the imminent departure of one of his more lucrative income streams. At Harry's request he reluctantly, but efficiently hailed the required taxis and waved the party on their way, carefully putting what he believed to be 10 francs in his pocket.

Closer inspection later lightened his mood as he unfolded a 50 franc note. He smiled to himself as he considered that his planned excursion to the Folies Bergère would be even more pleasant than he could have imagined. Madame Lepidus would also be getting her new coat.

***

Smith and Perkins, after leaving the British Embassy by the rear exit, spent the remainder of a rather pleasant Parisian afternoon visiting a number of tourist spots. Neither man had visited the city before, so they decided to take advantage of the opportunity that now presented itself. Just like regular tourists, they visited the Arc de Triomphe, the Eiffel Tower and finally Notre Dame.

Although the train to Berlin was not due to depart until 7.00pm, they decided it would be best to arrive well ahead of the departure time to lessen the chances of being seen. In order to avoid the necessity of visiting the buffet car during the long journey ahead, they purchased adequate food supplies whilst they were sightseeing. Without checking into their hotel as previously planned they arrived at the Gare de L'Est at 5.30pm.

The train was already waiting by the platform as they anticipated and after presenting their tickets to the platform guard, they were shown to their compartment by an overly eager carriage attendant.

The attendant assured them of his full attention during the journey. Should they require his services, nothing would be too much trouble, he asserted, as he proceeded to open the door to compartment 6c and stood expectantly as the two men took up occupancy.

'Merci beaucoup,' said Perkins as he closed the compartment door, almost trapping the outstretched hand of the expectant attendant in the process.

The deflated guard muttered a number of expletives under his breath and returned to his position at the head of the carriage to await the arrival of his next guests, who he hoped would be more generous. He decided that should the light from 6c show on his panel at any point in the journey, it would go unanswered.

***

The station clock was showing 5.45pm as two men approached the ticket barrier and presented their tickets to the platform guard.

They carried matching leather attaché cases, held firmly together by looped and buckled straps. The platform guard identified them immediately as travelling salesmen. He had seen thousands of similarly dressed men during his unfulfilled career on the railways. 'Guess the Occupation' was a game he liked to play. It helped to pass the time as he sat in his cramped, cell-like cubicle, watching the world pass him by.

As a small boy, he had dreamt of having a career as a train driver, but by an ironic twist of fate he discovered that he suffered from chronic motion sickness. With a deep sigh he motioned the two men on board and instructed them to proceed to carriage 6.

The carriage attendant greeted the two men with little of his customary enthusiasm. He too played the occupation game and knew instantly that there would be slim pickings from these gentlemen. He politely showed them to compartment 6d and opened the door for them to enter.

As the taller of the two men walked past him the attendant noticed that he had a duelling scar on his right cheek. This struck him as rather odd for a travelling salesman, but his attention was soon drawn away. As he went to close the door, the smaller of the men reached towards him and much to his astonishment, deposited a number of coins in his hand.

The occupation game was suddenly thrown into chaos as several passengers arrived simultaneously, carrying strangely shaped luggage. To add to the confusion there was also an eclectic mix of accents that the platform guard struggled to understand.

The passengers were clearly travelling together as all the tickets were for carriage 7 and they appeared to know each other very well, judging by all the back slapping, hugs and handshakes that were going on between them. The guard looked on open mouthed in wonderment. He had never seen so many black men in one place at the same time.

If truth be known he felt quite intimidated by their presence and for the first time in many years, he was rather pleased to have the relative security of his little cubicle around him. The men congregated together a few yards onto the platform, clearly waiting for someone important to arrive before they boarded the train.

On cue, a bear-like figure of a man in a camel hair coat marched towards the now crowded platform. Trailing in his wake were two much smaller men labouring under the weight of luggage which was obviously far too heavy for them.

'Whiteman,' the man boomed in the direction of the open-mouthed platform guard. In his confused state, he wasn't quite sure whether this was a declaration of the man's name or his ethnicity. He quickly viewed the ticket thrust towards him, together with those for the man's two companions, who were still labouring to reach the platform gate.

He quickly beckoned the camel hair coated man through and motioned to his companions that they should follow him. The baggage carriers struggled through the barrier with some difficulty, panting and sweating profusely under the weight of their loads.

'Whiteman' was clearly the man in charge, as he proudly marshalled his troops together and led them to carriage No.7.

The platform guard settled back into his cubicle after deciding that without question the party were some form of sports team. He thought most probably they played a popular American game that had read about in a discarded copy of L'Echo de Paris, called Baseball. Satisfied with his decision regarding their occupation, he settled back and waited for his next passengers to arrive.

**

Jimmy V sat in silence looking out of the window at the busy streets of the French capital. So many colourful people going about their lives, seemingly without a care in the world, and yet throughout Europe there was a growing unrest which they seemed completely oblivious too.

Lady Julia smiled as he looked across at her. He was such a lucky chap to have had such a woman as his travelling companion through so many adventures. A remarkably resourceful and intelligent woman, and also intellectually superior to most men of his acquaintance.

'James, are you quite all right?' remarked Lady Julia as she saw Jimmy V continuing to look in her direction across the taxi.

'Simply splendid. I was just thinking…'

'James. You know that is not such a good thing to do before dinner,' Lady Julia gently chided him.

'Indeed not,' he replied with a smile.

A few moments later, the taxi pulled up outside the station and the driver quickly opened the door for the couple to get out. Behind them, the second taxi had arrived and Harry was helping Mary to alight. Two very contented Parisian taxi drivers pulled away, after receiving a gratuity that equated to double the usual fare.

The two couples proceeded into the station and headed towards platform 5, where the train to Berlin sat gently making steam. Jimmy V carried his beloved trombone in its crocodile skin case, whilst his three fellow travellers scanned the faces of the people waiting in the station, hoping not to catch a glimpse of someone they might recognise.

Harry presented their tickets to a rather startled looking platform guard and the party were invited to proceed to carriage No. 1.

The platform guard slumped back into his seat. Had he missed the news that there was a black men's convention occurring in Paris? Or perhaps Berlin? Was there some major sporting event that he didn't know about? Harry? Must be a boxing champion. A strange day indeed. It would certainly give him something to tell his friends about later when he visited the Café Renoir. After all it wasn't every day that you met an All-Star American Baseball team, and the world heavyweight boxing champion…

Chapter 23

The giant station clock clicked on to 7.00 o'clock.

The guard blew his whistle and waved his green flag to the driver, who pulled the released the starting handle allowing the giant German built engine to spring to life. Its wheels began to grip the rails and slowly pull the long line of carriages away from the platform.

Jimmy V and Lady Julia had settled into their seats in the dining section of carriage No.1 and were choosing their evening meal as the train started to move. Jimmy V had chosen a bottle of 1924 Chateau Haut Brion for them to enjoy with their food.

'I think I will have the pâté to start, followed by the duck? What about you my dear?'

Jimmy V always started with pâté and invariably had duck when it was on the menu. Lady Julia smiled at his predictability.

'I think I will join you, James.'

'Splendid.'

An immaculately dressed waiter took their order and they settled back to await their meal.

Harry had arranged that he and Mary would dine together in the small servants' restaurant at the rear of carriage 3. The set menu this evening was Mushroom Soup, followed by Wiener schnitzel and new potatoes. For dessert, the couple had a choice between Raspberry Macaron or Orange Gelatin, a moulded sweet jelly containing orange slices - a dish that had become very popular in the finest restaurants.

In carriage No.6, Smith and Perkins also set out their evening meal. They had purchased bread, and a selection of cold meats and cheeses.

'The bread doesn't get any softer on the palette, Sir,' remarked Perkins, as he bit into a long sandwich he had created from the assemblage.

'Indeed it doesn't Perkins. I have often thought that the A.B.C. should open a few shops on the continent. I am sure they would make a killing.'

'Not to mention an acceptable cup of tea, Sir.'

'Indeed they could Perkins. Indeed they could.'

As the train approached the outer suburbs of Paris and began to increase speed, the two men in the neighbouring cabin also began to plan their evening meal. They had purchased bread and cheese, together with a packet of Leibniz butterkeks biscuits.

The two men ate in silence, each alone with his thoughts. As they looked out of the window, the remains of the day and the city gradually drained away in equal measure. Night would soon consume the last of the light, leaving them only the shadows of buildings and the silhouettes of trackside trees to look at until the morning.

In carriage No.7, the party was in full flow. The collection of musicians brought together to form the latest incarnation of the Paul Whiteman band was noisily renewing old acquaintances, or making new introductions.

The open plan nature of the 2nd class carriage ensured that very quickly everyone knew who was playing with the band. Before the train had left Paris, Buddy Bolden and Red Nichols had taken out their trumpets and started an impromptu 'Jam' session. They were soon joined by the bass player Wellman Breaux and the drummer Warren 'Baby' Dodds. The latter, like all drummers in the absence of regular drums, was playing the furniture, the tables, the glasses and anything else that came within reach of the sticks he always carried in his coat pocket.

The band members were the only residents of carriage 7, but very soon the sound of music had reached several others.

Josephine Baker appeared at the adjoining door, followed by her troupe of dancers, who were very keen to join the party. The two dancers who had been at the Ritz the previous evening waved enthusiastically at Wellman and Warren, who responded with broad smiles before striking up enthusiastically with yet another chorus.

Fufu Lamore followed the other dancers into the carriage. She looked much less enthusiastic than her colleagues. Her mind was awash with thoughts and concerns about the safety of her dashing commandant and the urgent mission on which he had been sent. These thoughts were soon banished, however, as a young trombone player with a wide, toothy grin stopped playing and approached her with a glass of absinthe in his hand.

'Could I invite you to join us, Miss?' he offered over the sound of the music.

'Thank you,' she grinned, 'that would be most pleasant.'

'What's your name?' she enquired with a smile.

'That would be Johnny 'The Slide' Williams,' he replied, flashing a smile that revealed a set of piano key white teeth. He offered her the largest hand she had ever seen, which she took willingly.

The carriage attendant marvelled at the stamina of the young people, as they continued to play and dance through the journey. His usual passengers were normally snoozing gently long before the train came to the border crossing into Germany. On this occasion, however, the music was still in full flow as the train came to a stop and two rather astonished looking border guards entered the carriage to check passports and travel documents.

Their arrival brought the session to a tumultuous, and somewhat damp conclusion, as Baby Dodds smashed a half full bottle of Martell cognac with his final, and rather too exuberant drum fill. The two guards stood in silence at the entrance to the carriage. Just like the platform guard at the Gare de l'Est, they too had never seen so many black men in one place, nor they considered, had they even seen so many beautiful young women.

Jimmy V and Lady Julia were just finishing their coffee and the rather excellent Belgian chocolates that accompanied it, when the train came to a halt and the border guard entered the carriage.

The guard looked disdainfully at the couple as he entered and slowly approached them. He had been a soldier in the war and had been severely wounded by shrapnel during the artillery bombardment that had proceeded the Battle of Passendaele. His wounds had left him with a pronounced limp. Every painful step that he took towards the couple reminded him of the deep loathing he held for all Englishmen.

'Tickets!' he demanded, in as commanding a voice as he could muster, thrusting his hand out towards the couple.

'I will ensure that the gentleman is given the appropriate documents, Sir.'

The guard swivelled remarkably quickly considering his injuries, alarmed by the booming voice that had suddenly erupted behind him. As he spun round, he found himself looking directly into the chest of Harry Pratt.

The guard's demeanour immediately changed as he stared up, open mouthed at the intimidating figure.

'Thank you,' he stammered, as he gingerly took the tickets and passports offered to him. Harry smiled as he observed the guards hand trembling as he held the documents.

'Splendid! Another chocolate my dear?' asked Jimmy V, as he held out the plate of Belgian chocolates for Lady Julia.

With the border formalities completed and the train resupplied with coal, water and food, the journey would soon recommence. Paul Whiteman had arranged with the train staff that a box would be brought to him when they stopped at the border. He knew the players in his band, and that this was going to be a long and thirsty trip to Berlin. Prohibition may apply in the USA, but in Europe there were no such restrictions.

Before leaving Paris, he had purchased the entire stock of absinthe and cognac from a rather startled, but very happy shop keeper in the Rue Grand Marché. As the train pulled away from the border he appeared at the door of carriage No.7 with Josephine Baker at his side. He was carrying the box which clanked invitingly as the train started to pick up speed.

'Gentlemen. I declare the bar is open,' placing it on the nearest table.

'Enjoy your evening, Gentlemen. I intend to enjoy mine.'

With a broad grin, Whiteman turned and headed back to his compartment followed by Josephine Baker.

Behind them, the party restarted with renewed vigour. The carriage guard slumped glumly in his seat as he contemplated the long night ahead. He was accustomed to enjoying an uninterrupted night's sleep on these trips. That was part of their appeal for him. Sadly he suspected this trip would be very different.

As the train passed over the border into Germany the party was in full voice. The size and composition of the band was reduced significantly, as various players gave in to fatigue or found alternative forms of entertainment. 'Slide' Williams hadn't been seen since the Belgian border.

Lady Julia had convinced Jimmy V that an early night would be advisable and had retired to her sleeping compartment very soon after they left the border. After enjoying a rather nice glass of cognac, Jimmy V had also retired for the night.

Harry and Mary were left alone. As the train moved on serenely through the shadows of the German hinterland, the lights in carriage No.1 were quietly extinguished.

Chapter 24

The sun rose spilling weak beams of light onto the brilliant blue livery of the speeding train. The long procession of carriages travelled smoothly, but noisily through the German countryside, startling horses and sheep as it passed by, the giant engine belching smoke and embers into the early morning sky.

With the time approaching 6.00 a.m., the train slowed down as it approached the station at Rathenow, an insignificant little town in the Brandenburg region.

The party was over in carriage 7 and the seats were now festooned with slumbering bodies, some still clutching instruments as they slept. The tables were littered with the detritus of the festivities. Half empty bottles and glasses were lying everywhere. The carriage guard shuffled uncomfortably in his seat, trying to catch up on long delayed sleep.

Smith and Perkins were awake. Neither man had slept particularly well, despite their fatigue. Thoughts of their mission and the unexpected complications conveyed to them by General

Carruthers the previous day made for a growing level of concern in their minds. They sat opposite one another, staring out of the carriage window in thoughtful silence at the German countryside, whilst consuming the last of their rations. As the train wound its way carefully around a long bend in the track, the outskirts of the small town came into view.

The station had few facilities to accommodate the needs of visitors. The schedule indicated that there would only be a short stop for the purposes of taking on more fuel and water for the remaining miles to Berlin. Few passengers would have taken advantage of the station facilities, even if such a thing had been on offer. The silence that now enveloped the whole train provided ample testament to the general sleeping state of its occupants.

The train came to a gentle halt. Smith noted that even if they had wanted to stretch their legs, the inadequacy of the platform's length meant they would not have been able to do so. The bend in the track allowed him a good view of the platform, which was only long enough to accommodate two carriages. The driver had positioned the giant engine, together with carriages 1 and 2, well ahead of the platform. With admirable efficiency, within seconds of their arrival a water pipe and coal shoot had been positioned above the tender.

Smith watched the refuelling operation with disinterest. A group of four men emerged from the station waiting room. The leading man opened the door to carriage No.4 and stood to attention by its side. A further group of eight appeared from the waiting room and marched purposefully across the platform. Without breaking step, they entered the carriage. The leather clad guards followed them onto the train and the carriage door was closed with a resounding thud. The platform once again stood silent and deserted.

The whole operation had been carried out with admirable, almost military precision. So quick that Smith had no time to alert Perkins to the scene. He did have time, however, to positively identify a number of the men involved.

'Why would so many prominent members of the NSDAP be in such a non-descript little town, Sir?' wondered Perkins, after he had been briefed.

'That's a question I have no doubt we will have to address at some point, Perkins. I feel that it may in some way intersect with our mission. For now, the most important thing is to ensure that

London is made fully aware. The presence of Focke, Junkers and Porsche alongside members of the NSDAP will be something of considerable interest, I am sure.'

Perkins nodded his agreement.

There was a shudder as the giant engine suddenly sprang back to life. Slowly, the line of carriages edged through the station and began the final leg of the journey to Berlin. In carriage No. 7 all remained quiet as its occupants slept on, blissfully unaware of the events of the past hour.

Smith and Perkins were not the only witnesses to the appearance of the train's new passengers. As they sat back in their compartment and thought about what had just occurred at Rathenow, elsewhere on the train there were others who were also deep in thought.

Chapter 25

A few minutes after the train had left Rathenow, the carriage guards began to move through the train waking their passengers.

Harry had already prepared breakfast for Jimmy V and Lady Julia before the appearance of the guard. Ascertaining they were already awake, he clicked his heels and marched off to disturb the sleep of other passengers further down the carriage.

Mary had laid out Lady Julia's clothes in preparation for their arrival in Berlin whilst she was in her bathroom. She was now busying herself repacking their clothes from the journey. She smiled contentedly as she packed her own perfectly folded nightwear.

'I hope you slept well, Mary?' enquired Lady Julia, as she emerged from the small bathroom cubicle.

'Perfectly well ma'am,' replied Mary with a smile.

'I believe that Harry has prepared breakfast in the salon. I shall complete the packing whilst you complete your meal.'

'Thank you Mary. Have you eaten?'

'Harry and I breakfasted earlier, Ma'am.'

'I see. Very good,' responded Lady Julia with a hint of a smile.

In carriage No.7 things were not so neatly ordered. Or polite. There was a general melee as heavily hung-over party revellers tried to pack away their instruments and collect together discarded bags. There was a rich and varied selection of curses and swearing as they constantly got in one another's way. The gentle sway of the train coupled with the largely inebriated state of the musicians made for quite a comical scene. The dancers had returned to their own carriage where they were giggling and excitedly exchanging stories and gossip from the night before.

'You look like you had an exciting night Fufu?' remarked Lucille Laporte, as she grinned across at a smiling Fufu Lamore.

'Better than average. Much! Much better than average,' she giggled in response.

'I think Josephine and one or two more of the girls may have also enjoyed their evening,' remarked Fufu, nodding towards the largely deserted seating area.

'I hope Miss Baker has arranged for breakfast when we arrive in Berlin,' said Lucille hopefully. 'I am starving!'

*

Smith and Perkins had finished the last of their rations and were making plans to communicate with London as soon as they arrived in Berlin. There must be reasons why the leaders of the NSDAP would be meeting with a group of leading industrialists in a small, insignificant town, in the middle of the German countryside. Rathenow was many miles away from any major centre of population or recognisable industry. They must report to their superiors as quickly as possible and get their instructions.

The two men in the next compartment had spent an extremely uncomfortable night in their cramped surroundings. Neither had been able to sleep, particularly as they had failed to bring sufficient food to sustain them through the journey. As the sun rose ever higher in the sky, the pangs of hunger had taken hold. They had been hoping to replenish their food supplies when the train made its scheduled stop at Rathenow.

Looking forlornly through the window as the train had stopped some way short of the platform, they too had witnessed the events. As the train resumed its journey they sat discussing the ramifications of what they had seen. They too would need to report to their superiors as soon as they reached Berlin.

Chapter 26

The train was a hive of activity as the first concentration of buildings that formed the conurbation of Berlin appeared. Passengers were either waking, eating, or packing away belongings with equal vigour, in preparation for their arrival at Lehrter Bahnhof.

In contrast, Jimmy V and Lady Julia were enjoying a leisurely breakfast. Harry and Mary with admirable and practised efficiency had completed the packing and were fully prepared for their arrival.

Harry had pre-arranged a number of taxis to transport both themselves and their luggage to the Hotel Adlon. The luxurious hotel occupied a site conveniently positioned on the corner of the Wilhelmstrasse and Pariser Platz. It was next door to the British Embassy and across the street from the French and American Embassies, both of which were located on the Pariser Platz itself.

Lady Julia sat patiently listening to Jimmy V outlining his itinerary for the coming day. She appeared to be as attentive as always. His excitement really was infectious she thought to herself, as he repeatedly stated how much he was looking forward to meeting his fellow band members for the rehearsal. She smiled as she listened, touched by his boyish enthusiasm.

The rehearsal and sound check had been arranged for the afternoon in the famous Europahaus nightclub, where they would perform for the first time later that evening. Lady Julia would take the opportunity whilst the rest of the party were occupied, to report to the Embassy. Harry was also making plans. He could be reasonably sure as soon as the rehearsal began, his services would not be required for several hours.

There were many seriously hung-over and exhausted musicians slumped in their seats further down the train. The enthusiasm of the previous evening's revelries had been replaced by a mixture of anticipation and alcohol induced fatigue. The musicians, as was always the case through the history of bands, had gravitated into small sectional groups.

At the trumpet table, Buddy Bolden and Red Nichols were busy cleaning the valves of their instruments, whilst holding a discussion about the relative values of the J B Arban Cornet Method versus the Louis Saint-Jacome Grand Method. Benny Carter and 'Si' James, the remaining members of the trumpet section, sat bemused by the discussion. They were both largely self-taught and hadn't heard of either.

The next table was occupied by the trombone section. Johnny The Slide Williams was dozing gently with his shoulder resting on the window. He slept with a broad grin on his face, seemingly resting from his exertions the previous evening. Pee Wee Hunt and Spiegle Willcox nodded in his direction and winked at each other as their colleague let out the occasional sigh of contentment.

Their conversation largely centred on the upcoming series of concerts in the German capital. Jimmy V, as the newest member of their section, also found his way into their discussion. Occasionally they glanced past their sleeping colleague and out of the window. The density of the buildings was noticeably increasing as they neared their final destination.

Across the central walkway Fud Livingston and Jimmy Noone, the saxophonists, were holding an in depth discussion regarding the relative merits of the long established Vandoren reeds and the latest products on the market from the newly founded Rico reed company. The youngest member of the section,

Jimmy Dorsey, was listening intently to the discussion, but knew better than to interrupt his more illustrious colleagues with his views even though, unknown to his colleagues, he had recently signed an endorsement contract with the Rico company.

Some distance from the main group, at a table on his own sat the pianist, Earl Hines. He was surrounded by piles of music. As the band's official librarian it was his job to make sure that each player had his charts in the order decreed by Paul Whiteman. Whiteman would erupt in magnificent style if his players did not have the necessary music immediately available when instructed. Having worked with him on several occasions previously, Hines was well aware of this and had no desire to be on the busy end of such an outburst.

At the final table in the carriage sat Wellman Brieux and Baby Dodds. They had decided that hair of the dog was required to conquer their hung-over state. Having found an almost full bottle of cognac, they were happily passing the remaining journey time by consuming its contents. Baby Dodds in the absence of his sticks, conveniently hidden away by his colleague, was tapping rhythms on the table with his fingers, much to the general annoyance of everyone around him.

Smith and Perkins were packed and ready for their impending arrival. In order to avoid any chance of detection they had decided to remain in their carriage for some time after the train arrived at Lehrter Bahnhof. They couldn't be sure that their presence on the train had remained a secret, despite the various precautions they had taken in Paris. Whilst they could have hoped to be lost in the crowd, they decided this was a risk that they could not afford.

In the neighbouring compartment, the two men had discussed their imminent arrival in Berlin. They had concluded that they would disembark immediately upon its arrival. If they stood by the carriage door as the train slowed down for the platform, they could alight as soon as the speed allowed them to do so. As they sat waiting in silence, the deafening noise generated by their empty and now deeply growling stomachs reminded them of their hunger.

Both men had already decided that despite the very obvious importance of what they had witnessed at Rathenow, they would first of all find the most convenient café and eat.

Chapter 27

The giant engine signalled its approach to the Lehrter Bahnhof with a loud blast on its whistle. The long line of carriages shuddered, as the train's speed began to slow, almost to a crawl. The two men from carriage 6, as planned, were in position and poised to leave the train as soon as the edge of the platform came into sight. With remarkable agility, both stepped off as soon as the train slowed down. They flashed their tickets towards a startled guard, before making their way towards the entrance to the U-Bahn and were out of sight within seconds.

As they descended the steps, they saw in the distance what they craved most, a Wurstbude. The smell of cooking hit them with the power of a gunshot as their stomachs applauded in recognition. A short time later, having each consumed a double helping of the giant bratwurst sausages on offer, they were safely aboard the underground train and heading in the direction of the Pariser Platz.

The considerable presence of Paul Whiteman, resplendent as always in his camel haired coat, appeared in front of his band members, as the train started to slow down on its approach to the platform.

'Gentlemen, welcome to Berlin. I am assured that our official tour bus will meet us outside the station. Look out for two buses with 'Kase Runfahrten' written on the side. The first is for us, the second for Josephine and her ladies.' His pronunciation of the latter word made the still hung-over musicians want to smile, but none of them had the courage to show it. They nodded in unison to confirm they understood the instructions.

'The instruments stored in the baggage car will follow us to the venue in a separate van,' he continued.

'Earl, you go with the instruments and sort out the charts ready for this afternoon. It'll give you chance to check out the piano. Buddy, Si and Slide, make sure all our bags and equipment are safely loaded.' Whiteman was a man who liked everyone to know who was in charge.

Glancing towards the table at the far end of the carriage, Whiteman was just in time to see his drummer, Baby Dodds, finishing the last of the cognac.

'Hey, Baby! You and Wellman can go along with Earl and sort out your kit ready for this afternoon.' he shouted over the sound of the train whistle.

'Wellman, try to sober him up!' Whiteman added with a sigh as he looked with disdain at his drummer. His blood-shot eyes effectively confirmed every drop of cognac that he had consumed.

'Gentlemen, rehearsal at 3.00pm, see you all there!' Without expecting or waiting for a response, he turned and left the carriage.

Paul Whiteman was quite probably the best band leader in the world. He was not one to waste words, nor was he in the habit of waiting for players to arrive. The musicians had all worked with him before and they all knew that. They would be in place by 2.45pm, ready to play and prepared for 3 hours' hard rehearsing. Whiteman always made sure he paid his musicians the best rates, but in return, expected that they earned their money.

Jimmy V and Lady Julia were enjoying a final cup of Blue Mountain coffee when the train's whistle blew to signal their impending arrival in Berlin.

'A pleasant journey?'

'Pleasant enough, James.'

'Harry?'

'Yes Sir?'

'Would you ensure that Ladybee and Mary are suitably cared for when we arrive, please? I feel it appropriate that I should have a chat with Mr Whiteman before we depart for the hotel.'

'My pleasure, Sir.'

'Splendid.'

'21, and it's only 9.30am!' thought Harry. Lady Julia saw the look that appeared on Harry's face and nodded knowingly.

The train came to a halt. The giant engine, as if to consummate its arrival, gently kissed the bumpers at the end of the track. The driver released the pressure valves and a loud hiss of steam brought it to a complete stop. Carriage doors were immediately flung open on their hinges and passengers began to spill out onto the platform like a myriad of seeds bursting forth from a giant pod.

The Bahnhof baggage handlers began their work immediately the train came to a halt. The red double doors of the baggage cars were pulled back and the loading ramp lowered onto the platform. A long queue of luggage trolleys was already in position, ready to receive the cargo as it was passed efficiently along by a line of immaculately dressed porters.

It wasn't long before the luggage of the Paul Whiteman band had been checked off by the designated players, loaded onto trolleys and was making its way noisily along the platform.

The musicians left the station as instructed and found the two open top buses waiting for them outside. Having loaded the instruments and luggage onto the waiting van, Wellman, Dodds and Earl Hines were crushed uncomfortably into the open front, next to the driver.

They sat waiting patiently for Paul Whiteman to make his appearance.

Harry supervised the loading of their luggage onto the waiting trolleys. These were now lined up behind one another in preparation for their onward journey to the Hotel Adlon. Jimmy V made his way down the platform where he saw the unmistakeable figure of Paul Whiteman walking towards him, with Josephine Baker on his arm.

'Jimmy! How good to see you again,' Whiteman exclaimed, holding his arms out wide as the two men approached each other.

'I hope that you and the chaps will join me for drinks after the concert this evening, Mr Whiteman? Of course the invitation extends to you and your dancers, Miss Baker.' Jimmy V added, looking towards her.

'I am staying at the Adlon. My man, Pratt, will arrange suitable transportation.'

'That is most kind of you Jimmy, I am sure that the boys will find that most pleasant.' answered Paul Whiteman, trying his best to be as formal as he could. He doubted that the boys in the band would object to another free night's drinking.

Paul Whiteman and Josephine Baker took their leave and left the station. Parked in front of the now loaded tour buses was a rather grand looking open top Durkopp taxi. The driver opened the door for the couple to take their seats. A theatrical signal from Whiteman gave notice for the procession to set off. Onlookers could be forgiven for thinking this was some kind of presidential parade moving towards the centre of the city, rather than the arrival of a band of musicians. In the band bus, Red Nichols had to fight an overwhelming urge to play some kind of fanfare as they pulled away from the station, but was dissuaded from doing so by Buddy Holden.

A few moments later, Harry had ensured their luggage had been safely loaded aboard the taxis and that they too could leave the station. Jimmy V collected his trombone and graciously led Lady Julia towards the exit and the waiting Autoruf taxis.

A full fifteen minutes passed before Charles Smith opened the door to compartment 6c and peered cautiously towards the platform. He was confident that the majority of passengers had now left the area and that he and Perkins could anonymously leave the train.

'We will take the U-Bahn Perkins I think.'

Perkins nodded his agreement.

The platform guard was surprised to see the two Englishmen emerge from the carriage so long after the main assemblage of passengers had left the area. He smiled ruefully to himself as he decided they must have slept through the arrival of the train.

He had always considered the English a lazy and inefficient breed. Like many men of his generation, he had served during the Great War and was deeply resentful of the impact the economic sanctions imposed by the war reparations were having on both him and his family. How could such a lazy and disorganised nation have triumphed in the conflict? He demanded their tickets with as much disrespect as he could muster with so few words and watched them as they proceeded towards the U-bahn.

The two Englishmen walked briskly to the steps where the smells from the Wurstbude immediately greeted them.

'Sausage, Sir?'

'Excellent idea Perkins! Make it two, I'm famished. Do they have tea?'

***

The platform was now deserted. The baggage porters had returned their trolleys to the storage bays and were dispersed around the station on various other duties. The platform guard was sorting the tickets he had collected and was quietly contemplating what his wife might have prepared for him today in his lunchbox. He so hoped that it was not sauerkraut again.

Outside the station, three large black Maybach W5 cars drew up. A tall man in a long black leather coat stepped out of the first of the cars and marched towards the station entrance.

He completely ignored the platform guard as he strode purposefully towards the waiting train. As he approached, a door was pushed open and two similarly dressed men jumped down from the train and joined him on the platform.

With the platform secured, a steady stream of passengers left the carriage in small groups. Each group followed one of the leather-coated men to the waiting cars which then left the station. The whole operation was completed with admirable efficiency. A few minutes passed before another Maybach drew up to the station entrance to collect the final passengers from the train.

The platform guard stood to attention as several officials from the NSDAP filed past him towards the waiting car. He had attended a rally addressed by their esteemed leader some weeks earlier and the power of his rhetoric had moved him greatly. He watched the small party get into the waiting car and leave, before he realised that he had not requested their tickets.

No matter. He would certainly have something to tell his wife when he got home.

Looking down into his lunch box his mood changed as he stared at the mass of over-fermented cabbage that awaited him uninvitingly for lunch.

Chapter 28

The Hotel Adlon was the most luxurious hotel in Berlin. It was, to be more accurate, the most modern and luxurious hotel in the whole of Germany. It had hot and cold running water feeding all its bathrooms, complete with the very latest showers. It boasted its own laundry, bakery and butchers department. It was also fully self-sufficient for electricity, having its own dedicated power generation plant.

Since its grand opening by Kaiser Wilhelm in 1907, its sumptuous lobby supported by huge square marble columns had welcomed many of the royal families of Europe. Jimmy V and Lady Julia were well accustomed to opulent surroundings, having stayed in many of the world's finest hotels. The splendour of the Adlon however, left them quite unashamedly stunned.

The journey from the station to the Adlon had passed without incident. Harry with his usual efficiency was ensuring that the hotel check in procedures were completed, whilst Jimmy V and Lady Julia looked around the lobby. They noted the various signs above large oak panelled doors. The ladies' lounge, music room, library and the smoking room. Adjoining the latter was a glass fronted cigar shop with a laminated neon sign advertising Cuban cigars.

A large number of guests were looking around the interior Japanese garden complete with various palms and a giant fountain in the shape of an elephant spraying water from its trunk.

'This would make an excellent venue for this evening Ladybee, don't you think?'

'I am sure so, James.'

'Splendid! I shall ask Pratt to make the necessary arrangements.'

To the side of the Japanese garden was a large group of people queuing patiently at the entrance to the restaurant. To the far side of the lobby there was a similarly large queue waiting for admission to the state dining room.

'I think we shall order lunch to be brought to our rooms, Ladybee. I do not wish to be late for the rehearsal.'

Lady Julia smiled in affirmation. She had her own plans for the afternoon and certainly did not want to be delayed waiting for a space in an overcrowded restaurant.

'Splendid!'

Harry found the couple, despite the vast number of people wandering around the lobby. He confirmed that their suites were ready and were located on the second floor of the hotel. Jimmy V was to occupy the Berliner Suite and Lady Julia would occupy the un-named adjoining suite.

The rooms were on the western side of the hotel overlooking the Pariser Platz. Both had self-contained servants quarters for Harry and Mary. Rather conveniently, there was a connecting door between them.

Harry had arranged for a light lunch to be brought to the Berliner suite. As always, he had already anticipated Jimmy V's requirements.

***

The Paul Whiteman Band, along with Josephine Baker and her dancers had checked into the Kurfurstendamm Gasthof. This comfortable but rather more basic hotel was located in the thriving, party heart of the city. Its principal benefit to the band was that it was within walking distance of the Europahaus.

After completing the checking in process, the musicians had quickly unpacked their belongings.

It was likely to be a long afternoon of rehearsals, so they were now dispersed along the length of the Kurfurstendamm Strasse in an effort to obtain cheap food and drink supplies to sustain them through the remainder of the day.

Whiteman had made it very clear when booking the members of his band that their fee would include hotel, transportation and breakfast. Anything else was down to the individual musicians to arrange. Whiteman was far too experienced as a bandleader to offer anything more than the minimum that was expected.

Breaux and Dodds had decided that sleep was the best option for them after the excesses of the previous evening and had retired to their room. The bottle shaped bulge in Dodds' bag, carefully liberated from the train journey, was no doubt some form of sleeping tonic.

The rest of the band had split into sectional groups as always and were now located in various cafés along the length of the Kurfurstendamm Strasse. Paul Whiteman and Josephine Baker had planned to have lunch at the hotel. Over the course of their meal, they discussed the order of events for the coming rehearsal. Josephine was anxious that her dancers should remain as fresh as possible and therefore insisted that her numbers should be rehearsed first. By the end of lunch, a plan had been agreed.

Unfortunately, the result of the discussion would mean that the order of the charts so carefully assembled by Earl Hines earlier would now be compromised. Paul Whiteman smiled to himself as he looked forward to his forthcoming eruption when the band had the wrong music on their stands. He was the boss, and what he said was all that mattered. He so enjoyed a good rant before a performance, he liked to keep his players on their toes.

***

Smith and Perkins travelled to the Pariser Platz and wasted no time in reporting to the British Embassy. The two men were quickly ushered through the public area and into the offices of the Attaché General.

Major General Sir William Blyth was the man in charge of covert operations in Berlin. He had received notification from General Carruthers to expect their arrival, but the communication did not enlighten him as to the purpose of their mission. As the two men outlined what they had seen at

Rathenow, however he became increasingly concerned.

He had received intelligence reports from various sources over the past few months suggesting that a number of prominent industrialists may have NSDAP sympathies, but he had no concrete evidence to suggest that any face to face meetings had actually taken place.

The growing economic problems caused by the war reparations were bringing increasing tension throughout Germany, but particularly in the wealthy classes. The NSDAP had openly sought support from the industrial community in their quest for power before, but if an actually meeting as discovered by Smith and Perkins was what had taken place, then this was a worrying escalation.

Blyth would seek instructions from London immediately and contact the agents at their hotel when he had news. He confirmed that rooms had been arranged for them at the Hotel Seifert on Budapester Strasse. This was within walking distance of the rear entrance to the embassy. Smith and Perkins feared they would not be spending much time in their room. They were both severely fatigued and hungry despite the double helping of bratwurst that they had enjoyed from the Wurstbude earlier. They doubted that the Seifert would have a restaurant or room service and they could not run the risk of detection by walking the streets of Berlin during the daytime. For now, they would have to suffer their hunger and rest in the hotel until Blyth contacted them.

***

Gaston Fermeneau and Pierre-Gerard Limoux had arrived at the French embassy within 20 minutes of leaving the Lehrter Bahnhof.

After identifying themselves to the receptionist, they were shown through to the offices of the military attaché, Commandant Jacques Clermont immediately.

Chapter 29

Although the Adlon was less than a mile from the Europahaus, Jimmy V was anxious that he wasn't late for the afternoon rehearsal. He insisted that Harry should arrange for a taxi to collect him at 2.00pm, a full hour before the appointed time. Harry, as always, acquiesced to the request. With typical German efficiency, the Autoruf taxi had drawn up in front of the Adlon at precisely the time requested. Jimmy V had already been waiting in the lobby, like an over-anxious schoolboy for 15 minutes.

He quickly climbed aboard and sat with his trombone case on his lap for the short journey along the Stressemann Strasse. Harry would remain at the hotel in order to ensure that everything was unpacked and arrangements were made for later in the evening. He also had a number of other tasks that he wished to complete during the course of the afternoon.

***

Lady Julia waited patiently in her room overlooking the Pariser Platz. As the taxi drew up in front of the hotel, she saw Jimmy V clamber aboard and drive off towards his rehearsal. She smiled as she saw how keen he looked, almost tripping over his trombone case in his rush to get away. She always admired and indeed loved his boyish enthusiasm for everything musical; one of his many charms, she considered.

Gathering her hat and scarf from Mary, she made her way out of her room and descended in the lift. She knew that Harry would be in the lobby area making arrangements for the party later in the evening and would observe her leaving the hotel. She was confident however, that if she crouched down as she moved through the lobby the large crowd of people that were always milling around the vast space would conceal her departure. She had taken the added precaution of dressing as inconspicuously as a lady of her stature could muster, in a plain tan coloured outfit.

As the ornate open lift slowly descended, she saw Harry being shown into one of the offices to the rear of the main reception desk. She breathed out in relief. This made her task of leaving the hotel undetected much easier. Feeling much more relaxed she strode purposely towards the hotel exit, unaware of a small group of people seated quietly beside the entrance to the Japanese Garden watching her as she moved through the crowd.

The woman was dressed in a long black coat with her face largely obscured by a large black hat and birdcage veil. The three men sitting with her were dressed in matching black suits and fedora hats. At her instruction, one of the three men stood and left the hotel.

Lady Julia walked through the large oak doors of the neighbouring British Embassy within minutes. She spoke quietly to the desk clerk and was quickly ushered through to the main offices. Looking through the doors from street level, the man watched as Lady Julia disappeared into the heart of the embassy. It was clear from the speed of her admittance that her arrival was expected. He returned to the Adlon to make his report.

***

Harry spoke to the duty manager. An area of the Japanese garden would be set aside and reserved exclusively for Jimmy V and his guests. Food and drink would be provided to the party as requested. After bidding the manager farewell, Harry left the office and walked towards the front of the hotel. He stepped aside to allow a man in a dark suit, who was clearly in a hurry to enter. The man nodded his appreciation of the gesture before he entered the

Japanese gardens and joined a party of people already seated there.

Having left the hotel, Harry walked the short distance across the Pariser Platz and entered the American Embassy. Moments later he was seated in front of a large walnut desk looking appreciatively at its ornate splendour. The inlay work on the desktop was truly a work of art with a mesmerising display of marquetry featuring woods of many colours making up the bald eagle emblem of the United States.

The door to his left opened and the ambassador, accompanied by the military attaché entered the room. Harry rose and shook the outstretched hands of the two men. The military attaché, Colonel Maxwell Stokes was the first to speak.

'Harry, it's good to see you again. How long has it been?'

'Constantinople in 1917 I believe, Sir.'

'How can we be of service Mr. Pratt?' enquired the ambassador.

Chapter 30

NSDAP Headquarters, Leipziger Strasse, Berlin

'Welcome to Berlin. It is good to see you again.'

Valette Simone, Countess de St.Augustin sat in a large leather chair in the office of the Gauleiter of Berlin-Brandenburg, Dr. Joseph Goebbels.

'I believe that you have some information for me, Countess?'

After leaving Paris, she had travelled by taxi to a small landing strip on the outskirts of the city. Waiting for her was a Focke Wulf A16 in which she had flown to Berlin. The flight had been quite traumatic in what was an experimental aircraft, but as hoped it had allowed her to arrive in Berlin well ahead of Paul Whiteman and the rest of the party.

He listened with interest as she talked about meeting Viscount James Stanley, Lady Julia Mortimer and Harry Pratt in Paris. She reported that she had seen the latter two individuals making visits to their respective Embassies.

Goebbels had been made aware of the visit of Paul Whiteman and his orchestra to Berlin and unbeknown to the countess, had received his orders some weeks before the visit. He had become quite a fan of jazz music, and owned several records featuring the Paul Whiteman Band. He first encountered jazz music during his studies at the University of Heidelberg.

Following his appointment as the Gauleiter in Berlin, he had become a regular visitor to the Europahaus and was also fond of visiting the popular Berberina dance hall, where he had listened on many occasions to the resident orchestra led by the Jewish bandleader Efim Schachmeister. He had learnt to keep his musical tastes to himself. If it were to become general knowledge that he was a follower, and of a Jewish exponent in particular, he was sure that his tenure as the Gauleiter would be a very short one.

Jazz was not the most popular of music with senior members of the party. The party chairman in particular was very open with his views. He considered the music grossly decadent and ill disciplined; much preferring the classical music of his beloved Richard Wagner.

As the Countess continued with her report Goebbels became increasingly concerned. The number of foreign powers at work in his territory was something of which he had not been aware. His briefing had not covered the fact that agents from several countries were going to be in Berlin at the same time. This added potential complications to the mission that had been assigned to him.

He was not naïve enough to have believed that this situation would not arise at some point. The signatories to the Treaty of Versailles knew the continuing effect that the payment of war reparations was having on the German people. They knew there was open and growing dissent on the streets of many cities. It was only a matter of time before they sent agents to find out how severe this had become.

The rise of popular support for the NSDAP had coincided, and in many ways had driven and thrived on the dissent that reparations had created. He sat castling his fingers as he contemplated the options available to him. What would be the best course of action to take? Just as importantly, what actions would further his own ambitions within the party? Could he risk going ahead with his mission with so many agents around? What if he were caught? What were the likely consequences for him if he failed?

Countess St. Augustin completed her report and sat back in her chair waiting for the Gauleiter to respond. After many moments of silence, Goebbels leant forward towards her.

'Countess, your report is very thorough. It is clear to me that we must maintain a close watch on this situation. Your past relationship with Lady Mortimer could be very fortuitous for us. I believe that you can use this to successfully infiltrate the group without suspicion.'

He sat back and waited before delivering his next statement.

'I am convinced that the agents are here on an intelligence gathering mission as you have intimated. It is unlikely that they are aware of our plans for the coming days.' He spoke slowly, emphasising his choice of words to create what he believed was dramatic effect.

'It is vital for the future of the NSDAP that the information they gather is the information we wish them to believe. They can learn nothing of our true plans.'

She nodded in recognition.

'I will speak to my superiors. But I intend to go ahead with my plan and be in attendance at the

Europahaus for this evening's performance. I will rely upon you to ensure that suitable introductions are arranged, Countess.'

Her audience with the Gauleiter was now at an end. As she stood and prepared to leave, she observed for the first time how short in stature the Gauleiter was. As he moved towards the door to show her out, he walked with a pronounced limp which he worked hard to conceal. The Countess had been trained to see such things. She had no doubt that he perceived his deformity as a sign of weakness and in his position he could not afford to show any frailty, in either mind or body.

The Countess was aware of this little man's high ambitions within the party. She was not without ambitions of her own, nor was she above using his quest for increased power to suit her own ends.

Chapter 31

Jimmy V was the first to arrive at the Europahaus.

After leaving the taxi, he presented himself at the stage door where a doorman showed him into the theatre. He had earlier assisted the drummer with his kit and two of his colleagues with the rest of the stage layout, but had not been expecting any of the other musicians to arrive quite so early.

Jimmy V assembled his trombone and settled down to look through the charts that had been placed, in set list order, on his stand. It was a full 30 minutes before the first of his colleagues arrived.

He knew most of the players from his regular visits to America and had performed with many of them in the past. A number of them had attended his party in Paris.

As each group appeared, the excitement inside him seemed to grow in anticipation of the sound that would be created. At 2.40pm, a harassed looking Earl Hines arrived and started handing round small scraps of paper he had hurriedly written out on his way to the theatre.

At 2.45pm, Paul Whiteman arrived, along with Josephine Baker and her dancers. The theatre management was on hand to greet them as they stepped through the stage door. The stage doorman looked on with disinterest; he was not a fan of Americans or jazz music.

At 2.55pm, with the pleasantries completed, Paul Whiteman took off his Chesterfield coat and stood in front of his band for the first time.

'Gentlemen, welcome to the Europahaus,' he boomed, opening his arms out wide.

'We will begin with one of Mr Berlin's new charts, Blue Skies.'

He grinned maniacally as he waited for the musicians to start frantically searching their stands for the correct chart, but all was calm. Earl Hines did his best to hide a smile as he waited for Whiteman to start the count in, his hands poised in anticipation above the pure white ivory keys of the Rosewood Model O Steinway piano. He chanced a glance across the stage towards Lucille Laporte waiting in the wings with her fellow dancers. She winked back at him.

As Whiteman worked through the set list that he had agreed earlier with Josephine, he became more and more angry. The band already had the correct music in place, almost before he could announce it. By the time the band played the final chart of the dancers' set, his face had taken on the hue of a sailor's favourite sunset.

Jimmy V was in paradise. The rehearsal had been magnificent and he felt assured that he had risen to the challenge. Paul Whiteman's fearsome reputation for his aggressive approach to rehearsal seemed not to have materialised, most probably due to the pencilled note from Earl Hines giving the amended set list.

'Break!' boomed Whiteman, as soon as the dancers had left the stage.

'15 minutes! Earl! A word, please!'

Earl Hines gingerly closed the lid of the Steinway and reluctantly followed the disgruntled bandleader, as he strode towards his dressing room. The rest of the band with the exception of Baby Dodds, made their way to the coffee table. This had been laid out for them in the well of the theatre. Dodds, as always, had brought his own refreshments.

Only five minutes passed before a smiling Earl Hines reappeared.

'Still got all your fingers Earl?' enquired Red Nichols with a grin.

'We all owe you a drink Earl!' said Slide Williams, displaying a broad, tooth filled grin.

'Quietest rehearsal I've ever known. Good on you Earl,' added Wellman Brieux, as he offered him a cup of coffee.

Hines accepted the thanks of his fellow band members. It helped to dissipate the less than praiseworthy words which Paul Whiteman had just imparted to him. He knew that Whiteman would find something to criticise, no matter how smoothly the rehearsal had gone; that was part of what made him one of the world's top bandleaders. On this occasion, all that he could think to complain about was the height of his stand. Hines was more than happy to accept this as his only complaint and would sort it out easily with the theatre management, as soon as the remainder of the rehearsal was completed.

When Paul Whiteman returned to the stage, his mood had lightened considerably. This had probably been facilitated by a visit from Josephine Baker. She had joined him in his dressing room immediately after Hines had made his relieved exit.

The remainder of the rehearsal passed without incident.

Jimmy V's excitement had grown with every chart the band played. He sat back and admired the soaring trumpet sounds of Buddy Bolden and the incredible, note-filled solos of Fud Livingston on his tenor saxophone. Slide Williams was proving to be a great section leader and his lyrical jazz improvisation was right up there with the very best he'd ever heard. When the rehearsal finally came to its conclusion, Jimmy V felt that it had gone well. He had played his part and was happy that he knew exactly what was expected of him later in the evening.

'Gentlemen. Thank you for this afternoon. Earl has the detailed arrangements for this evening. See you all later.'

With that, Whiteman left the stage and strode towards his dressing room. The band watched his back disappear, before they breathed a collective sigh of relief and started to pack away instruments and re-order their charts back into the original set lists. Earl Hines set out details of the itinerary for the evening ahead.

They would not be required on stage for their first set until 9.30pm. The second set was scheduled for 11.30pm, with a third and final set starting at 1.00am. In between there was a variety of cameo performances from other performers. One name amongst the acts in particular was very familiar to Jimmy V and his fellow musicians.

Anita Berber was a much celebrated, but deeply controversial and extremely risqué burlesque dancer. She had performed almost exclusively in Berlin. Perhaps he might be able to persuade Lady Julia to come to the theatre earlier than required, so he could see her act....

Packing away his trombone, he realised how exhausting the level of concentration he had needed during the afternoon had been. He considered that for now, a nap might be his best plan. Having bid farewell to his new band colleagues, he set off to walk the short distance back to the Adlon. Walking along the Stresemannstrasse he thought about the events that had just taken place. He could not remember when he had enjoyed himself so much in an afternoon.

Behind him, two men walked slowly in the same direction. Occasionally they slowed down, glancing into various shops by the road side, making sure they didn't catch him up.

Chapter 32

Lady Julia sat in the British Embassy listening to Major General Sir William Blyth, as he recounted the information received earlier from Smith and Perkins.

It soon became abundantly clear that the fears she'd heard expressed in London concerning the rise of the NSDAP in Germany could be very real indeed. There might be many reasons why senior figures from German industry would be meeting with officials from one of the prominent new political parties in the country, however at a time when tensions were beginning to rise in many parts of mainland Europe, the development was very concerning. The attaché came to the end of his report and sat back in his chair.

'What do you make of it, Lady Mortimer?'

Lady Julia sat in silence for a few moments as she collected her thoughts.

'I agree with Captain Smith - the key to this mystery clearly lies somewhere in the area around Rathenow. I would recommend that he and Sergeant Perkins are sent there as soon as possible.'

Major General Blyth nodded in agreement.

'I suspect that the NSDAP will have taken precautions. They will have informants within the train authorities on the alert for any requests to travel to such a small town, particularly by foreign nationals, General. I suggest that it may be safest to travel by road. Do you have a car available?'

'I will ensure that a suitable vehicle is supplied, Lady Mortimer. I will contact Smith and Perkins at their hotel and inform them of your instructions immediately.'

Lady Julia stood and shook hands.

'Please pass on my regards to the Ambassador. Will he be attending the Europahaus this evening?'

'I am afraid that he is otherwise engaged this evening, Lady Mortimer. I am led to believe that Dr. Josef Goebbels, the NSDAP Gauleiter for Berlin will be present this evening. He is a very dangerous man with great ambitions, I am informed.'

'Thank you, Sir. I will be prepared. You will be aware, of course, that Harry Pratt will be present this evening?'

'Our large American cousin?'

'A valuable ally, Sir. Particularly in the absence of Smith and Perkins,' she continued, completely ignoring the attempted humour from the General.

'You may be correct Lady Mortimer, but I think that it is perhaps wisest not to make him aware of all our activities outside Berlin. The Americans have shown themselves to be less than supportive lately. They are taking this neutrality business very seriously.'

Lady Julia nodded and made her way towards the door.

'General, London needs to be fully briefed on this matter as soon as possible. I believe that General Carruthers needs to be made fully aware of these recent developments.'

'I agree, Lady Mortimer. I will ensure that a suitable communiqué is prepared and signalled as soon as possible.'

'Thank you, General. Please contact me should there be any further news.'

Lady Julia left the room and made her way to the rear of the embassy. She was met by one of General Blyth's aides, who opened the security door that led to the alleyway running along the rear of the Adlon. She pulled her hat down as she walked smartly past the staff entrance and out on to

Stresemannstrasse. Turning to her left, she was back inside the hotel lobby within seconds.

The large Brocot et Delettrez wall clock positioned above the reception desk showed the time was 3.15. She smiled as she thought how Jimmy V would be feeling right now, playing in the Paul Whiteman band for the very first time.

'Lady Julia, can I be of assistance?'

Turning abruptly, she came face to face with the large figure of Harry Pratt. She was always surprised how quietly he could move, for such a big man.

'Harry, I am pleased to see you. Shall we have coffee? I have a number of things I need to discuss with you.'

'That would be most kind Lady Julia. Shall we go to the Japanese Garden? I believe that will afford us some privacy.'

In the few moments since she had left the embassy, Lady Julia had decided to ignore the concerns of General Blyth and go ahead with her plan to brief Harry on the events that had occurred on the train journey. Harry, in return, briefed Lady Julia on the information that he had received during his meeting at the American embassy.

The Americans had also received information concerning clandestine rendezvous, but as far as he knew they had no knowledge of any activities taking place in Rathenow, or indeed anywhere else outside of Berlin. He would make sure his superiors were made aware of developments and that they afforded whatever assistance they could.

***

In the French Embassy, Gaston Fermeneau and Pierre-Gerard Limoux had briefed Commandant Jacques Clermont on their observations in Paris and Rathenow. He listened and considered his response carefully.

'Gentlemen, we are aware that the British and Americans are taking an uncommonly close interest concerning matters in Berlin. As far as you are aware, no one else observed the events at Rathenow?' The two men nodded an affirmation.

'I will ensure that you are supplied with suitable transportation. I require you to leave Berlin within the hour.'

The Commandant rose from his chair and left his office. In his absence, the two men discussed their imminent departure. They were disappointed to be missing Josephine Baker and her dancers, particularly Fermeneau, who had not had the opportunity to see the show when it was in Paris. Limoux on the other hand, much to the envy of his colleague, had seen the show on four occasions.

A few minutes passed before the Commandant returned and confirmed he had acquired an Adler Standard 6 for their use. The vehicle would be fuelled and ready for them within thirty minutes. They would not have time to go to their hotel; he had therefore arranged for them to refresh themselves at the embassy.

Thirty minutes later, they were driving through the streets of Berlin on their way to Rathenow. They had no idea what they were looking for, nor had they any idea of what they might find. They were certain, nevertheless, that whatever was lurking in the town, it could be of great importance. Their journey through the suburbs passed in silence.

Chapter 33

Jimmy V arrived back at the Adlon after a pleasant walk through the busy streets of Berlin, carrying his beloved trombone. His mind was still full of the sounds from the afternoon's rehearsal. He entered the lobby and made his way to the lift without pausing.

Two men in dark suits followed him into the hotel and stood by the side of the elephant fountain, watching as he made his way towards the lift. As the lift doors closed, one of the men left and hailed a taxi. His colleague entered the Japanese garden and calmly ordered coffee.

'Harry! What a splendid time I have had this afternoon. Truly splendid!'

'Very good, Sir.'

'I am required to be at the theatre this evening at 8.00pm. I am sure that I can rely on you to make the necessary arrangements, please?'

'My pleasure, Sir.'

'Splendid. I must speak to Lady Julia. I am sure she will want to know all about my afternoon. Perhaps she would like to join me for tea? I trust that we have satisfactory supplies?'

'Of course, Sir. I took the precaution of packing your usual blend in more than sufficient quantities.'

'Splendid!'

After notifying Lady Julia that Jimmy V had returned from his rehearsal, Harry set about preparing tea and ordered a selection of cakes for the couple. A few moments later, Lady Julia appeared at the door.

'Ladybee! How splendid to see you. I cannot wait to tell you all about the wonderful time I have had this afternoon. Simply splendid.'

'That would be marvellous James,' replied Lady Julia, trying to ensure that her voice displayed the requisite amount of enthusiasm.

'Tea, Ma'am?' offered Harry, with sympathy in his voice.

Chapter 34

Captain Smith and Sergeant Perkins were seated in the British Embassy waiting for Major General Sir William Blyth. They had been shown into the office by the General's aide, James Carrstairs, who stayed with them and remained standing silently in the corner of the room, as the General began to brief the men.

'Gentlemen, I have received some rather alarming intelligence reports following your visit earlier. Enquiries have confirmed that there has been a considerable increase in vehicular movement in and around the Rathenow area over the past few months.'

Smith and Perkins looked at each other, as the General continued with his update.

'The activity appears to be principally to the east of the town. This area is very heavily forested, seemingly only popular with local hunters. It appears that, much to the annoyance of the locals, a large area of the forest is in the process of being cleared and a series of barbed wire fences has been erected to prevent prying eyes.'

'Are there any reports of what the purpose of this activity might be, Sir?'

'None that I have been able to confirm, Captain. But I think it is safe to assume in the circumstances that in addition to the fences, there are most likely a number of additional security measures in place.'

The General steepled his hands, as he had a habit of doing when thinking.

'Gentlemen. We need to know precisely what is going on in Rathenow. I have arranged for suitable transportation to be made available to you.'

Smith and Perkins rose and prepared to leave the office.

'The NSDAP are a very dangerous organisation. I believe that the stated ambition of their leader, to restore Germany to its former status, knows no boundaries and by their actions recently in Munich, they have already proved themselves to be ruthless in their pursuit of power. I have no doubt they will defend their secrets with whatever force they see fit.'

'Thank you for your concern, General. Perkins and I will take suitable precautions. We are quite happy to defend ourselves, if it becomes necessary.'

'Good luck, Gentlemen.'

'Thank you, Sir.'

The two men shook hands with the attaché and left the room.

As soon as the door closed, the aide spoke.

'You didn't inform them about the intelligence reports concerning the activities of the French, Sir?'

'No, I chose not to, Carrstairs. In my opinion it would be safer for them to work independently for now. I am not sure that we can altogether trust the French in this. The information you reported recently has left me with grave concerns regarding one of their agents.'

James Carrstairs nodded in agreement.

Chapter 35

'Sir, I believe you mentioned taking a nap before this evening's performance?' interrupted Harry, after an hour and 17 further 'splendids' had elapsed. The daily count was already approaching 40, with the record now firmly in sight.

'That sounds like an excellent idea, James, I could do with a little rest myself. I want to be fully refreshed before this evening's entertainment. From your detailed description, it promises to be a wonderful performance.' Lady Julia did her best to hide her gratitude for Harry's timely intervention.

Ordinarily, she would have adored listening to Jimmy V's enthusiastic rhetoric, but she was genuinely fatigued. She also feared that that she may need to be fully alert and focussed during the course of the evening.

'Splendid idea, Ladybee. Until this evening - 7 o'clock?'

'I think 7.45pm would be more suitable, Sir.' suggested Harry.

'7.15pm it is then. Let's split the difference?'

Harry and Lady Julia nodded their agreement.

'Splendid!'

*

NSDAP Headquarters, Leipziger Strasse

Valette Simone, Countess de St. Augustin sat alone in the black leather armchair in the office of the Gauleiter of Berlin-Brandenburg. On the desk in front of her was a silver framed photograph of the NSDAP leader. Standing by his side as he delivered one of his stirring speeches, was a smiling Dr. Goebbels. A messenger had visited Valette at her hotel 30 minutes earlier with a rather short, but very precise message.

'Countess, thank you for returning.'

Goebbels entered his office, followed by the two men who had been with the Countess earlier at the Adlon.

'After our meeting earlier today I received reports of several agents arriving and subsequently departing from the embassies of France and Great Britain. Their presence in Berlin troubles me greatly. It is vital that I find out the purpose of this unexpected increase in activity as soon as possible. '

Valette nodded in agreement.

'Countess, I intend to attend the Europahaus this evening as your companion. I understand there will be a party afterwards at the Hotel Adlon. I would very much like you to secure an invitation for us to this gathering.'

'I will ensure that an invitation is made, Herr Gauleiter.'

*

Harry left the hotel as soon as he could be sure that Jimmy V was sleeping soundly in his suite. It was imperative that he pass on the information given to him by Lady Julia to his embassy as soon as possible. He assumed the hotel would be under surveillance by the authorities and therefore took the precaution of using the service lift. This led to the laundry room and from there, gave access to the basement. He could then leave the hotel using the staff exit.

Once outside he took a circuitous route to the rear entrance of the American embassy, where he made his report to the military attaché, Colonel Stokes.

The Colonel listened as Harry explained the actions taken by the British agents. Harry was acutely aware of the long standing American policy of neutrality, which he personally considered to be ill-judged and he knew that the Colonel, along with much of the military were also fervently opposed to the country's position.

It was inconceivable in Harry's opinion that if war once again erupted in Europe, the USA would be able to maintain its position for long. The Colonel had to be concerned about the direct involvement in German affairs by an American agent being discovered, however. This could leave the position of the United States greatly compromised.

The Colonel also held some rather grand political ambitions and had no wish to put these in jeopardy by becoming part of some wild goose chase instigated by the British. He had fought under British command in the last year of the war, which had left him with a well-developed loathing of the race.

'Harry, I feel that we should not become too embroiled in this matter. In my view, our position should be to maintain a watching brief and see how matters develop.'

Harry sat in silence. He had expected that the Colonel would instruct him to offer as much assistance to Lady Julia and her colleagues as possible. The orders he had been given were diametrically opposed to his expectations. After a pause, the attaché continued,

'The neutrality of the USA must remain central and paramount in this matter. You must ensure that you do not become involved in actions that could be construed by the German authorities as being in support of the British.'

'Sir…'

'Harry, I mean it! Whatever the agents discover at Rathenow, it must remain their problem and not ours.'

The Colonel leant forward in his chair. He placed both hands on the desk, as if grasping the wings of the magnificent eagle seal.

'Harry, Europe may be marching headlong towards another damaging conflict, but the United States of America has no wish to be a part of it.'

He leant back before he continued,

'In my opinion, it is very unlikely that whatever is going on - if anything, at Rathenow, will directly threaten the security of the United States. It is a European problem and under no circumstances should it become ours. Do I make myself fully understood?'

This was an argument Harry knew he couldn't win and therefore he nodded in feigned agreement at the Colonel's comments.

'Harry, I know you have a deep sense of loyalty to this aristocrat of yours, but I trust that your loyalty to your country will outweigh your desire to help him, or his friends?'

'I know where my duty lies, Sir.'

Harry rose and shook the Colonel's hand before leaving the office. He took another, longer route back to the hotel to allow himself time to consider the implications of the meeting and the consequences that might arise, should he decide to go with his own instincts and disobey the orders that he had just been given.

By the time he passed through the staff entrance some 20 minutes later, he had decided exactly where his loyalties lay.

Chapter 36

Fermeneau and Limoux arrived in Rathenow as the sun was beginning to set. They had decided it would be less suspicious and most likely more productive to explore the town and its environs during daylight hours. With this in mind, they had found the Gasthaus Klaus, one of the many small inns that lay on the outskirts of the town. The inn only had a few rooms, which were basic, but ideally suited to the needs of the many travelling salesmen by whom they were generally occupied.

As they drove through the rolling countryside of the German hinterland, they had discussed plans for the coming days. So many new people visiting such a small town would not have gone unnoticed, particularly the number of important strangers the agents had observed getting on the train. It was also likely that many of the local population might also be connected to, if not directly involved in, whatever was going on.

There would no doubt be a wealth of gossip circulating in the town. If they were careful and prompted the local gossips in the right way, bought them the odd drink or two, they had no doubt people would be more than willing to offer their opinions concerning any unusual goings on. The agents positioned themselves in the centre of the inn's small bar and started to listen to the various conversations taking place around them.

It appeared that there were a great number of tales to tell around and in this outwardly sleepy little provincial town. They listened in amusement as two men talked about a burgeoning scandal concerning the pastor's wife and the butcher's delivery boy.

Apparently, she was an attractive and buxom lady, considerably younger than her rather austere and studious husband, who spent much of his time in his church, or visiting his parishioners, leaving her alone. It was only to be expected therefore, that she had sought out her own form of entertainment in the guise of the delivery boy.

They overheard several conversations concerning the state of the economy and how prices had doubled, trebled, and generally shot through the roof over recent months. The overwhelming opinion of the townspeople was that it was all the fault of the French, although a great deal of abuse and vitriol was directed towards the inability of the Weimar government to stand up to the unreasonable demands of the war reparations. The men sat in silence as the conversations became quite heated at times. They didn't have long to wait before they heard what they were hoping for.

A group of locals dressed in rough-cut hunting clothes were drinking large steins of beer in the bay window of the bar. Lying at their feet, each had a large hound of some nature. As they drank from their glasses, they were discussing the erection of high fences in the forest to the east of the town. They were clearly incensed about the presence of these fences, which had been put there without any prior warning, cutting across several hunting tracks that had been in use for hundreds of years.

The eldest man in the group appeared to be the leader. He was very vociferous with his objections and used wide arm gestures to emphasise his point as he ranted on and on about having reported the matter to the mayor, but having not as yet received a response. He was convinced the mayor was on the payroll of the people working in the forest.

One of the men complained about several large, horse-drawn wagons that were passing his home every evening, carrying away loads of felled trees. They all sympathised with him, someone adding that he also heard the wagons on occasions returning late into the night, loaded with cargo concealed under tarpaulins.

A small, round hunter in a leather waistcoat joined the conversation, commenting on the number of patrolling guards he had seen when he was out in the forest. He believed that they were trying to pass themselves off as some kind of park rangers by carrying shotguns, but from the amount of noise that they made as they moved through the forest, he knew they could not be experienced woodsmen.

One of the men suggested that the guns were perhaps more for the guards' protection from the wild boars. He was soon shouted down by his colleagues.

The leader finished his beer and wished his colleagues a good evening. His wife was preparing their evening meal and he needed to be home soon, he explained. The group all guffawed at his admission, but they all knew his wife and in his position they would have all left the bar some time ago.

Within ten minutes, many more of the early evening customers had made their way home, wishing the innkeeper a good evening as they left.

Eventually, there was only one of the hunters remaining; the youngest of the group.

'Good evening, young man. May we join you? Can I get you another beer perhaps?'

Fermeneau approached the young man and in impeccable, but heavily accented German, tried to initiate a conversation.

'My colleague and I are visiting your lovely town for a few days. Perhaps you could help us with some directions on where we might go?'

The young man looked at them with some suspicion. He was accustomed to seeing a great many visiting salesmen in the bar, but these two looked very different to the any he had seen before. Most of the salesmen had been rather overweight and poorly dressed. Through their tailored suits and pressed white linen shirts, he could see that both of these men had well-toned physiques. Despite his misgivings, however, he was more than happy to accept their hospitality, after all a few extra free beers at the end of a long day were always very welcome. Besides which, he wasn't at all looking forward to going home to his mother with the news that his day's hunting had been less than fruitful.

***

Smith and Perkins set off from Berlin some hours after the two French agents. They decided to stay overnight a few miles from Rathenow, in the small village of Kotzen, where Major General Blyth had recommended a small inn that he used. He assured them that in his experience, the innkeeper could be very discreet. The two men had smiled as they exchanged views on which of the Major General's secretaries might have been the subject of this discretion.

Kotzen was eight kilometres from Rathenow and located on the edge of the forest that lay to the east of the town. They believed it quite likely, given its proximity to the area, that any unusual activity in the locality would not have gone unnoticed. After finding the inn and checking in, the two men wandered along the main street of the town towards a tavern they had passed as they entered the village.

Taverne Willi was on the main street next to the post office. They ordered coffee and took a table outside on the small terraced bar, which was surprisingly full of local men enjoying an early evening drink, no doubt before they made their way home after a day's work. Judging from the clothing that the men wore, it appeared the majority of them were manual workers. Smith had seen a small trailer tethered to a rather bored looking mule a short distance away from the bar, loaded with a number of axes and double handed saws. He thus concluded that at least some of the men were woodsmen.

From the information received via the embassy informants, it was quite likely that these men were involved in the clearing of the forest area.

The workers were talking about various items of local gossip, mostly surrounding the activities of a number of rather promiscuous women in the town. The men were more than happy to make remarks about one of the women in particular, who appeared to have enjoyed the attention of a number of their company. Smith and Perkins smiled as they noted some things never change when a group of men gathered together in a bar. Their nationalities might be different, but the ability of workmen to lust after women remained a universal trait.

The conversation died down, as a slim young woman dressed in a bright red cardigan and matching court shoes walked slowly past the Taverne. The men's eyes followed her every step as she glided serenely along the street, fully aware that she was being watched. As soon as she was out of earshot, various suggestions were made as to what each of them thought they would like to do with her.

After a few minutes and many bawdy suggestions, the theme of the conversation changed. One of the group was asking the others how long they thought it would be before they had finished the clearing in the forest they had been ordered to create. A large man dressed in Lederhosen and smoking a clay pipe remarked that if the weather remained kind, they would be able to clear the remaining trees and flatten the ground within the next few days.

One of the younger men asked him if he had any idea what such an area of ground could be used for. The leader said he had no idea, but then leant forward and lowered his voice, as he warned his men that it was perhaps best not to ask questions or talk about such matters in public.

The conversation stopped as another young woman passed by the Taverne, this time walking in the opposite direction. Several sets of eyes once again followed her motion. Smith and Perkins noted that she too was clearly aware of the attention and doing everything she could to ensure the men noticed her. The sway of her hips as she passed the post office elicited deep sighs from a number of them.

The agents ordered another cup of coffee as Willi passed their table. They sat back in silence as they pondered what they knew they would have to do later.

.

Chapter 37

Jimmy V was wide awake long before 6.30pm. He couldn't sleep, despite his fatigue. He checked for the third time that his trombone slide was suitably greased, and that his mouthpiece and mutes were all in his case.

Hearing that Jimmy V was awake and moving around, Harry knocked and without waiting for a response, entered the bedroom.

'Sir, would you care for tea?'

'Splendid idea, Harry.'

Jimmy V walked into the lounge and sat down in one of the armchairs overlooking the Pariser Platz.

'Harry, I am really quite nervous about this evening.'

'Yes, Sir.'

'These chaps are at the very top of the profession. I was very flattered when I was asked to perform with them. But… I can't help wondering whether I am good enough and why I was asked to come along.'

Harry remained silent and patiently waited for the water to boil.

'I am sure he could have asked so many other trombone players. There are so many who are higher up the pecking order than me, Harry.'

Harry poured a small amount of hot water into the tea pot and gently rotated it, expertly allowing the pot to warm. The art of tea making was one of the many skills he had learnt since taking on his role.

'It is very odd, Harry. But I have to confess that I am rather pleased he thought to ask me. I am so looking forward to what I am certain will be a simply splendid evening.'

Harry added four teaspoons of Darjeeling leaves to the now warm pot and then added the boiling water. He waited patiently for the tea to brew. Jimmy V continued to look out over Pariser Platz, deep in thought.

'Your tea, Sir.'

'Thank you, Harry.'

'I have arranged for a taxi to collect yourself and Lady Julia. The taxi will arrive at 7.15 as agreed.'

'Thank you, Harry'

'I have arranged to accompany Mary to the theatre a little later. Lady Julia has requested that she attend this evening's performance.'

'Splendid Harry. Thank you'

Harry looked at Jimmy V as he continued to stare blankly out of the lounge window. He had seen his nervousness prior to giving performances on many occasions, but he couldn't remember ever seeing him quite so apprehensive before.

Seeing the anxious state of his employer, Harry felt a tiny pang of guilt that he was responsible for instigating the invitation. How else could he have engineered the opportunity to travel to Berlin?

When he had received the initial intelligence reports indicating that the NSDAP were planning some form of international demonstration, he knew that he must be in Berlin to prevent it. The intelligence suggested the NSDAP intended to set up some form of newsworthy event and the Weimar government would be implicated as being complicit in the act. The NSDAP intended then to lay claim to having thwarted it.

The upcoming tour by one of the world's leading black American performers, accompanied by a largely black American jazz orchestra, was a potential prime target.

Given his previous relationship with Josephine Baker, and the undoubted skills of his employer, it was simple to formulate a plan whereby Harry could ensure his own legitimate presence in Berlin. He knew that Jimmy V would not be able to resist the opportunity to play with the Whiteman Band, and he had been proven right.

***

Lady Julia had also been unable to sleep; she had far too many thoughts flying around in her head. Having spoken to Harry earlier, she had not been surprised that the American embassy wished to have no involvement with any of the unfolding events in Rathenow, given their strict neutrality policy. In Lady Julia's experience, the Americans were only likely to act where one of their citizens was directly threatened, or where it was likely to be of tangible benefit to themselves.

She felt that she needed an additional pair of eyes during the evening's proceedings and had taken the unusual step of requesting that Mary should accompany her.

Mary was more than happy to acquiesce to Lady Julia's request. She had loaned Mary one of her gowns, which the maid had then spent much of the afternoon shortening.

Mary knocked on the bedroom door and entered.

'Mary, you look quite stunning. I believe that you will turn many heads this evening. Harry will be quite speechless when he sees you.'

She smiled and giggled as she saw her maid blush deeply.

Chapter 38

Jimmy V and Lady Julia arrived at the Europahaus at 7.20pm, fully 5 minutes after the Autoruf taxi had collected them as arranged. The stage-door attendant was still at his post. He yawned deeply as the Englishman signed into his book. He certainly woke up when he saw Lady Julia, however.

He stared at the elegantly dressed young English woman and like all men, he was struck by how very tall she was. She wore one of her new Coco Chanel figure hugging gowns in which she looked quite stunning.

Whilst the door attendant was admiring Lady Julia, Jimmy V took his trombone to the band dressing room, where he left it in what he hoped would be the capable charge of Baby Dodds, who was sitting in the dressing room preparing for the evening's concert with a bottle of Schnapps.

He expressed vehemently his dislike of the taste, but as he explained to Jimmy V, despite exhaustive efforts earlier, which involved visiting numerous bars and liquor stores, he had been unable to secure a bottle of his favoured scotch anywhere.

Jimmy V returned to Lady Julia and together they entered the club from the back-stage area. The door attendant followed them with his eyes, before slumping back into his chair with a sigh. Mathilde, he remembered, had been a bright young thing with a waspish waist when he had married her in 1900, just like Lady Julia. But three strapping lads and twenty seven years later, time had taken its toll, unfortunately.

Jimmy V and Lady Julia were surprised to see so many people already seated in anticipation. Very different to the night time trends of London and Paris, where people attended the theatres much later in the evening.

A myriad of waiters, dressed in long white, heavily starched aprons extending to below knee level and tied in a theatrical knot at the front, scampered effortlessly between the tables, each carrying ridiculously overladen silver trays held expertly with one hand above their heads. Large steins of beer and plates of food tottered precariously, before they were delivered to the waiting customers.

Jimmy V was thankful he had the forethought to arrange a table with the theatre management earlier in the day, from which Lady Julia would have a good view of the stage.

'Herr Jimmy!' bellowed the theatre manager as he approached them, smiling broadly through a thick moustache.

'Your table is this way, Sir.' He gestured theatrically with his hand as he guided them to a table set in a private booth, offering not only a good view of the stage, but more particularly of where the trombone section would be sitting later in the evening.

'This will be splendid!' remarked Jimmy V, as he pulled back a chair facing the stage for Lady Julia to take her seat.

'Shall I take your coat, Madam? A waiter will take your order shortly.'

Jimmy V pressed a bank note of some description into the man's hand as he took the coats to the cloakroom. He wasn't very good with the new German currency, but the manager seemed very impressed with the gratuity which he quickly put into his pocket. This was going to be a good night indeed he thought, as he calculated that the tip he had just received represented the best part of a day's wage.

Jimmy V sat back and drank in the atmosphere of the Europahaus. The general ambiance was very different to the nightclubs and concert venues of London. Closer, perhaps, to the venues in which he had performed in America, but somehow not quite the same. The atmosphere seemed altogether more casual in some ways, but this did nothing to dispel his anxieties about his upcoming performance.

'Julia, how good to see you!'

'Valette!' answered Lady Julia in surprise.

'I had not expected you would be in Berlin? You didn't mention it when we saw you in Paris.'

'I hadn't intended being here. However, after meeting Mr Whiteman and Miss Baker at the Ritz I simply could not miss the show. I caught the mid- morning train and here I am! Viscount, how good to see you again.'

'Countess, how splendid to see you. Would you care to join us?'

'Thank you, but I have no wish to intrude. I have arranged to meet with some old and dear friends. We are all very excited at seeing your performance this evening.'

'How very kind,' replied Jimmy V with a smile

'Perhaps you would care to join us later? I have organised an after show party at the Adlon. As a friend of Ladybee, you would be most welcome. Please bring your friends along too.'

'That is most kind,' replied the Countess, suppressing a smile.

'Splendid! We will look forward to seeing you later.'

Lady Julia watched the retreating figure of the Countess, as she made her way through the throng of tables towards a dimly lit booth at the back of the theatre. She was unable to make out the identity of any of the three men that greeted her return, but she was reasonably sure they were not the same men that had accompanied Valette the previous evening.

Her view was interrupted by the appearance of a waiter, who took their drinks order. Jimmy V, much to her surprise, ordered an orange juice for himself.

Lady Julia smiled. How nervous he must be about the evening's performance, his anxiety almost made him even more endearing to her. His nervousness added a certain vulnerability, which she found wholly alluring. She looked across as he shifted nervously in his seat. Jimmy V, in a nightclub, without a Martini in hand. This was an occasion worthy of note in the Melody Maker.

She glanced around the room. There was certainly a cosmopolitan mix of people slowly gathering for the evening's entertainment. The rich assortment of colours and fashions worn by the women was matched by the wide variety of eveningwear worn by their male counterparts. Whilst there was no formal dress code at the Europahaus, like elsewhere in Europe there was a certain convention that men were expected to follow when attending evening engagements and for the most part, this was being followed, although she quickly lost count of the number of garishly coloured bow ties sported.

Her gaze was drawn to a group of men seated together at a table on the very outside edge of the theatre across from her position. They appeared to be having a rapturous time.

Their attire was anything but conventional, with the majority of them wearing richly coloured velvet jackets, accompanied by a variety of pastel coloured cravats or silk scarves in place of bow ties. Many of them wore large brimmed hats adorned with long feathers from either pheasants, or possibly even peacocks.

The table in front of them was full of glasses containing drinks of a vivid green colour, which she took to be Absinthe. They had clearly embraced the spirit of the bohemian lifestyle she heard so much about, from what she saw, she was thankful the infectious culture had not made its way across the English Channel to London as yet.

What would her mother make of them? As for James' mother? Thank the Lord they were not here. She could only imagine the level of horror the two ladies would have felt.

The background music being played by the house band came to a stop and the lights slowly began to dim, to signal the start of the evening's entertainment. What was to follow would give Lady Julia a whole new meaning for the word 'Bohemian'.

Chapter 39

Smith and Perkins returned to their room as soon as they were satisfied they had learned as much information as they could in the Taverne Willi. They were very wary of arousing too much suspicion by lingering for too long. After a short discussion, they agreed on a plan and were now waiting for the cover of darkness before they set out.

They had undertaken many covert operations together in the past and acknowledged that all operations carried an element of risk. The cover of darkness would help, but regardless of this, both men were aware they were very much going into unknown territory, against a foe whose strength and location was also not known to them.

On the face of it, this was a simple recognisance mission; enter the forest, see what is happening and then return to the inn. Experience, however, told them it was never that simple. If the forest was concealing a secret that someone wanted to hide, it made sense that whoever that someone was, they would want to protect the area more closely at night time. This was when it was most likely that unwelcome eyes might come along snooping around.

The workers that had been talking in the tavern were obviously part of the daytime labour force and would have little or no knowledge of whatever security measures were in place once they left. It appeared from the conversation they overheard that the men had no clear idea of why they were carrying out the task they had been assigned.

The two men knew it would have been dangerous, and most likely pointless to ask too many questions. The result would only have been to draw unwanted attention towards themselves.

They dressed in silence.

The dark coveralls that they had brought with them were concealed in hidden pockets sown into the lining of their overcoats. They would put these on as soon as they entered the forest. Light and sound discipline would be essential in the nocturnal environment and neither man had anything that would rattle or reflect the light from the moon.

Each carried a Luger Parabellum M17 pistol. In the event either of them was killed during the mission, the presence of a standard issue German pistol would not point directly to them being foreign agents. Each also carried false papers, provided by the embassy, which identified them as farm machinery salesmen working for the Mengele Agrartechnik company based in the Gunzburg area of Bavaria.

The time ticked slowly by as the last rays of sunshine began to trickle through the upper fronds of the pine trees visible from the windows of their room at the edge of the forest.

From what they had learned earlier, the area of most interest was a number of kilometres away. They intended to set off as soon as darkness fell and make their way through to the clearing as quickly as possible.

They sat in silence, alone with their thoughts as they waited for darkness to fall. Perkins had stripped down the Luger and was oiling the mechanism for the third time that day. Smith was repacking his equipment into his rucksack, making sure that nothing would rattle and give their position away.

***

Several miles away on the other side of Rathenow, the two French agents had spent a very tedious hour talking to the young hunter about the citizens of the town with whom he thought they could discuss their merchandise. The agents were acting as knife salesmen, a role that came naturally to Gaston Fermeneau, who had held such an occupation before the war.

Patience was essential if they were to find out the information they sought and after three more steins of beer, the young man was showing clear signs he had reached his limit.

'So Hans, you enjoy hunting in the forest?' asked Fermeneau, casually.

The young man nodded, placing his empty glass on the table.

'You have been having a few problems recently I heard you say,' added Limoux.

The young man nodded as Formeneau ordered him another beer. He explained in detail what had occurred over the last six months, recounting event after event that he'd witnessed or heard about, following the arrival of the 'strangers' in town.

The agents sat in silence and listened as the young man talked, punctuating his words frequently with a rich array of expletives, as he told them of the effect each event had on his livelihood, which seemed to centre entirely on the hunting of wild boar.

The agents learned where in the forest the fences had been erected, most of which appeared to intersect with the long established runs of several families of boar. In the young man's opinion, this was done solely to prevent him earning his living.

The agents thought that this was unlikely to be the case, but knew it was best to keep their opinions to themselves.

The sun had almost set as the agents concluded they had learned as much as they were likely to from the young hunter and thanked him for his help. As they prepared to leave, the young man took hold of Fermeneau's arm and spoke very quietly behind his hand, so that nobody would be able to hear him.

'I think it is the French. My father, before he was killed in the war, he told me that you should never trust the French.' He looked round to make sure that nobody was listening before he continued.

'I think they have built a secret sausage factory in the forest.'

The two agents nodded in feigned agreement as they took leave from the bar. When they were out of earshot, Fermeneau turned to Limoux.

'I suspect, Limoux, that a French sausage factory is not what we will find in the forest.'

'I believe that your suspicions may prove to be correct, Sir,' he replied with a smile.

Chapter 40

The lights were fully dimmed at the Europahaus, leaving only the table lamps to softly illuminate the faces of the audience waiting eagerly for the show to begin. After a few moments, the house band started to play again.

With a crash on the cymbal, several male dancers rushed on to the stage dressed in voluminous Turkish style trousers covered in what looked like goose feathers. From the waist upwards, they were completely naked.

Their upper torsos had been covered in some form of oil, to which had been applied several layers of glitter which shone in the stage lights, giving them a luminescent glow as they completed various leaps and turns. Every time one of the dancers performed an entrechat, a plume of feathers was displaced from his costume and sent floating up into the air, where the feathers caught in the swirling lights before spiralling to the floor.

The attention of the cravat wearing men was absolute as they cheered bawdily and applauded the dancers' every movement. Lady Julia smiled as she watched their feathered hats bouncing along in time to the music. Several of them held bank notes aloft as the dancers gyrated in front of them.

On stage, a curtained box was quietly wheeled into place by the stage crew, now dressed in smart dinner suits.

As the music gained in momentum, the dancers gradually moved away from the audience and surrounded the box at the centre of the stage.

With a cymbal roll and a crash, the band went silent. The dancers dropped to the ground, and a hush descended on the audience. The curtain was pulled back and a tall, slender woman dressed in a tight fitting, man's evening suit, complete with tailcoat, stepped elegantly from the box and on to the stage.

The men crawled along the floor, leaving a snail trail of glitter and yet more of their plumage in their wake. As they reached towards her, their hands were kicked aside. She descended serenely towards the dance floor, leaving them floundering theatrically behind her.

The house band struck up a song introduction as she descended the last step onto the main arena.

Anita Berber was the toast of Berlin. She started to sing in a soft, sultry voice as she moved towards the middle of the dance floor. After completing the first verse, she was joined by the dancers who surrounded her adoringly as she completed the chorus. As the final notes sounded they held aloft a blue silk canopy, which obscured her from the view of the audience.

The house band started the second verse, and the dancers dropped the canopy to the floor to reveal Anita Berber in all her burlesque glory. She now wore a sparkling blue thong, and very little else, it appeared. To retain some semblance of modesty, she held two large ostrich feather fans in front of her breasts.

The dancers continued to gyrate at her feet in time to the music. Most of their plumage had been displaced and either floated towards the front tables, or lay in untidy piles around the edge of the dance floor.

Lady Julia looked across at Jimmy V. He seemed to be completely engrossed in the show, despite his earlier nervousness. She smiled to herself as she wondered what was going on his mind. Had he even noticed the dancers, or was he still planning his first solo for later in the evening?

On stage, Anita Berber was building towards the finale of her opening number. The dancers collected at her feet and reached up towards her bare breasts. With a flourish, she lifted her arms to reveal a matching pair of blue sequined tassels attached to her nipples, as she sang the final note. The audience applause was immediate and rapturous. The house lights dimmed and the dancers left the stage.

When the lights came back on, a small army of stagehands was at work sweeping the floor to clear the carnage that had taken place. Smears of oil and glitter were all that was left after the feathers had been swiftly collected into small sacks. The house band returned to playing background music.

'Well, that was somewhat different Ladybee. If they perform like that every evening they must get through a great many sacks of feathers. It must provide a good supply of duck for the menu.'

Lady Julia smiled at the thought. No mention of Anita Berber's near nakedness, only how many ducks or geese would be sacrificed to provide the necessary supply of feathers.

'Splendid music.'

A few moments passed before the house lights once again dimmed and it was time for Anita Berber to reappear. Lady Julia could not begin to imagine what might be coming next.

As the house lights came back to life, a small enclosure had been erected at the side of the main stage. Inside it were several sheep grazing on a bale of hay. Their wool had been dyed in a rich variety of luminescent colours and sprayed with glitter. This shone brightly, as it was caught in the glare of the stage lights.

Above the stage, swinging on a trapeze adorned with flowers, was Anita Berber. She swung back and forth over the top of the enclosure as the house band played the introduction to her next song.

To the cheers of the cravat men the dancers reappeared, this time clad in lederhosen shorts. Their upper torsos appeared to have been liberally reapplied with oil and glitter during the break.

Looking up at Anita Berber, Lady Julia could think of nothing else except how very uncomfortable it must be to sit on a trapeze in a thong, particularly as it appeared to have no form of padding.

Jimmy V still appeared to be engrossed in the show, as he sat staring into space. He was not looking up at the swinging form of Anita Berber on her trapeze; his thoughts were now clearly focussed on his own performance.

At the back of the Europahaus, Valette Simone sat alongside the Gauleiter of Berlin, Dr. Goebbels flanked by his ever present bodyguards. They were dressed in the brown shirts that had become the trademark uniform of the NSDAP. The shirts did not match the black suits and ties they wore but neither man seemed too concerned about the lack of dress sense, as he surveyed the scenes around him.

It was most unlikely that they would be called upon to protect the little man seated between them, however they were armed and ready to act if a threat appeared.

Goebbels was a cautious man who considered himself far more important than he most likely was. There was no doubt that he possessed the ambition and the desire to show that he could be a valuable asset to the hierarchy of the party. This evening he might just have the chance to show exactly how capable and valuable he could be.

The Gauleiter considered himself to be something of a ladies' man and was a great admirer of Anita Berber. He had seen her show many times and never tired of seeing her disport herself in front of him. His thoughts on this occasion, however, drifted away from her performance and firmly towards his plans for later that evening. Looking down at his briefcase leaning against the leg of the table, he allowed himself a wry smile.

Chapter 41

The birds completed the final refrains of their songs as the last strands of light left the canopy of trees. Smith stared through the small gap he had left in the curtains of his room, towards the forest. He estimated that they would have about four miles to cover through the trees, with only the light of the moon to guide them before they reached the area where he believed the clearing to be located. He was anxious to set off, but experience told him it was far too early. There would still be people out and about in the village.

He heard a nearby door open and the muffled sound of voices in the distance, as someone took their leave from a neighbour's house. The door closed and footsteps echoed on the stony ground as the guests moved off down the street. A few moments passed in silence before he heard the barking of a small dog as another door opened and closed a little further away.

The closing door sounded like a rifle shot in the stillness that now enveloped the village.

Perkins had completed the cleaning of his weaponry and was lying on the bed.

'Sir, have you any idea what might be going on here?'

'I don't want to assume anything, Perkins. It would appear that the locals are not involved, other than as manual labourers. That leads me to believe that whatever is going on must require some expertise. Expertise that is not available locally.'

'It must have something to do with the NSDAP, Sir. The reports we've been getting in London indicate that since the release of their leader from prison, they have become increasingly active.'

'I have read the reports, Perkins. However, there is no mention of them being involved in anything other than politics. Whatever we discover this evening, I very much doubt it will be related to politics.'

They drifted back into silence once again, as they waited for night to descend outside the window.

***

On the other side of Rathenow, Fermeneau and Limoux finally left the bar and made their way back towards the centre of town. The market square was still busy and a rich variety of music was drifted from a number of street cafes.

The many tales relayed to them by the young hunter confirmed there was clearly a mystery to be solved in this outwardly sleepy town, and the Frenchmen needed to know more than they had learned so far.

Some of the people involved directly in the forest activities could well be out and about in the town. Given the animosity that the arrival of the visitors had clearly created, it was likely that they would stand out from the crowd.

It was not long before their patience was suitably rewarded. After ordering coffees in only the second venue they visited, they noticed a group of four; two men and two woman, seated in a booth inside the café. Their dress alone marked them as different from the rest of the customers.

The women wore dresses and hats that were far more suited to the city than a small rural town and both men wore well-tailored suits with starched collared shirts and ties. Most of the local population dressed in home manufactured work clothes. Rather conveniently, within a few minutes of their arrival, a table became free close to the booth. The agents quickly claimed the table for themselves and called over the waiter.

They ordered a light supper of meats and cheeses from the menu and settled back in their chairs to take in the night scene in the centre of the town, their well-trained ears focussed on the conversation taking place in the booth behind them.

***

The comfort of darkness had now completely enveloped the village of Kotzen. Smith and Perkins slipped out of their rooms and quickly entered the sanctuary of the forest. They stopped and listened for a few moments for any sign of movement that might indicate they had been observed and followed. To their relief, they heard nothing except the gentle evening breeze rustling the leaves of the trees.

Smith checked the dial of his compass. The direction points glowed brightly thanks to the tiny specks of radio luminescent paint applied to them. After a few seconds, they moved off again as quietly as they could, through the thick forest. After about 100 yards, they were relieved to come across a trackway. Smith consulted his compass once again. It appeared the path led in the direction they wished to travel. It was extremely narrow - most probably a hunter's path thought Smith. It was unlikely they would come across such an individual in the darkness; however, they decided that light and sound discipline should continue to be exercised.

***

Fermeneau and Limoux ordered a fresh pot of coffee. The conversation from the table behind them was proving rather banal. The two men were from Munich, and were married with children. One of the women was from Dusseldorf and the other from Heidelberg. Both were unmarried. They listened with waning interest as the group talked about their respective families.

Suddenly the conversation took a new direction.

'Have you completed your re-calculations after yesterday's testing, Helga?'

'Yes, I completed them this afternoon. Only a slight adjustment is required. I have passed the changes to the engineers. The new shaft should be ready for testing by the end of tomorrow,' replied the woman from Heidelberg, now identified as Helga.

'Excellent!' replied Munich man.

'Herr Focke will be pleased with our progress. We will remain on schedule to demonstrate the fully functional engine when he visits at the end of the week,' added his colleague.

'That would be fantastic Heinrich. But are you sure the engineers can have it fully mounted by then?' replied Munich man.

'I am certain, Rolf. They are all aware that in order for us to meet Herr Udet's deadline, we must have the engines fitted and working by the end of the week.'

Fermeneau and Limoux listened as the party discussed technical data relating to their work. They slowly drank the fresh coffee brought to them and looked out over the central square of Rathenow. A town seemingly oblivious to the secrets in its forest.

***

Smith and Perkins followed the hunter's path, pausing occasionally to check for sounds and to consult the compass. An hour passed before they caught sight of something glinting in the moonlight ahead of them. They bent to a crouch, as they once again checked their direction. Creeping forward, they came to the fence which cut right across the path, exactly as the young hunter had described.

Smith pointed to his right and the two men left the path and made their way slowly into the undergrowth. Their way was now much more difficult, blocked off here and there by fallen trees covered in slippery moss and lichen. Overhead, the silence was punctuated by the hoots of an owl as it stood vigil over their progress. Perkins looked up at the canopy of trees but couldn't see from where the sound originated.

After about 200 yards, the two men turned left and once again headed towards the fence. Perkins extracted the wire cutters packed into one of his pockets and started to quietly cut a hole through the thick wire. It seemed that after every snip of the cutters the owl hooted in alarm, as if trying to sound an alert to passing guards. Perkins paused after each link was cut, listening for any sound. Smith remained on guard, his Luger pistol now in his hand.

After fifteen minutes, Perkins had created a large enough hole for the agents to be able to slip through. The perfect arc of fencing lay to one side, ready to fit back into place. The precision of Perkins' work meant that once replaced, it should withstand all but the closest of inspections.

The two men slipped through the fence. In front of them was a sharp incline, leading to a ridge about thirty feet above their current location. Smith caught hold of Perkins' arm before he could start to make the climb. Looking up, he caught sight of a silhouette. The shape of a man carrying a rifle came slowly into view as the two British officers couched beside the trunk of a fallen tree.

The man looked around in silence. Had he heard the sound of the wire cutters? Had he been alerted by some hidden tell-tale attached to the fence some way off? Had the hooting of the night owl given Smith and Perkins' presence away? They felt the tension in their bodies as the guard stood still in the gloom.

They controlled their breathing, thankful that the night was warm and that the steam of their breath in the night air would not reveal their location. After what seemed like an eternity, the man slowly moved off the ridge and descended noisily through the trees on the other side. A few seconds later, they heard him curse as he tripped over some hidden obstruction in the darkness.

Smith and Perkins waited patiently for a long time before beginning their climb. Moving cautiously and silently forward, checking ahead as they went, careful not to create any noise, they crept forward on all fours. It was a full ten minutes before they reached the top of the incline and could look over. They stared at the scene that greeted them.

Chapter 42

Jimmy V sat nervously, waiting for the clock to tick around. He had watched the performance of Anita Berber with interest, but his mind was focussed more firmly in his own world. The musicians of the house trio played a succession of nameless background music as the Paul Whiteman Band assembled behind the heavy draped stage curtains.

The stage crew had removed the multi-coloured sheep and herded them into their temporary holding pens erected in the basement of the theatre. It had taken some time for them to clean up the droppings and hay. Jimmy V was somehow disappointed that the droppings were not also multi-coloured.

He smiled to himself as he recalled one of his favourite childhood games alongside his brother Charles. The boys had made crude catapults from the limbs of fallen saplings, strung with strong elastic they found in their mother's sewing box. They had taken it in turns to try and fire dark brown sheep dung pellets into their sister Melissa's baby carriage. Their dear old nanny, Miss Jenkins, had a habit of falling asleep on one of the estate benches, which meant she was always blissfully unaware of the two boys collecting ammunition from the estate grounds. She could never quite grasp how the sheep dung managed to accumulate in the baby carriage.

'Must be crows!' she once said to one of the house maids, after a particularly good day for the boys. Dear Miss Jenkins. He had been so sad when she died.

His mind was soon brought back to the Europahaus when the stage crew started spraying the area where the sheep had been with a rather sickly, sweet smelling perfume of some nature. Coupled with his nervousness, Jimmy V began to feel quite heady.

'I preferred the smell of sheep,' Slide Williams commented, as he arranged his mutes underneath his music stand.

'Me too,' agreed Red Nichols, holding his nose as he sorted through the charts that had been placed on his stand by the ever efficient Earl Hines.

'Doesn't go well with my allergies,' he continued before sneezing loudly.

The band was fully assembled and ready to perform by the time Paul Whiteman appeared from his dressing room. He was resplendent in a white tuxedo and red bow tie, carrying his trademark long conducting baton proudly as he strode towards the stage.

'Gentlemen, Whiteman's here. Let's get this show started!' he bellowed, as he reached the centre of the stage.

For the next hour, Jimmy V was in musical heaven. He sat in awe of the unfailing standard of the players around him. A standard that he emulated time and again, as his confidence grew through the performance. Lady Julia sat alongside Harry and Mary as a succession of charts were played by the band. It seemed to her that every song seemed to just get better and better.

In all the years she had heard Jimmy V play, she had never heard him perform as well as he did that evening. His solo in the Paul Whiteman song 'Wonderful One' was truly magnificent. When the band played the Paul Whiteman hit 'When the one you love, loves you' she was almost drawn to tears by the wonderfully lyrical solo the young Viscount played. The band concluded their first set with a rousing version of the 'Whiteman Stomp' with solos from Earl Hines, Red Nichols and Slide Williams.

Joseph Goebbels had paid particular attention to Josephine Baker and her dancers. She sang a number of songs during the first set that captivated the audience. To the Gauleiter, it was Josephine Baker's undoubted beauty that attracted his eye. Glancing at his briefcase he reflected that he had his instructions. He would follow them to the letter.

There was a forty minute break between sets and Jimmy V decided to return to Lady Julia in the auditorium.

'James! That was truly magnificent. You must be so pleased.'

'Thank you Ladybee. It was rather a special experience. Truly splendid!'

Harry smiled.

'Harry, are the arrangements for later this evening complete?'

'Yes, Sir. I have also arranged for a number of taxis to transport your guests. They will be by the stage door as soon as the performance finishes.'

'How thoughtful. Thank you, Harry.'

Lady Julia smiled as she saw that the earlier nervousness had vanished and her Jimmy V had most definitely returned. Further confirmation came as he summoned a passing waiter and ordered drinks for the party, including his customary martini.

The second and third sets were performed with equal aplomb by the band, to an increasingly appreciative crowd. Josephine Baker concluded her set with her famous Banana Dance, which elicited demands for several encores from the audience. Lady Julia noticed that the 'Cravat' table had remained stoically silent throughout her performance.

By the time the band played its last encore 'Say it with Music', the clock had ticked around to 1.00 am. The crowd bayed for more, but the show was over and Paul Whiteman bowed theatrically, but with an undoubted sense of finality as he left the stage. The theatre announcer thanked the audience and proudly proclaimed that the band would be performing again the following evening. Lady Julia looked at the clock and smiled at his inaccuracy.

The taxi ride back to the Adlon was a short one during which Jimmy V talked excitedly, recounting every chart in detail. He was still talking as the taxi came to a stop outside the hotel, seemingly not noticing its lack of motion.

'James! We have arrived.'

'Of course we have my dear. Did you hear the final chorus of Love be a Lady? What a sound from the trumpets Ladybee! Have you ever heard such a noise?'

Jimmy V handed the driver a note in payment of the fare and proceeded with his commentary. The taxi driver looked down in amazement when he realised that the note he had just received was the equivalent of an entire evening's fares.

The hotel concierge greeted the couple as they entered the building, confirming that a substantial area of the oriental garden had been set aside. Food and drinks would be served as soon as the remainder of his party arrived. Jimmy V paused briefly to acknowledge his statement before continuing with his recollections of the evening.

Chapter 43

Smith and Perkins peered over the crest of the hill.

Below them, a substantial area of the forest had been cleared and an assortment of sizeable buildings had been erected. Immediately to their left, the trunks of several dozen trees had been stacked neatly into pyramids awaiting collection. There was another perimeter fence, topped with coils of barbed wire and in the distance, pin pricks of light shone from several windows, indicating that they were occupied.

Stretching away to their right was a long corridor of land that had obviously been newly cleared, as a large number of felled trees still lay where they had fallen, strewn like motionless bodies on a battlefield. As the two men continued to survey the scene, a guard appeared from the nearest building with a hunting rifle casually slung over his shoulder. He started to rummage through the pockets of his coat. A few moments later they saw the spark of match, as he lit his pipe.

The orange glow of the tobacco illuminated the lower half of his face as he inhaled the smoke. He walked slowly in the direction of one of the other buildings. Smith and Perkins held their breath, as he suddenly paused and looked up the hill directly towards them. He appeared to be listening for some unheard noise from within the forest.

Through the gloom of the night, he seemed to be looking directly into their eyes as the glow of his pipe once again lit up his face. A noise that sounded like thousands of shuffling feet suddenly erupted from immediately below them, which made the guard turn and take the rifle off his shoulder.

A large boar had appeared and was moving noisily through the undergrowth, looking for food. The guard was now at full alert as he brought his rifle into the firing position, aiming towards the source of the noise.

Smith and Perkins looked on helplessly, unable to move for fear of attracting attention, as the boar continued to push through the fallen leaves and rotting timber below them, foraging for food. The sound stopped suddenly, as the boar caught the scent of man on the breeze. Whether it was the guard or Smith and Perkins that it could smell was uncertain, but it sensed danger.

A high pitched squeal punctuated the clear night air as the boar made a bolt for the safety of the deeper forest. The guard lowered his rifle as he realised the source of the noise. He walked over to the nearest pile of logs and relieved himself. The steam rose skyward as it mingled seamlessly with the smoke from his pipe.

Smith and Perkins started to breathe again as they watched the guard walk back towards the second building and without further alarm, enter and close the door behind him. They waited a few more minutes before shuffling backwards away from the ridge.

A number of hours later, as the first signs of dawn began to appear on the horizon, they were sitting in their rooms at the Pension, their return journey thankfully passing without incident.

'We need to know what is going on in those buildings, Perkins.'

'The large building on the outer edge of the compound looked like a hanger of some nature. That could be the key to the entire operation, Sir.'

'Tomorrow night, Perkins, we will return and find out.'

'Yes, Sir. Tea?'

'Excellent idea, Perkins. Earl Grey?'

'Only Darjeeling, Sir'

'In that case milk and two sugars please, my man.'

Chapter 44

A line of taxis began to appear at the Adlon, giving the impression of forming a convoy, as a plethora of guests began to arrive. Inside, Jimmy V and Lady Julia were waiting to greet their guests.

'Has the special order arrived, Harry?'

'Yes, Sir. The table in the corner, next to the large bonsai tree.'

'Splendid.'

'Warren,' Jimmy V announced as Warren Baby Dodds, the drummer emerged alongside his ever present companion Wellman Breaux, from one of the first of the fleet of taxis.

'I have a surprise for you chaps. Please come along with me.'

A small table had been set aside, in the middle of which was a single bottle of amber coloured liquid.

'I hope you will find this more to your taste?' remarked Jimmy V, as he motioned Baby Dodds towards the table.

'Jimmy, I could kiss your scrawny little English butt!!' exclaimed the drummer, as he caught sight of what awaited him. A bottle of Grant's finest

Scotch whisky sat in the centre of the table, resplendent in its very distinctive tricorn shaped bottle. Two fine lead crystal glasses were set on coasters, waiting to be filled.

'That won't be necessary, Warren,' replied Jimmy V, with a smile,

'Enjoy your evening gentlemen.'

Jimmy V left the two musicians to enjoy their drinks.

'Sir, will you be requiring my services further this evening?' enquired Harry.

'I don't think so, Harry. Thank you as always. Splendid arrangements!'

Harry took his leave and headed towards the staircase leading to the upper floors. He had arranged an equally pleasant evening of his own.

The majority of the band had chosen to leave their instruments at the Europahaus in anticipation of the following evening's performance. Paul Whiteman, ever the showman, had decided that he and Josephine Baker should return to their own hotel first of all to change and thus make a grand entrance to the after show party.

The Countess de St Augustin and her party arrived with some ceremony in the large black

Maybach W5 car, driven by a chauffeur dressed in the brown shirt of the NSDAP. The wing mirrors were festooned with flags bearing the swastika emblem of the party, which stood to attention proudly on the front of the vehicle.

The hotel concierge and his staff reacted very differently to the arrival of the Maybach, remaining stoically still as the occupants disembarked and the cars pulled away.

Lady Julia was looking out of the window as the car stopped in front of the hotel entrance and the door was opened. The reaction of the hotel staff as the Countess and her companions alighted and entered did not go unnoticed.

Valette Simone, Countess de St. Augustin was clearly not a woman to be taken at face value and Lady Julia was becoming increasingly aware she was not a friend to be trusted. She smiled at the small, schoolboy like figure of the Gauleiter, as he tripped along at the side of the statuesque figure of the Countess.

She recognised him immediately from the pictures she had seen at her briefing in London. He was trying to hide an obvious limp which made him favour his left side. Her well-trained eye could see he had a weakness on that side. People might have mistaken this as a legacy of some brave act during the war, but Lady Julia was aware it was an accident of birth. He certainly didn't hold himself like a military man.

Why would he be carrying a briefcase to the party? Perhaps he had arrived at the theatre directly from his duties at the NSDAP Headquarters? They certainly made for an odd couple as they arrived at the Oriental garden. The three bodyguards who exited the car with them remained in the lobby, as the couple made their way to the festivities.

'Countess, I am pleased you were able to come.'

'Julia, thank you for inviting us. May I introduce you to my good friend, Dr Joseph Goebbels?'

'Good evening, Lady Mortimer. The Countess has told me so much about you. I am pleased to be able to meet you in person.'

Lady Julia towered over the diminutive figure of the Gauleiter, as he offered his hand.

'I am pleased you were able to join us, Dr. Goebbels. Would you like me to arrange for your case to be taken to the cloakroom?'

'Thank you. That won't be necessary,' he replied, a little too forcefully.

'But thank you for your very kind offer,' he added quickly, in an effort to diffuse his previous comment.

'Please help yourself to drinks and canapés. I believe you may remember some of the musicians from Paris, Valette?'

'Is Miss Baker here yet?' enquired the Countess,

'Joseph would like so much to make her acquaintance.'

'I believe she will be arriving shortly with Mr Whiteman. I will let her know when she arrives that she has a new admirer.'

Lady Julia moved on to greet another party of guests that had just entered the hotel. The arrival of further taxis had been delayed as they waiting for the Maybach to leave the front of the Adlon. Slide Williams and Fufu Lamore emerged arm in arm.

'Julia!' exclaimed Fufu, excitedly.

'Now this is what I call a Hotel. Look at the elephant, Johnny!'

'Welcome, Philomena.'

'Please Julia, call me Fufu. Everyone does.'
She laughed as she slipped her arm through that of
Slide Williams and wandered off towards the
fountain and the rest of the band.

Lady Julia noticed that Jimmy V was
circulating as always, showing his well practised
skills as a party host. What a perfect team they made
at such gatherings she thought to herself. Like a well
oiled machine, she met the guests as they entered the
hotel and he greeted them warmly into the party. It
had been this way for as long as she could remember
and so, she hoped with a smile, it would always be.

The final taxi pulled up outside the hotel and
the unmistakeable figure of Paul Whiteman emerged
in his camel coat. For such a large man, he moved
remarkably quickly as he opened the opposite door
for his companion to disembark.

Josephine Baker emerged in a new outfit
that was quite stunning. The myriad of sequins that
covered the slender gown was mesmerising, as they
sparkled and shimmied in the lights of the hotel
canopy. Paul Whiteman had the broadest grin that
Lady Julia had ever seen as he led her into the hotel.
The atmosphere stood still as they walked slowly
towards Lady Julia and the oriental garden, where the

assembled crowd burst into a spontaneous round of applause.

'Miss Baker, Mr Whiteman, I am so pleased that you could join us. Miss Baker, you look quite stunning.'

'Thank you Lady Julia. I want to out-sparkle that German bitch. Is she here?'

'I believe so. I think she arrived long before the show actually finished. She is seated over there.' Lady Julia indicated a table close to the fountain at the end of the garden.

'In that case, we shall go over here.' Josephine turned abruptly and set off in the opposite direction with Paul Whiteman following in her wake. Perhaps Josephine Baker had been less than impressed by Anita Berber's performance. She was accustomed to being the star attraction, and clearly did not take kindly to being the support act.

'Ladybee, what a splendid party. Martini?'

Looking around, Lady Julia saw that Valette and her companion had taken a table on the edge of the bar area, but there was no sign of the bodyguards from earlier. From the position they had taken up, they had a perfect view of the whole of the oriental garden, which was now awash with partygoers.

Paul Whiteman was talking animatedly to Earl Hines, presumably about some indiscretion he had committed on the charts. From his demeanour, it appeared that he had not fully forgiven him for spoiling his fun at the rehearsal earlier. Hines was trying his best to look suitably chastised, whilst inwardly he knew his actions had received universal approval from his fellow musicians.

Josephine Baker was talking to Lucille Laporte, who, it seemed, was always now within touching distance of Hines.

As Jimmy V returned with a freshly made Martini, Lady Julia excused herself and approached the group.

'Miss Baker, may I introduce you to an old acquaintance of mine and her companion for the evening? I understand they are both great admirers of yours.'

Josephine Baker was always pleased to meet new fans and readily accepted the invitation. She was also quite pleased to leave Whiteman to his rantings.

'How pleasant to meet you, Miss Baker. I have heard so much about you from a number of my colleagues who have seen your show in Paris. I have to say, their comments failed to do you justice. Your performance was quite magnificent this evening.' Goebbels took hold of Josephine Baker's hand and kissed it gently, looking up into her eyes as he bent forward.

Josephine Baker mentally recoiled, but hoped that her revulsion didn't show as she looked at the slippery toad of a man who had just spoken to her.

'Thank you, Sir. How very kind of you.'

'I can also inform you that our glorious leader, Adolf Hitler is a great admirer. He has asked me to present to you a signed copy of his memoirs.'

Goebbels reached down into his briefcase and removed a slim package that had been carefully wrapped in red tissue paper tied with gold thread. A label bearing the party emblem hung from the centre of the package.

'That is most kind. Please pass on my thanks.'

There was a loud shout from behind her at the bar.

'Hey, Josephine! Come and tell Earl what you told me earlier about that chart.'

Josephine Baker gratefully excused herself from the conversation and moved back to Paul

Whiteman who was busy berating Earl Hines again. The Gauleiter watched as she walked away. What a pity. Such a great beauty… but his task was complete.

***

Later in the evening, Fufu Lamore emerged from the bathroom of her room. Slide Williams was lying on the bed in his shorts, reading a book.

'What have you got there?' she enquired,

as she casually sprayed perfume on her wrists.

'I found it on a table when we were leaving the party, it must have been left by someone.'

'What's it called?'

'I don't know. I can't read. I think it's in German anyway and it don't have pictures! I've been through every page and there are no pictures. What kind of book don't have pictures?'

'Never mind. You won't be needing pictures tonight.' Reaching over, she casually turned off the light.

Chapter 45

The occupants of the Kurfurstendamm Gasthof were awakened by the sound of ear splitting screams coming from inside room 101. Buddy Bolden and Red Nichols were the first on the scene and were hammering on the door, as Fud Livingston and Jimmy Noone appeared from further down the corridor. With a splintering of wood, the door lock finally gave way and the four men burst into the room.

Kneeling on the bed with a sheet around her was Fufu Lamore, screaming hysterically.

'Johnny!! Wake up Johnny!!'

The four men looked at the prostrate and motionless figure of Johnny the Slide Williams, lying sprawled out on the bed. His face had taken on a deathly dull pallor and his tongue hung limply out of the corner of his mouth. His eyes were wide open, staring blankly at the ceiling.

'Do something!!' screamed Fufu, as the men stood like long petrified statues staring at the scene. The hotel manager came rushing along the corridor and pushed his way through the crowd, as they stood helpless in the doorway.

'What is happening here?' he shouted, as he pushed past Fud Livingston.

'Make way! Make way!'

He fell silent when he saw the weeping figure of Fufu Lamore laid across the inert body of Slide Williams, his lifeless eyes now staring directly back at the hotel manager. The shock made him spring backwards, knocking into Red Nichols as he let out a curse in German.

'I shall call the Police,' he called, rushing away from the room. The musicians continued to stare helplessly, as Fufu continued to sob. Fud Livingston broke the silence.

'Fufu, you can't help him now.'

'He's gone, Fufu' added Buddy Bolden.

'Come with us. We can wait for the Police next door,' said Red Nichols, as he moved forward to comfort Fufu. It took the persuasive powers of the four musicians to prise Fufu away from the body of Slide Williams and lead her out of the room.

Behind them, a uniformed hotel maid appeared in the corridor. She stood with her head bowed, unseen, as the three men led a weeping Fufu past her. As the door to Red Nichols' room closed, she entered room 101 and covered the body with a white sheet. She put on a pair of black leather gloves and looked around the chamber. From the bedside table, she carefully slipped something into the pocket of her apron.

She stepped out of the room and made her way towards the service stairs, where she disappeared out of sight. Her departure, just like her appearance, went unnoticed.

A Black Maybach W5 pulled away from the alleyway at the rear of the Gasthof a few moments later and joined the early morning traffic along Kurfurstendamm Strasse. In the rear seat, the maid handed over the copy of Mein Kampf to the diminutive figure seated next to her and took off her gloves. The man carefully placed the book and gloves in his briefcase, took off his own gloves and closed the lid with a satisfying snap. It was done.

Chapter 46

The police arrived within 10 minutes. They paid no heed to the Maybach as they passed it along the Kurfurstendamm Strasse, their alarm bell sounding out noisily as they forced their way through the early morning traffic. Inside the Maybach, Goebbels nonchalantly thumbed the catch of his briefcase, whilst Valette Simone, still dressed in the maid's uniform, looked straight ahead. The sight of Slide William's eyes, staring accusingly back at her as she slipped the sheet over his lifeless body was so unnerving it was playing on her mind.

Two police cars drew up outside the Gasthof and four officers, two uniformed and two in suits got out and entered the hotel.

Fufu Lamore was still sobbing as the two uniformed officers attempted to talk to her. Although she spoke perfectly adequate German, she was of little help to the police in her hysterical state. Josephine Baker and Lucille Laporte had arrived on the scene just before the police and were able to comfort Fufu and give what little information they knew to the officers.

One of the suited detectives had entered room 101 and examined the body, his colleague remaining in the corridor. The absence of blood and no obvious wounds suggested that foul play had not been involved, but he would have to rely on the expertise of the doctor when he eventually arrived through the traffic, before he could declare this an unfortunate, but natural death.

The second officer went to talk to Fufu. Judging from the reaction of the uniformed officers who sprang to attention on his appearance, he clearly had seniority over the others. In broken English, he announced

'I have called a doctor and an ambulance to remove the body.'

The cold, clinical tone of his voice set Fufu off once more wailing in grief.

'We need to establish how this man died. The doctor will be able to tell us.'

Fufu continued to sob in response.

'We will need to speak to anyone who has had contact with the deceased in the last 24 hours. My colleagues will take statements.'

Turning to the hotel manager he continued,

'You will arrange for a suitable room to be available?'

The manager nodded confirmation and hurried off to make arrangements.

'I will remain here and take a statement from the Fraulein.'

***

The doctor arrived and completed a very brief, visual examination of the body. Fufu was still sobbing as she was led back into the room a short time afterwards.

'I believe that it was a problem with his heart, Detective. I will examine the deceased more closely when he has been taken to the hospital. I do not suspect that foul play is responsible in any way for this man's death.'

The delivery of the doctor's verdict did nothing to placate Fufu, who continued to wail, comforted by her colleagues. The detective thanked him for his diagnosis as the doctor nodded his head and left the room.

A short time later, the three other policemen returned after taking short and largely meaningless statements from the other band members, which all said more or less the same thing. They had finished the concert, gone to the party and returned to the hotel. As the detectives continued to make notes and talk, two ambulance attendants arrived, carrying a stretcher.

'The body is next door.'

The detective issued his instruction with a shake of his hand, before returning to the conversation with his colleagues.

'Fraulein, it appears that this is an unfortunate accident, but I will conclude my investigation when I have received Herr Doctor Dobbertin's report. The body will be released to you as soon as possible. I would ask if you could please inform your embassy. The ambulance will take the deceased to be examined in the mortuary at the Koningen-Queen Elisabeth Hospital.'

With this, he clicked his heels together, nodded his head and left the room with his three colleagues following in his wake.

'What a cold, heartless bastard of a man!' blurted Lucille, after the bedroom door had been closed behind the departing group.

'Typical German over efficiency,' observed Josephine.

'He was so very young,' said Lucille.

'And strong,' added Fufu

'How could such a young man have a heart problem? Such a thing is surely not possible.'

*

Elsewhere in the Gasthof, Paul Whiteman was deep in discussion with Earl Hines and Wellman Breaux. As the most senior players in the band, he felt it appropriate to obtain their opinion on what they should do about the rest of the week's scheduled performances, however he had already made a decision.

'I think Slide would want us to carry on with the shows Mr. Whiteman,' offered Earl Hines.

Wellman Breaux nodded his agreement.

'We can't do anything to change what has happened,' he added

Again Breaux nodded.

After a short pause, Whiteman spoke.

'The show must go on? I will consult with Miss Baker and confirm to you all by lunchtime.'

The two men nodded and agreed to let the rest of the band know the situation.

'What about Jimmy V, Mr Whiteman? Does he know about Slide?'

'I will try and telephone him,' agreed Whiteman.

'I'll tell him he'll be playing lead for the remaining shows.'

***

Harry took the call from Paul Whiteman whilst Jimmy V was once again doing battle in the bathroom with the shower contraption. The last of his guests had departed the Adlon at around 3.30am. Harry, having heard him enter the room a little after 4.00am, had decided to allow him to sleep longer than he would normally have done.

Harry was shocked by the news and all manner of thoughts tumbled through his mind. Was this an unfortunate coincidence? If it were a heart attack, could it just be one of those things? Over exuberance in the bedroom after too much drinking? Or had something triggered it? Could Slide Williams have been the intended target all along? Had the intelligence got it wrong? What kind of significance could the murder of Slide Williams, an ordinary black American musician hold? If it were murder, how could it have been engineered? There could not have been any obvious signs of a murder, or surely the police and most definitely the doctor would have said something. There would have been arrests.

A sudden exclamation from the bathroom indicated that Jimmy V had once again failed to regulate the shower at a comfortable temperature. This brought Harry's thoughts sharply back into focus. He needed to inform his embassy as soon as possible and Lady Julia would no doubt need to speak to her superiors.

Chapter 47

Jimmy V was shaken by the news broken to him by Harry. He sat silently at his breakfast table for a long time without touching the food, staring out of the window, as the life of Berlin continued below him, unaffected.

'Such a waste, Harry. A charming chap. A truly gifted trombone player.'

There was a long pause before he spoke again.

'Did Mr Whiteman indicate what would happen now?'

'He said to inform you that you would have to play lead, Sir'

'Of course.'

'Yes, Sir. As a tribute to Slide. He was certain this is what he would have wanted.'

Harry was not certain that Jimmy V heard his final comments. He simply nodded his head and continued to look out of the window.

'I have spoken to Lady Julia, Sir and informed her of the situation. As you are aware, she is acquainted with Miss Lamore. I believe she has left the hotel with Mary and will be offering her condolences.'

*

Major General Sir William Blyth had heard the news concerning the death of the American trombone player long before Lady Julia arrived, having already being contacted by his opposite number at the American embassy. The two men had concluded, not surprisingly, that the death, if foul play were involved, was most likely a case of mistaken identity. The intelligence had been very specific that a high profile member of the party was under threat and Slide Williams was not likely to be the principal target of any assassin.

The General's inside contact at the hospital had confirmed that the doctor's initial conclusion relating to the cause of death was unlikely to change. Doctor Dobbertin had several important operations to perform that day and therefore would not examine the body again, despite his conversation with the detectives earlier. He would base his report on his initial diagnosis.

The police would be happy with the doctor's analysis as this would enable them to close the file quickly, release the body and move on to more important crimes. The death by natural causes of an unknown foreign national, warranted little investigation.

As cold as this seemed, Lady Julia was forced to conclude as she travelled to see Fufu Lamore that even in London, the sudden death of an unknown American musician would go largely unreported. All her senses, however, screamed that this could not have been a natural event.

The attaché had agreed and instructed her to make whatever enquiries she felt necessary to establish the true circumstances surrounding the incident.

*

Lady Julia arrived at the entrance to the Kurfurstendamm Gasthof, where there was an eerie silence in the deserted entrance lobby. The reception desk was unmanned and despite ringing the reception bell over and over again, it was several minutes before the hotel manager appeared. He summoned a sleepy looking bell boy from the basement and ordered him to fetch someone from the Whiteman band to come and meet her.

The manager was deeply troubled she had found out about the sudden death of one of his guests so quickly. He had hoped he could keep it quiet for as long as possible. After all, the death of a guest on the premises, regardless of cause, was never good for business.

Josephine Baker appeared with the bell boy. She had dressed and collected her thoughts in the few short hours since the events of the morning. She accompanied Lady Julia to room 103, where Fufu sat with two of her fellow dancers. She had stopped sobbing and was dressed, but judging from the redness around her eyes and the puffiness of her face, she was clearly still in a very distressed state.

Lady Julia had hoped to be able to discuss the events of the previous evening with her old school friend, however the presence of so many other people made this impossible, if she were to avoid arousing suspicion.

Mary stood by the doorway as Lady Julia talked to Fufu, before quietly slipping along the corridor and entering room 101. Not surprisingly, given the earlier presence of the police, her search yielded nothing of any value.

*

'He was such a nice man, Julia. Such a gentle man, despite his size.' Lady Julia nodded, as Fufu started to talk about Slide.

'He had no education. Music was all he knew. He couldn't read or write English, let alone German.'

This last comment struck Lady Julia as quite an odd remark, but in the circumstances she let it pass without comment.

*

Paul Whiteman judged that calling a rehearsal for the afternoon would be pointless; it was unlikely that anyone would be in the mood for playing. The band members collected together in the small bar that occupied much of the ground floor of the Gasthof, where they spent the morning and much of the early afternoon chatting quietly in small groups. Josephine Baker decided she would sing in the evening performance, but that under the circumstances her dancers should stay behind in the hotel and comfort Fufu. Paul Whiteman had agreed and requested Earl Hines to amend the set lists accordingly.

Hines completed the task with little enthusiasm, especially when it came to sorting out the charts for the trombone section. At the suggestion of Whiteman, the lead trombone music was sent by taxi to the Adlon.

In Jimmy V's rooms, the music lay on the sitting room table unopened. Under normal circumstances, he would have been overwhelmed to play lead trombone with one of the finest bands in the world and would have spent the entire afternoon inspecting every note, accent, and dynamic change indicated on every single one of the charts. But these were far from normal circumstances.

Harry knew his master too well to interrupt him in his thoughts, but he knew with some confidence that when the time came, Jimmy V would rise to the occasion. He always did.

*

In Rathenow, the day passed agonisingly slowly for the two French agents as they prepared for their evening's exertions. They wandered around the small town, trying to remain as inconspicuous as possible, whilst listening to any snippets of information they could from the locals.

To their surprise, whatever was happening in the forest, nobody in the town was aware of, or particularly wanted to be concerned about it. The town had become accustomed to visitors, but it was very clear to them that the residents were not at all happy to discuss the local activities, particularly with two more strangers with strong non-German accents. As long as they spent their money in the local shops and cafes, they were tolerated.

*

In Kotzen, Smith and Perkins formulated their plans for the evening. Unlike their French counterparts, they now knew the location of their target and following their visit the previous evening, had a good idea of the security measures in place. The largest building appeared most likely to hold the answers they were seeking. This was located on the outer edge of the clearing, on the opposite side of the compound from their initial position. They would be able to scout around the compound without too much trouble, but they would have to set off much earlier than the previous night.

After preparing and carefully packing the equipment they decided they might need, they spent much of the day sleeping, in preparation for what they suspected could be a long night ahead.

Chapter 48

Smith and Perkins were woken from their afternoon sleep by an unexpected knocking at the door. Perkins answered it, whilst Smith stood ready with his pistol drawn, out of sight. They were not expecting visitors. The owner of the pension clicked his heels and stood to attention, before informing them that a visitor had arrived from their head office and wished to speak to them. Perkins thanked the manager for informing him.

A few moments later, the two men approached the reception area, where they were greeted by the aide they had met at the embassy a few days earlier, James Carrstairs. After exchanging pleasantries, Captain Smith suggested coffee at the Taverne Willi. Once safely on the main street, Carrstairs informed them of the death of Slide Williams.

They were shocked to hear that matters had escalated so quickly, and even more shocked to learn that it was one of the musicians who had died. They rapidly reached the same conclusion as that reached in Berlin; the death was undoubtedly an unfortunate accident.

'There's no doubt that the intelligence was very clear,' repeated Perkins, as the three men took up seats in a quiet corner of the terrace outside the tavern.

Smith ordered coffee from the waiter, as he stepped onto the terrace and, rather reluctantly it appeared, approached the table. The three men were the only customers in the tavern, it being the middle of the day and the waiter had been dozing gently before their arrival, as he leant on the corner of the bar.

Carrstairs continued to brief the two agents on the events of the previous evening, before listening as they explained their journey into the forest and discoveries they had made.

'We would have to deny all knowledge of your involvement here, of course,' he offered needlessly, as Smith completed his report.

'We don't exist, Carrstairs. There are no records to link us with any embassy. We are the original invisible men, who carry no papers. We have no distinguishing marks. We are travelling salesmen, or whatever we choose to be,' continued Smith.

Carrstairs did not have sufficient security clearance to have been made fully aware of the existence or purpose of the department for which the men worked, and had been briefed by the attaché that he should not ask any questions.

He should not attempt to discuss any ongoing operation, unless the men offered the information to him, should not make notes, nor must he under any circumstances, discuss his meeting with anyone except the attaché. An hour after arriving in Kotzen, Carrstairs got into his small unmarked Opal Puppchen and drove away from the town, back to Berlin.

Smith and Perkins paid the bill and returned to the pension to await the cover of darkness. They hoped that the events in Berlin had nothing to do with the goings on in the forests of Rathenow; however, the death of Slide Williams could not be ignored, given the original purpose of their mission.

If they had been in Berlin, could they have prevented it? They would never know. Was his death the result of a heart attack, or was there another, more sinister cause? For now, they needed to concentrate on their mission. There would be time enough later to find answers to the questions posed by events in Berlin.

The afternoon passed slowly, as each man tried unsuccessfully to sleep. Their thoughts were constantly drawn back to Berlin with a deep concern that their mission may have been compromised before it had even begun.

*

Gaston Fermeneau and Pierre-Gerard Limoux sat in their hotel room. They were confident they had gleaned enough information from the huntsman the previous evening to be able to find the location of the 'sausage' factory complex with relative ease. Hans had informed them that if they headed east following the old logger's road, they would come across the first check point about 10 kilometres into the forest.

Their plan was simple. They would drive their Adler to within 2 kilometres of the check point and then turn off the road and hide it. They would hike through the forest in a north easterly direction and approach the compound well away from the check point. If the directions they had been given were accurate, they should be able to find what they were looking for with little trouble.

Hans had been careful to inform them that there were several wild boar runs around the area, which had been cut off by the fences, so their plan was to locate one of these heading in a generally easterly direction and follow it until they reached the fence. Hopefully without encountering one of the boars, whose habitat had been disturbed.

Gasthaus Klaus was located on the eastern edge of Rathenow, but some way from the forest road indicated by Hans. They had therefore relocated their car some distance from the hotel during the course of the afternoon. It was now parked close enough to the forest road to enable them to leave without arousing suspicion.

The sun was dropping gently below the line of the forest canopy as the two men left the Gasthaus and walked nonchalantly towards the centre of town. Turning left, they located the Adler and drove steadily out of the town. Fermeneau kept a steady watch on the odometer as it ticked around and as it reached eight kilometres, he tapped Limoux on the arm and indicated that they needed to pull over as soon as possible. Locating a suitable gap in the trees, he carefully manoeuvred the large car off the road.

As the engine ground to a stop, the two men listened for any sounds around them that would indicate they had been seen. Except for the gentle rustle of the branches above them, the night was still.

In the distance, an owl hooted as it started its early evening search for food under the canopy. A gentle breeze moved the trees, occasionally allowing the weak light of the moon to penetrate. The two men gathered arms full of fallen branches and camouflaged the rear of the car. Satisfied that they had concealed its location, they sat in silence and waited for nightfall.

*

Smith and Perkins left the pension as the last strands of sunlight dipped below the treeline. As they entered the forest, they could hear the sounds of the workmen returning to Taverne Willi. They were talking loudly, bragging about how many logs they had created that day and how many journeys it would take to move them from the storage yard.

One voice suddenly boomed out above the others.

'Your brother and his gang will have to work all through the night, Helmut, if they are to clear the logs by daylight. Perhaps you should give him a hand?'

Helmut was clearly not impressed by the offer and sounded out a string of expletives in response. This drew raucous laughter from the other workers.

'Lots of activity at the site could be to our advantage, Perkins.'

They knew the distance they had to cover and were sure that they could retrace their steps in half the time it had taken the previous evening without fear of being discovered. This should allow them more than enough time to locate a suitable entry point at the other side of the compound. They very quickly found the hunter's path and moved along it at double speed, confident of the path's direction and that based on the previous night, it was highly unlikely they would meet anyone along the way.

Within an hour, they reached the point where the fence cut across the path and turned to locate the area they had cut into the previous evening. They were relieved to see their handiwork had not been discovered, quickly removed the clips holding the wire in place and slipped quietly through the gap. They were once again faced with the climb up the small incline that overlooked the site.

Conscious that this was where they encountered the guard the previous evening, they proceeded at a more cautious pace. But there was no alarm this time.

Looking over the ridge, they could see why this might be the case. The site was a veritable hive of activity. Large lights that reminded Perkins of the floodlights at the new Wembley football stadium illuminated the scene below them.

The entire area was now clear of trees, which were stacked in pyramid piles along the side of a man-made trackway. As they had suspected the previous evening, the area was being prepared as a runway. Four large mechanised tractors were moving along the ground dragging huge plough-blades behind them. A second tractor followed with a heavy roller attached that was gradually levelling the area.

Scurrying behind them like an army of ants on the move, were a number of smaller machines with deep front mounted buckets. These were collecting the spoil from the levelling machines and loading it onto horse drawn carts.

Two horse drawn trailers with long metallic arms attached to their sides, giving them the appearance of upturned spiders, were parked near the stockpile of logs. Two gangs of about a dozen men were busy loading logs.

'Brother of Helmut?' motioned Perkins.

Smith nodded in affirmation. The two men moved carefully away from the ridge so they could talk through their plan of action.

'With so much activity it is tempting to just walk through the middle of them all,' Perkins offered.

'They are rushing to get the site completed in time for something. There is obviously something of significant interest in that building. We will continue with the original plan, Perkins.'

Chapter 49
Berlin

The atmosphere within the Paul Whiteman band as it arrived at the Europahaus was subdued in the extreme. It was clear that nobody really wanted to be there, but out of loyalty to both Slide Williams and Whiteman, the band had assembled at the arranged time as usual.

Anita Berber had already completed her act by the time the band started to arrive and was sitting, partially clothed, in her dressing room alongside her close friend Susi Wanowski. The two friends were sitting giggling and sharing stories.

Having arrived at the theatre considerably later than the previous day, Jimmy V and Lady Julia walked past the door to her dressing room

'I was sorry to hear about your friend,' she shouted, as she caught sight of the couple.

'So tragic when someone dies so young. That is why I choose to live my life to the full. A million miles an hour, like my friend Susi,' she continued, as she placed a hand on the thigh of her companion.

'Would you care to join us?'

Jimmy V looked into the room at the two women. Between them, on a low coffee table, sat a white bowl with an upturned white rose, soaking in some kind of liquid. There was a powerful and quite overwhelming aroma pervading the air. Lady Julia was aware the two women were clearly about to indulge in one of the new designer drugs of the day.

The practice entailed eating a selection of rose petals, after they had been left immersed in a mixture of ether and chloroform. This was proving to be a very dangerous combination indeed, and one that had already claimed the lives of a number of young people on the continent. She quickly took hold of Jimmy V's arm.

'Thank you, but James is just about to perform, Miss Berber. Perhaps later.' Lady Julia moved off, gripping Jimmy V tightly.

'What was that smell, Ladybee?' he enquired as they reached the dressing room.

'It rather reminded me of a hospital ward.'

'Play well, James. Make Slide proud,' she said, as she left him at his dressing room door and made her way into the theatre.

Baby Dodds and Wellman Breaux were already sitting in the dressing room when Jimmy V arrived, between them, an unopened bottle of scotch.

'This is going to be a tough night. I ain't played sober since 1910. It didn't go well.'

Wellman Breaux nodded sagely to his friend. Fud Livingston came in and placed his case in the corner of the dressing room.

'You guys ready for this?' He looked round the room at the empty eyes staring back at him for a response, but none came.

'Me neither. But hey man, the show goes on. Time to make music.'

He grabbed his saxophone and left the room which gave the cue to his colleagues that it was time for them to follow him onto the stage. What followed next was one of the most emotional nights that anyone in the band, the audience and in particular Lady Julia could ever remember witnessing.

All the soloists were on top form. Josephine Baker sang like an angel. Out of respect for Slide, and in the absence of her fellow dancers, she had chosen not to perform the Banana dance. All her numbers were received with long and sustained applause from the audience.

Even the cravat table stood to applaud as she completed her final song, the wonderful Irving Berlin chart entitled 'Always'.

The band played wonderfully well and Lady Julia knew that the Honourable James St. John Smyth, 3rd Viscount of Stanley had produced the performance of his life. The look of respect he had gotten from the other members of the band every time he stood to play a solo would have been worth more than gold and diamonds to him. Paul Whiteman had been right to make the band perform. It was what they all needed to do, not just for Slide Williams, but for every one of them.

Thankfully, Anita Berber had left the theatre by the time the band completed their final set and so avoided another embarrassing scene between her and Josephine Baker. The two women clearly despised each other.

The taxi ride back to the Hotel Adlon was a quiet one. As the taxi drew up to the entrance of the hotel, Jimmy V looked over at Lady Julia.

'Are you alright Ladybee?'

'Yes James. Are you?'

'I think I will be now. Thank you for being there this evening. Thank you for being beside me.

You know how very much I appreciate you being with me, don't you?'

'I think so, James.'

'There can never be anyone else. You do know that, Ladybee?'

Lady Julia smiled as she got out of the taxi and made her way into the lobby of the Adlon. Ascending to the second floor suites, Lady Julia looked across at Jimmy V still clutching his beloved trombone case and smiled. She turned as she reached the door of her suite.

'I know James. Thank you.'

'Splendid.'

The first of the day. Jimmy V was going to be okay.

Chapter 50

Inside the Adler Standard 6, the two French agents were drifting into semi-consciousness, when their senses were brought back into focus by a distant rumbling. The sound grew in intensity as it got nearer and nearer. The whinnying of a disgruntled horse indicated that something heavy was being transported along the road behind them.

A series of what appeared to be twinkling eyes appeared in the darkness, as they looked in the rear view mirrors they had been careful to leave available to them.

The noise built until the first of a gang of horses came into view, pulling a trailer piled high with logs, which were poorly hidden underneath a dark tarpaulin. Candled lanterns swung from the harnesses of the lead horses and at intervals along the side of the trailer, giving the impression the assemblage was some form of multi-eyed prehistoric monster, lumbering through the forest.

The horses struggled to cope with the enormous weight and took every opportunity to inform the two man crew of their displeasure by whinnying and tossing their heads in a form of equine chorus.

The two men remained statue-still inside their steel hideout, as the trailer slowly passed them by, the rumble of wheels gradually fading into the night air, and the gentle hooting of a stalking owl once again became the only thing to break the darkened silence.

In the distance they could hear the sound of another rumbling, as a second assemblage began its journey along the road. It was time to leave their sanctuary and make their way towards the source of the noise. There was no way of knowing just how many more wagons were likely to pass by and the comment from one of the huntsman in the café the previous evening, that they been disturbing his sleep throughout the night, made the Frenchmen think it would foolish to wait any longer.

They quickly moved through the undergrowth within sight of the road, in the knowledge that any sounds that they made would be covered by the noise of the horses. They paused briefly as the next trailer passed them by, these horses just as unhappy as their companions, straining with the weight as they dragged their burden of logs through the night.

Further away, they heard the sound of a gate closing and the rattle of a chain being pulled into place, signalling that they must be close now to the perimeter fence. Fermeneau motioned to his colleague to move deeper into the forest, where they could approach their objective some distance away from the main gate. Within twenty metres, they had located a pathway that was heading in the direction that they wished to travel.

'A hunting trail?' questioned Limoux, in a hushed voice,

'Or a boar trail. Either way, we will follow it.'

The pathway was well used and soon led them to the fence they hoped for. Moving a few metres away from the path, Limoux produced a set of wire cutters and expertly snipped a hole in the fence just wide enough to crawl through. Looking up they could see a glow in the night sky, which seemed to be coming from just beyond the tree line at the top of the ridge. Moving more slowly now, they came across an outcrop of rock. Fermeneau pointed upwards and the two men climbed and peered over the top of the rocky platform.

Laid out below was the compound they had expected to find, but they were shocked by the amount of activity taking place in front of them. Dozens of men were busy loading logs onto waiting wagons, or wielding axes as they trimmed branches from felled trees.

Looking down out over the ridge, they saw a hint of movement in the trees beneath them. Moving slowly and soundlessly, two shadowy figures were making their way around the outer rim of the compound. Fermeneau pointed to his colleague, but he had already spotted them. They waited until the two men were within a hundred metres of them, before they pulled back from the rock's edge towards the forest.

'Someone else is interested in this area,' said Limoux

'And they do not wish to be seen.'

'Professionals, from the stealth of their movements. Not local hunters. We are fortunate - they wouldn't be expecting anyone to be observing them from up here,' added Fermeneau.

They looked in the direction the men were heading. In the distance they could still see the progress they were making, but their disturbance of the forest was almost imperceptible. Unless you were looking specifically for them, it was unlikely they would be seen from within the compound, particularly with the glare of the overhead lights doing its best to turn night into day.

As Fermeneau continued to look, the two men reached the corner of the fence nearest to the largest of the buildings visible from his vantage point and stopped.

A few more minutes passed, before he saw movement from inside the fence and the shape of two shadowy figures quickly pass over the 5 metres of dead ground and flatten themselves against the side of the building.

A few seconds later, they located a door at the side of the building and disappeared from view.

Inside the compound, the night shift workers continued with their tasks, completely oblivious to the intruders.

*

Smith and Perkins entered through an unlocked outer door, which led to a small storage room full of unmarked wooden boxes. They edged forward to peer through one of the windows into the main part of the building.

The interior was cavernous and in its centre, laid out in line, were three large, mono-winged aircraft. The first two had four engines which had clearly recently been fitted, as the scaffolding needed to complete the fitting of the side cover panels was still in place.

The third aircraft was undoubtedly a single seat fighter plane. The huge engine remained unfitted and was on a moveable gurney to the side. Looking beyond the fighter and to the rear of the building, Perkins pointed at a huge square box of metal, which was in the process of being fitted with some kind of suspension system.

'That looks like the new Christie Suspension system, Sir,' whispered Perkins.

'Top secret American design. I saw the blue prints for it a few years ago. It will revolutionise the thinking on all tank design according to Boney Fuller.'

'Would that be Commander Fuller, Perkins?'

'Yes, Sir. I served under his command in 1916.'

The two men continued to stare through the window at a plethora of work benches containing a myriad of parts and weapons in various stages of design or construction. Smith's attention was drawn to a much smaller vehicle nestling neatly behind the fuselage of the first aircraft.

'Is that a small car?'

'I don't think so, Sir. The engine seems to have been installed in the boot. If that's the bodywork,' he continued, pointing at an array of parts stacked beside the chassis.

'It looks rather like a woodlouse, Sir'

'Or a beetle?' added Smith.

There was a noise to their left, which made them both duck down instinctively. German voices were approaching from the front of the building. As they got nearer, it became apparent they were two workmen talking about their inability to sleep with all the activity going on outside, because of which, they had decided to return to their work.

They intended to carry on with their preparations for the fitting of the engine to the fighter. This could mean they would need access to the storeroom… It was time for the two agents to make their escape.

As Smith and Perkins stood outside a few seconds later, they heard the internal door to the store room open and saw a light go on. One of the workmen collected a box of parts and returned to his colleague. The British men nodded to each other knowingly, before returning to the gap they had cut in the fence and finding safety in the thick undergrowth.

*

From the rocky outcrop, Fermeneau and Limoux saw the two shadows leave the building moments before a light went on near to where they left. Had the men been discovered? They watched anxiously but after a short pause the light went off again and the two shadows moved back to the fence and disappeared into the forest.

The Frenchmen decided to return to the car before the mysterious intruders had time to pass below them again. Looking over to the yard where logs were being loaded, they could see that another trailer was nearing completion. If they retraced their steps through the forest quickly, they would be able to use the noise of its movements to disguise their own.

As they joined the hunter's trail, there was a loud squeal from their left and a huge boar careered along the path. Fermeneau leaped quickly to the side to avoid the onward rush of the animal, but having been standing behind him, Limoux couldn't react in time and was thrown high into the air by the frightened creature as it dashed headlong down the path and straight into the fence.

The fence held firm as the startled animal once again let out an ear piercing squeal of alarm and shot past the two men, back along the track to the safety of the forest. Fermeneau rushed breathlessly to his colleague and found him lying in a crumpled state at the side of the path. His battlefield first aid training kicked in and he felt along his colleague's body for signs of any obvious wounds. His arms were intact and his head, but as he moved his hands along his right leg his hand suddenly became wet. Limoux groaned as Fermeneau touched him, his heavy canvass trousers had been split wide open.

The boar's tusk had created an ugly gash just above his knee which was now bleeding profusely. Fermeneau quickly removed his thick leather belt and formed a makeshift tourniquet around the top of his colleague's thigh to stem the flow of blood.

As he sat back, he instinctively stiffened as he felt the barrel of a gun being pressed into his shoulder blade.

Chapter 51

The noise of the boar careering into the fence had alerted someone to their presence in the forest. Fermeneau froze, waiting for his assailant to speak, but there was only the rustling of leaves to break the silence. It would be suicide to try and disarm him; he sat helpless. A bead of cold sweat gathered on his brow and rolled slowly down the side of his face as he waited to die.

'You really need to be more careful, Gaston. If you must go for a stroll through the forest at night, please avoid annoying the local wildlife.'

Fermeneau smiled as he recognised the voice. He turned slowly and looked up at the face of Captain Charles Smith, looking down at him and grinning in the gloom. He still had his Luger Parabellum held threateningly in his hand.

'Limoux is injured.' Fermeneau pointed to his colleague.

'Perkins, would you attend to this poor chap.'

Perkins appeared from the side of the path where he had been hiding and knelt over Limoux, who was only semi-conscious and groaned in discomfort as his wounds were examined.

'The wound appears to be superficial, Sir. It will require a number of stitches and will undoubtedly leave a nasty little scar, but the man will live.'

Limoux suddenly stirred and opened his eyes. His vision was disturbed, but he saw a dark figure leaning over him and instinctively lunged limply towards Perkins, catching him a weak, glancing blow on his shoulder. Fermeneau quickly reassured his colleague that all was in order.

'Limoux, are you able to stand?'

'I think so, Sir,' replied his colleague, still groggy from having been knocked out.

'We should leave the area as soon as we can Gaston. If Perkins and I heard you thrashing around in the undergrowth, then it is quite possible that a patrol or guard may have also heard the commotion.'

Picking up Limoux between them, the party moved off quickly and in silence along the hunter's path. After walking for about ten minutes Fermeneau risked a hushed conversation.

'We have a car, Charles.'

'Have you indeed. Now that is going to save a great deal of foot slogging. Where exactly is it you've parked?'

Fermeneau took the lead, whilst Smith and Perkins took over helping Limoux. A further fifteen minutes passed before they reached the spot where the Adler was parked. Much to their relief, it had not been discovered.

'What was your escape plan for returning to the town, Gaston?' enquired Smith, as they loaded Limoux into the back seat.

'We would wait for a trailer to pass and then follow it at a safe distance. The noise of the horses and the wheels should successfully drown out any sound of the engine. Two kilometres back towards Rathenow is an unmarked side road that leads through the forest and then approaches the town from the east.'

'Now there's a coincidence. I believe you are going our way.' Smith smiled as he heard the first rumblings of a trailer beginning to make its way along the road.

*

Forty five minutes later and without further incident, the four men were sitting safely in the

Pension at Kotzen. Perkins produced a suturing kit from his luggage and set to work on Limoux's leg, whilst Smith and Fermeneau sat talking, each man trying to extract as much information from the other without giving up any of his own secrets.

'I see you still have the duelling scar, Gaston.'

'Yes, but thanks to you that is all I have. Without your intervention that evening in Madrid, I believe the young Count would have taken out my eyeball. I owe you my life.'

'After your dalliance with his sister, I am not sure it's your eyeball he would have been concerned with.'

Both men laughed.

Limoux let out a subdued cry as Perkins inserted another stitch into his wound. After a pause, Fermeneau dropped his voice and spoke quietly to Smith.

'We both have an interest in the contents of that building, Charles, and we have worked together many times before. I am sure we can do so again. Limoux and I saw you enter the building. I know you are aware of what it contains and I am sure that whatever it is you have discovered will ultimately prove to be of grave concern to both our governments.'

Smith remained non-committal in his responses. After a long pause he looked candidly into the eyes of his French counterpart.

'The contents of that building I believe, Gaston, could have consequences for the entire world, but you understand my position. We will be returning to Berlin in the morning and I would suggest that you and your colleague do the same. I intend to report to my embassy immediately on our return and inform them of my findings. I will also inform them of your involvement, of course.'

Smiling at the Frenchman, he added,

'I feel certain they will not want any unsupervised Frenchmen lumbering around in the forest, upsetting the local wildlife. The fact that you know of our meanderings this evening will, I am sure, precipitate our working together on this matter. It will be my recommendation that we do so. I will contact you as soon as I get the necessary go ahead.'

Perkins had completed his work on Limoux's leg and was packing away his kit.

'Our paths will cross again soon, Charles, of that I am certain. Adieu!' Fermeneau shook Smith's hand and helped Limoux into the Adler.

Chapter 52

Lady Julia woke before 9.00 a.m.

With no after show party, she had retired to her bed relatively early, although she slept fleetingly, the parting words from Jimmy V still resonating in her mind.

She ran herself a bath and boiled the kettle in readiness for her customary pre-breakfast cup of Darjeeling. At the sound of the kettle boiling, Mary appeared from her room looking a little flustered and confused.

'Ma'am I am so sorry. I must have overslept, I do apologise. Are you quite well? Did you have an unsettled night? You should have woken me.'

'No, Mary, I had the most wonderful night. Sad, of course, in so many ways, but simply wonderful in others.'

'I am pleased and relieved to hear it, Ma'am,' replied Mary, recovering a little of her composure. Behind her, there was the muffled sound of a door closing.

'I shall prepare breakfast.' Mary added quickly, as Lady Julia smiled.

*

Smith and Perkins left the Pension early and covered the seventy kilometres back to Berlin in under two hours. They parked the large black Mercedes on Pariser Platz and walked the short distance to the embassy, arriving almost as the large oak doors were being opened.

Major General Blyth was surprised to learn that the men were in his office so soon after he had dispatched Carrstairs to speak with them. He sat listening to Captain Smith deliver his report, occasionally drumming his fingers together as he concentrated.

'You are quite sure that the smaller aircraft could only be for military use?' he asked, as Smith outlined their findings.

'Most certainly, Sir'

'You saw weapons?'

'No sir. Weapons had not been fitted at the time of our observation, however there were several weapons in various states of construction on the benches in the hanger. From the experience I gained working with Mr. Mitchell on single seat, mono-winged aircraft, I am satisfied that what I saw was designed to be a military fighter and not a Schneider trophy entry The wings are too deep and have clearly been designed to be fitted either with an array of machine guns or possibly even cannon.'

Blyth paused before responding.

'You do realise the implications of what you are saying, Captain Smith?'

'Yes, Sir.'

'Sir, the suspension system that I saw could only be intended for a tank. The chassis and the form of construction were most definitely based on plans I viewed in America by one of their top people, J. Walter Christie,' Perkins added to the discussion.

'I believe that he called it a helicoil suspension system. According to Boney Fuller, the system will revolutionise tank design.'

'That would be Major General Fuller, Perkins?' interrupted the attaché.

'Yes, Sir. My apologies. I served with him when he had the rank of Captain, just before the Battle of Cambrai,' replied Perkins.

'I have no idea how the Germans could have found out about it, but what I saw was definitely a tank chassis fitted with a Christie suspension system.'

'The development of any form of military aircraft or tank would be a clear breach of the

Versailles treaty,' began Blyth, more a statement than a comment requiring a response. Smith and Perkins nodded an acknowledgement, but sat impassively as he considered his next words.

'We need to be very certain of what we are looking at here, gentlemen, before we consider any further visits to Rathenow. I need to consult with the Ambassador before we take any action in this matter. He is not due back from London until the end of the week, but given the severity of the situation, I will try and contact him immediately. The involvement of the French in this matter is unfortunate, Captain Smith. I fear that it may unnecessarily complicate any actions we take,' continued Blyth.

'I can personally vouch for Gaston Fermeneau, Sir. I have worked with him in the past and can confirm that he is a greatly experienced, and skilled operative.'

'I am aware of your past dealings with Monsieur Fermeneau, Captain, not least with that unfortunate business in Spain. His colleague, on the other hand, is unknown to us. We need to be certain of his validity.'

'Is there information that leads you to believe that may not be the case, Sir?'

'Nothing specific, Perkins but we have received intelligence that gives me cause to be concerned about his involvement with this matter. We will deal with this as and when I have spoken with my counterpart at the French embassy.'

'What about our primary mission here, Sir?' asked Captain Smith

'Do we know anything more about the death of the American musician?'

'I am expecting the body of Mr. Williams to be released to his embassy later today. The authorities still maintain that the cause of death was a heart attack.'

'Given the original intelligence reports, I find that difficult to believe,' said Smith.

'The Americans have arranged for their own doctor to complete an examination of the body, when it arrives. We will no doubt know more after that has been completed.'

'Miss Baker and the Paul Whiteman Band will be performing their final show this evening, Sir.'

'That is correct, Perkins.'

'If an attempt is to be made on Miss Baker's life, as the original intelligence reports seem to indicate, then this evening would appear to be the most likely time. I think it prudent that Perkins and I be there, Sir.'

'I will arrange for a suitable table to be reserved, gentlemen. It is my intention to inform Lady Mortimer of your findings later today.'

'Thank you, Sir. Perkins and I will be at our hotel awaiting your instructions.'

'Thank you, Smith, I will contact you as soon as I have spoken with the Ambassador. I will leave the Mercedes at your disposal. Gentlemen, the involvement of the NSDAP in this matter suggests that our fears regarding the ambitions of this organisation are well founded. The Gauleiter for Berlin, that's the name given to their administrative leader in a district, Dr. Joseph Goebbels, was present at the Europahaus and was also a guest at Lady Mortimer's after show party. Whilst I have no direct evidence to link him with the death of Mr. Williams, I cannot rule out that there may well be a causal link.'

'Is Lady Mortimer acquainted with this gentleman, Sir?'

'I believe not Captain Smith, although she was introduced to him by a French Countess, an old friend of Lady Mortimer's by the name of Valette, Countess de St. Augustin.'

'Do you believe the Countess to be involved?' enquired Perkins.

'I think we must work on that assumption, Sergeant. She is certainly close to Herr Goebbels and for that reason alone, she is not to be trusted.'

Smith and Perkins shook his hand and left the office. As they made their way out of the embassy, they saw Carrstairs talking to one of the secretaries. He looked towards them as they left, clearly surprised to see them again so soon after his meeting the previous day.

Chapter 53

Lady Julia sat opposite Major General Blyth, listening in silence as the details of the visit to Rathenow were relayed to her.

'Captain Smith is certain what he saw was for military use?'

'Of that he has no doubt, Lady Mortimer.'

'I assume you have contacted London with regards to this matter, General?'

'I have, but as yet I have not received a response.'

There was a knock at the door. The attaché closed the file he had been reading. Carrstairs entered the room and acknowledged Lady Julia.

'Sir,' he began,

'My apologies for the intrusion, but I thought you would want to see the results of the American doctor's examination of Mr. Williams immediately. They have just arrived, courtesy of our contact at the American Embassy.'

'Thank you, Carrstairs,' replied Blyth, taking the file proffered to him. Without being invited, Carrstairs took up his normal position in the corner of the room, whilst Blyth read the report before offering the file to Lady Julia. She took it and looked at the final few words written by the doctor.

Cause of Death: Aconitum poisoning. Source unknown.

Lady Julia looked up from the report.

'Poisoned?' said Blyth

'So it would appear, Sir. But how? And why?'

'I think we can at least be certain now that Mr. Williams did not die from a natural cause as indicated by the German authorities, Lady Mortimer. How he was poisoned is perhaps not as relevant as why.'

'I would disagree, Sir. I think that how and why are of equal importance. Regardless, I feel that this report confirms fully what we had suspected all along - this was a tragic case of mistaken identity. The poison was most definitely intended for someone else.'

Lady Julia sat back in thought.

'Slide Williams was drinking bottled beer at the party, as were most of the band. I can't imagine how the poison could have been ingested in that way.'

Blyth nodded, as Lady Julia continued to look over the doctor's report once more. The young man had been in excellent health according to the examining doctor.

'He also ate the same food as the rest of the guests at the party.'

'Could the young lady who was with him have administered the poison?' enquired Carrstairs, speaking for the first time.

'I think that is highly unlikely. I was at school with her and in my opinion, she could not be responsible.'

'Poison is usually a lady's method of choice.'

'Carrstairs, I think you may have been reading too many of Miss Christie's novels,' replied Lady Julia.

'Although according to the writings of Strabo, Cleopatra may have used an ointment made from Aconitum to commit suicide,' offered Blyth, exhibiting his knowledge of ancient Egypt, gained from his degree in Classical Studies at Cambridge.

Lady Julia looked up at the General before she continued to consider the doctor's report. A few more minutes ticked by before she looked up.

'May I speak with our embassy doctor, Sir?' she enquired, thoughtfully.

*

Lady Julia left the embassy a short time after speaking with the doctor and hailed a taxi, instructing the driver to take her to the Kufurstendammstrasse Gasthof where 20 minutes later she believed she had the answers she needed.

Chapter 54

Lady Julia arrived back at the Adlon in time for afternoon tea. Jimmy V had spent much of the morning reading the newspapers in the opulent surroundings of the Berliner suite. The outpouring of emotion the previous evening had left him drained. Harry had ensured he was suitably supplied with Blue Mountain coffee, whilst he read both the English and German newspapers.

It was precisely 4.30 p.m. when Lady Julia appeared at the door of the Berliner suite, where she was greeted by Harry. As he opened the door, Lady Julia looked at him and said simply,

'Poison.' before handing him her coat and hat. Mary smiled at Harry as she followed Lady Julia into the room.

'Thank you, Madam. Viscount James is in the sitting room. I will serve tea presently.'

'Mary, perhaps you would assist Harry?' said Lady Julia, with a mischievous smile.

Lady Julia found Jimmy V seated in one of the armchairs, staring out of the window. He got to his feet and smiled as she wandered across the room towards him.

'Ladybee. How splendid to see you. Have you had a productive day?'

'Very informative, James. Very informative indeed.'

'Splendid. Shall we have tea?'

*

Smith and Perkins had received the coded message requesting they return to the embassy shortly after 4.00 p.m. As they parked the Mercedes on Pariser Platz, they saw Lady Julia making her return to the Adlon. The embassy was all but deserted as they sat waiting and for the first time, they noticed the huge chandelier that dominated the ceiling of the lobby. Perkins was still looking up as Carrstairs approached and invited them through to the office area.

'General Blyth is currently on the secure line to the Ambassador, gentlemen and has requested that I show you through to his office.'

The two men had barely taken their seats when the attaché appeared at the door.

'Gentlemen, I have just spoken to the Ambassador and after briefing him on the present situation, we have agreed on our next course of action. I have a number of instructions to give you. In the meantime, Carrstairs, I will rely on you to ensure that business is dealt with here at the embassy. Please ensure that the doors are closed on time this evening.' Somewhat reluctantly it seemed, Carrstairs left the room.

'The Ambassador has asked me to convey to you his profound concerns with regards to what you have discovered. He is communicating the facts of the matter to the Prime Minister as we speak. He is concerned that nothing happens to Miss Baker or any other member of the Paul Whiteman Band this evening and has asked me to personally oversee tonight's security operation.'

The two men nodded as he continued.

'The Americans have discovered, following their own examination of the body, that the unfortunate Mr. Williams was poisoned. Lady Mortimer has a theory on how this may have been achieved, which she is currently pursuing.'

'We saw her returning to the Adlon as we parked the car, Sir.' confirmed Captain Smith.

'She may have some answers. The Ambassador agrees with my view that Mr. Williams was not the intended target. Captain Smith, I would like you to contact Monsieur Fermeneau and invite him to attend the theatre this evening.'

'An extra pair of eyes could be useful, Sir. Shall I brief him with regards to the purpose of the invitation?'

'I expect he will only assist if you explain why, but be careful to brief him only on the subject of Miss Baker. Under no circumstances should you reveal the details of your observations at Rathenow.'

'What about Limoux, Sir?' enquired Perkins.

'We would prefer that he was not in attendance this evening, Sergeant, but I suspect that Fermeneau will insist. In which case, we will need to keep a very close watch on him.'

'What is the situation with regards to the Americans, Sir?' enquired Smith.

'I think we can safely assume that Harry Pratt will be in attendance as usual, alongside the Viscount. I will ensure that a message is conveyed to Lady Mortimer as soon as possible, so she can make sure he is fully briefed. I think it prudent in the circumstances that we concentrate on one operation at a time. We will have to delay dealing with your discovery at Rathenow to another occasion. For now,

I need to go through the finer details of this evening with you.'

An hour later, the three men had agreed their plan of action for the evening. During the course of the meeting, the Ambassador received a telephone call from London on the secure line, which confirmed that the Prime Minister had been informed and was aware of events.

He would fully support whatever actions were necessary, including deadly force, in order to safeguard the lives of everyone involved in Berlin.

Chapter 55

Jimmy V arrived more than customarily early at the Europahaus. His personal performance the previous evening had been an unqualified triumph and he was determined to make sure the final performance of the week was even better.

Kid Ory had instilled in him from an early age that preparation was the key, and his early arrival was necessary to make sure that he was fully prepared; Kid Ory's words 'Preparation brings the Perfect Performance... the three Ps!' rang soundly in his ears.

He had travelled alone, as Lady Julia informed him during afternoon tea that she needed to rest following a rather hectic day's shopping, before their departure. It was her intention to remain at the hotel and follow him later, accompanied by both Harry and Mary.

Jimmy V entered the stage door for the final time and warmly acknowledged the doorman as he had done every night, before walking the short distance to his changing room. The door to Anita Berber's dressing room, as always, was ajar but he quickly rushed by rather than risk another encounter.

If truth be known, Miss Berber and her friend with their so called 'bohemian' behaviour frightened the life out of him.

Wellman Brieux and Baby Dodds were already in the dressing room. Seated at the table, the two men were enjoying a pre-performance drink, or several by the look of things. A half empty bottle of the scotch he had procured for them sat between them, with its cork on the side. Jimmy V smiled to himself as he observed them, two truly world class musicians, alive and well in their natural environment.

'Hey Jimmy!' shouted Baby Dodds

'Can we offer you a drink?'

'Thank you. But I'm fine.'

'I tried the sober thing last night, Jimmy. I didn't enjoy it as I knew I wouldn't. Once was definitely enough,' laughed Baby Dodds.

Jimmy V smiled. Dodds and Brieux exchanged banter whilst he carefully unpacked his mutes and cleaned his slide once more, ready for the performance. He looked up at the clock as he heard the house band strike up and checked his charts at the side of the dressing room. He heard the voice of Anita Berber speaking uncharacteristically quietly in the corridor outside. She was talking to two strangers whom he assumed probably to be two of her 'well oiled' dancers. He decided it was perhaps advisable to remain where he was for the time being, rather than risk interrupting her.

*

Lady Julia waited in her suite for Jimmy V to leave for the theatre. As soon as she saw him get into a taxi, she made her way to the rear exit of the Adlon. The coded message she received during the course of the afternoon had instructed her to use the rear entrance to the embassy, as it was well after normal business hours and would attract less attention.

Harry emerged from the shadows as she neared the embassy and greeted her. Carrstairs opened the door as he saw Harry and Lady Julia approaching and without breaking stride, they entered the building and were shown straight through into Major General Blyth's office. He was not alone.

'Lady Mortimer, thank you for coming. I think you may have already met Colonel Stokes, my opposite number from the American Embassy?'

'Lady Julia, a pleasure to meet you again,' answered Colonel Stokes as he shook her outstretched hand.

'May I introduce you also to Commandant Jacques Clermont, a colleague from the French Embassy.'

'Charmed, Mademoiselle,' he answered, taking her hand and kissing it theatrically.

Blyth turned to his aide, who was still standing by the door to his office.

'Carrstairs. We are expecting a number of other guests. Kindly show them through to my office as they arrive, and ensure that we are not disturbed.'

The aide acknowledged the instruction and closed the door behind him. Five minutes later, Smith and Perkins appeared, accompanied by Gaston Fermeneau.

With everyone present, Blyth outlined the course of events that had led him to call the meeting, being careful to exclude any mention of the events at Rathenow. Smith and Perkins, assisted by interjections from Harry and Lady Julia, brought everyone up to date on what they believed to be an assassination attempt on the life of Josephine Baker, to be made that evening.

'But why would the NSDAP do such a thing, General Blyth?' enquired Clermont.

'Our understanding, Commandant, is that the NSDAP wish to destabilise the Weimar government. You will be aware of the Munich Uprising of 1923? I believe it has become known as the Hitler-Ludendorff-Putsch.' The Commandant nodded his recognition of the event.

'Their leader was arrested and imprisoned following that, I understand?' enquired Colonel Stokes.

'That is correct, Sir. Although he has now been released,' confirmed Smith.

'We believe that the ambitions of the NSDAP now extend considerably further and they have the desire to create an international incident. The murder of such a prominent artist as Miss Baker, and quite possibly other artists, including a leading member of the British aristocracy with ties to the United States, here in Berlin, under the very noses of the Weimar government, would represent such an event.'

Lady Julia was horrified by General Blyth's last statement. It had not entered her mind that Jimmy V could be a potential target. How could she have been so naive? With his title, his links to the royal family, his grandfather's wealth and influence in the United States, it was obvious. Why hadn't she realised that? If an attempt was made on his life, it would be front page news across two continents.

She looked across at Harry, whose steely resolve was clear. The revelation had brought a new and quite alarming dimension to the evening's proceedings for both of them, as Blyth continued with his briefing.

'We also believe that items of incriminating evidence, confirming the duplicity of the Weimar government will be fed to the press in the United States and England. The intelligence we received indicates that the NSDAP intend to use the resulting international furore as a means of seizing power here in Berlin, and ultimately across Germany.'

There was a silence in the room, as the full implications of the General's words were absorbed. Colonel Stokes was the first to speak.

'We must work together to ensure that there is no loss of life at this evening's event.'

'I agree,' confirmed Clermont.

'And so do I, Jacques. I believe we have the advantage, and are indeed very fortunate to have our best agents here in Berlin at the same time. Captain Smith, could I ask you to now complete the briefing and outline your plan of action for this evening?'

Turning to his two colleagues, Blyth continued.

'I am confident that we can leave our agents to act appropriately, gentlemen. Shall we have tea?'

The three men rose and left the room.

*

NSDAP Headquarters, Leipziger Strasse, Berlin

'Countess, I am afraid our failure at the Hotel Adlon has not gone unnoticed by our superiors. I have been reminded that considerable resources have been dedicated to this matter across the globe. We cannot fail again.'

The Gauleiter had nervously returned to the room, after completing a rather unpleasant telephone call to his superiors in Munich.

'Joseph, I can assure you that I have two of our best men in place at the Europahaus. They will not miss.'

'I hope not, for both our futures, Countess.'

The Gauleiter shifted uncomfortably in his chair. His childhood foot deformity always caused him pain when he was anxious.

'We will attend the Europahaus together this evening and make sure that all goes as expected.'

Valette Simone nodded her agreement. It had been her intention to be many miles away from Berlin by the time the evening events unfolded. It was her aim to put as much distance between herself and the Europahaus as possible, should anything go wrong.

She want to avoid any potential link being established between her and the men involved, despite having been seen in their company on several occasions over the past few days.

If she were many miles from Berlin, she could more easily claim she had no knowledge of their intended actions. The Gauleiter's insistence on her attendance now made this plan completely untenable.

Chapter 56

The mood amongst the musicians of the Paul Whiteman Band as they sat on stage, waiting for the curtain to rise, was mixed. The death of Slide Williams had touched them all in different ways, with some wanting to leave Berlin immediately, whilst others were adamant they should complete the tour in the memory of their colleague.

As it happened, all of them agreed that the performance the previous evening had been the right course of action to take and that it had turned out to be amongst the best gigs any of them had ever been involved in.

For that, they had the persistence of Paul Whiteman to thank. It had been he who insisted the best tribute to Slide was for the show to go on, and now that they faced the final night of the tour, there was a sense that the bond they had formed in the face of adversity was soon to be broken.

Paul Whiteman appeared as the stage announcer was introducing the band to the audience. In the wings, Josephine Baker stood with her dancers. Earl Hines looked across the stage at Lucille Laporte, as she stood ready to perform, and they exchanged smiles.

The curtain lifted as the band struck up with their first chart and within a few bars, Lady Julia could tell that the standard she'd heard the previous evening would be maintained. Paul Whiteman smiled broadly at each of the band members, as he directed them with as much aplomb and showmanship as he could muster.

Josephine Baker was wonderful in her first song, and her dancers, who had been absent the previous evening, performed brilliantly. Fufu Lamore managed to complete the first dance before breaking down in tears as she left the stage and fell sobbing into the arms of Lucille Laporte. The remainder of the first set passed without incident.

In the auditorium, Lady Julia sat alongside Harry and Mary; all three facing the stage but on full alert. Occasionally, Harry scanned the room for any potential threats.

Smith and Perkins had been given seats near to the cravat men. The raucous noise emanating from their table during the performance of Anita Berber left them quite bemused, but the distraction the table unwittingly provided was useful in enabling the two agents to scan the audience in an attempt to try and identify where any attack might come from.

Gaston Fermeneau was standing at the back of the auditorium, his positioning allowing him a good view of the Gauleiter and the Countess. He was surprised to see they were alone, as in the briefing earlier, Smith and Perkins had indicated that they could be accompanied by a number of brown shirted body guards. The absence of guards, for some reason, gave him an uneasy feeling.

The three military attachés sat at different tables in separate parts of the auditorium. Lady Julia noted that, as planned, the Europahaus auditorium had been quite neatly been divided into sectors, each being watched over by one of the interested parties. During the interval between sets, Jimmy V left the backstage area and came to sit alongside her, taking a seat vacated by Harry, who had thoughtfully ensured that a Martini was waiting for him.

Harry stood by the side of Jimmy V and took the opportunity to study the audience. Across the room, he could see Smith and Perkins doing the same from their vantage point on the opposite side of the dance floor. As they made eye contact, it was clear that nothing was giving them cause for concern.

Could the intelligence be wrong? Perhaps the presence of so many agents had already discouraged any would-be assailant? Harry looked to the back of the auditorium, where he saw Fermeneau observing Goebbels and the Countess from the standing area, close to the bar. A barely perceptible shake of his head indicated that there had been no movement from the pair.

Jimmy V returned to the back stage area in readiness for the second set and Harry resumed his seat as the house lights dimmed and the Paul Whiteman band struck up with their opening number.

Outside the Europahaus, a large black car quietly pulled into the alley at the rear of the building. The driver turned off the engine and extinguished the lights. Through the windscreen, there was a flash and an orange glow, as the driver calmly lit a cigarette.

High above the stage, hidden amongst the multitude of ropes connected to curtains and pieces of scenery, two dark figures carefully moved into position armed with Czech built Ceska Zbrojovka vz. 24 rifles.

Their orders were, after completing their mission, to leave the weapons where they could be easily discovered by the police, before making good their escape.

Their discovery was intended to implicate the involvement of Czech dissidents in the events that were about to take place. The Weimar government had actively encouraged a policy of appeasement towards the Czechs.

The assassins were experienced operatives and knew they would have to be in position for some time before they could take their shot. They needed to wait for the audience to have consumed sufficient alcohol to ensure mass panic when they opened fire. The ensuing confusion would enable them to successfully make their escape.

Below them, the Paul Whiteman Band finished their opening number. In the wings, they could see Josephine Baker and her dancers waiting to take to the stage.

The band struck up with the opening bars of 'Blue Skies' and the audience applauded enthusiastically as Josephine Baker strode confidently on to stage. Following in her wake were her dancers, swirling long ribbons above their heads. High above them, Gunther Prest relaxed his shoulder muscles. It was a routine he gone through on many occasions in the past, when he had been a highly successful sniper in the trenches of Ypres, with over 30 confirmed kills.

He gripped his rifle and carefully adjusted the sight aperture. Across the gantry, he could see his colleague, Erik Brune, going through the same procedures. The Countess had been very specific in her briefing earlier.

At the start of the second verse, the dancers would exit the stage, leaving Josephine Baker on her own to complete the song. At this point, she always walked down the steps and across the dance floor towards the first table on the left hand side of the audience, Prest was then to take his shot. Like his colleague, he had two targets. Josephine Baker was his primary target and the tall, slim English woman seated at that first table was to be his second. Brune's targets were both in the orchestra and should be stationary and clearly visible to him from his vantage point. The lead trombone player and the bandleader were to be shot in that order.

The first verse was coming to an end and the music was building towards the chorus.

Gunther Prest felt the familiar tension growing in his wrist, as his finger hovered over the trigger guard. He could see the arms of the dancers moving in sequence across his line of sight, the ribbons making it difficult for him to fix his primary target in the cross hairs of his Fiedler gun sight. The sight was not the best, he would have much preferred to use the Voigtländer that had served him so well in the war, but the Fiedler was more widely available and would point to the assassin being a non-professional.

The dancers were not dispersing towards the side of the stage as he had been told they would. Prest pushed the rifle hard into his shoulder, but looking through the sight, he could see only a profusion of hanging ropes and swirling ribbons. He had no clear shot and would need to wait.

Erik Brune was focused on the lead trombone player and had clear line of sight. His target was perfectly in the cross hairs, but he must wait to hear Prest take his first shot before pulling the trigger. The bandleader was just to his left and he would be able to take his second shot within seconds.

The chorus finished and the bridge into the second verse began. On stage, Josephine Baker started to move towards the steps that led down onto the dance floor. As she descended, Prest regained sight of his target. He braced himself, preparing to pull the trigger but suddenly he became aware of movement to his left as the dancers followed the singer down on to the dance floor. He would need to act before she moved away from the first table.

Two of the dancers were now protecting the back of Josephine Baker, with swirling coloured ribbons making it difficult for him to focus; the dancers were also unwittingly obscuring his view of the secondary target. Could he afford to wait for them to move? Should he take the shot and risk missing his primary target? He looked towards Brune, who was in position and clearly waiting for his lead. Prest repositioned his elbow on the gantry. Looking back through the scope, he suddenly had a clear shot.

He pulled the trigger.

Chapter 57

The noise of a shot echoed around inside the Europahaus.

Harry Pratt was the first to react; in one movement he threw himself across the table and used his enormous arms to wrestle both Lady Julia and Mary to the ground. Grabbing the table with his free hand, he dragged it across the three of them. His speed of movement was remarkably agile for a man of his size and stature.

As soon as he was sure of the women's safety, he sprang forward and dragged a stunned Josephine Baker to the floor and behind the protection of another table that had been upturned in the melee. A bullet splintered the wood next to his hand as he ducked down.

People were screaming and running in all directions as a third shot rang out. Jimmy V, on stage, had been bending down to reach under the stand for his plunger mute as the first shot was fired. His downward movement had saved him as the third bullet ripped into the chair immediately behind where his head would have been, narrowly missing his trombone. There was a crash, as music stands and stage scenery were kicked in all directions by the musicians, in their rush to escape the stage.

In the gantry above, Prest and Brune quickly realised they had failed in their mission and instigated their escape plan. Prest hoped that the drugged up Anita Berber had remembered to unlock the window they had identified. If not, they might have to fight their way out. Both men abandoned their rifles as planned and drew their pistols, as they looked to get away from the Europahaus whilst they still had the chance.

Smith and Perkins ran as soon as they heard the first shot and reached Jimmy V just as the bullet ripped through the back of his chair. Dragging the stunned Viscount backwards towards the edge of the stage, they made sure he was safe under the canopy, before heading towards the backstage area, where they hoped to confront the would-be assassins.

Panic stricken people were rushing in all directions, as Harry risked looking up from behind the table. Fufu Lamore sat in the middle of the dance floor cradling Lucille Laporte in her arms. Several seconds had elapsed since the last shot and Harry expected that the delay meant that the shooters would be making their get away. He moved forward to help Fufu.

Lucille Laporte had been hit a glancing blow in the shoulder, from which she was bleeding profusely. She looked very pale, and her breathing was shallow with the shock, but the bullet appeared not to have hit the bone and whilst she was unconscious, she was alive. Earl Hines came running from the stage as soon as he realised it was Lucille that had been injured and immediately took over from Fufu, cradling her in his arms, whilst Harry continued to examine the wound.

Harry ripped one of the linen table cloths into strips and began to dress the wound as best he could to stem the flow of blood. Fufu was covered in blood but was unhurt; she sat on the dance floor behind Hines, shaking and rocking backwards and forwards in shock.

Lady Julia and Mary made sure that Josephine Baker remained safely behind the table with them, until they could be certain the coast was clear. People were still running around the dance floor, screaming in panic.

At the back of the Europahaus, Fermeneau had heard the shots, but realised he was too far away to have any influence on what was happening, so he remained in position, watching the Gauleiter and the Countess.

As the scene played out, he observed the couple get to their feet so that they had a better view of proceedings. He was struck by how short and weak looking the Gauleiter appeared next to his female companion. The Countess, being much taller, was attempting to see what had happened through the mass of panicking people, but was having to give Goebbels, who had no chance of seeing, a running commentary on the scene; through the melee all she could see was a figure lying in the arms of one of the dancers, and a pool of blood.

She bent down and said something to the Gauleiter, who smiled in response. Shortly afterwards, the couple joined the throng of people rushing to leave the theatre, Goebbels clearly labouring to keep pace with the crowd, due to his deformity.

Fermeneau believed there was little to be gained from following them into the street and quickly moved towards the backstage area, hoping to get access to the rear of the building, where he expected that the assassins would try to make their escape. He patted the side of his jacket as he ran, where he knew he would feel the comforting shape of his Lebel revolver.

It took him some time to push through the crowd of people desperately trying to move in the opposite direction, but eventually, he reached the side of the stage where he saw Smith and Perkins in the opposite wings looking up into the tangle of ropes and scenery, searching for the source of the shots. They caught sight of Fermeneau and pointed up into the darkness.

*

Outside the theatre, two men climbed out of the second floor window which, to their relief, had been left open as they hoped, and quickly descended the rope they had prepared earlier in the evening. As they reached the alleyway, the window closed behind them.

They quickly loaded the rope into the open boot of the car parked in the alley and clambered into the back seat. The driver calmly drove away from the theatre.

*

Fermeneau couldn't see anything above him in between the ropes and curtains. He strained his eyes looking for any hint of movement, but there was nothing. He decided to go to the back of the stage, which would give him a different angle of view, but there was still nothing. Anita Berber came down the stairs as he approached the rear stage doors and screamed hysterically in alarm as she caught sight of the agent brandishing his gun. The cloudy appearance and lack of response from her eyes clearly indicated she was under the influence of drugs.

'Mademoiselle, have you seen anyone in this area this evening who shouldn't be here?' shouted Fermeneau, hoping that she would be able to understand him, but not expecting anything positive. She quickly turned away and screaming, ran into her dressing room and slammed the door.

Fermeneau ignored her and continued to look up into the roof of the theatre, but still nothing moved above him. Smith and Perkins came to join him.

'Nothing?' said Perkins,

'Nothing. Is Miss Baker badly injured?' enquired Fermeneau.

'Miss Baker was not hit. I am afraid that it was one of her dancers,' confirmed Perkins.

'Did Goebbels or the Countess see exactly what happened, Gaston?' enquired Smith.

'I believe not, Charles. I think they saw only what I saw. That someone had been hit, but in the confusion and panic, they would not know whom.'

'In that case, we may have bought some time. We need to speak to Lady Mortimer,' concluded Smith.

Chapter 58

A short time after the shooting, a group of men was gathered together in one of the dressing rooms at the Europahaus. Perkins and Fermeneau stood guard outside the door, to make sure nobody could hear the conversations taking place inside.

Anita Berber had long since left the building, still screaming hysterically about armed men in her dressing room disguised as penguins, no doubt the continuing effects of a large dose of rose petals.

Inside the room, Captain Smith was outlining his plan to the assembled group.

'You are confident that you can achieve this objective, Captain Smith?' enquired Major General Blyth.

'I am certain the Gauleiter will be convinced his plan has been successful, Sir. This gives us a window of opportunity to get Miss Baker and the others we believe to be in danger safely out of Germany.'

'This is a bold plan, Captain Smith,' commented Commandant Clermont.

'Lots of unknowns, Captain,' added Colonel Stokes.

'The longer we delay, the more chance there is that the truth will become known. We currently have the advantage, but in my estimation, that may not last for long. There were a lot of people in the theatre who could have witnessed exactly who was shot, any of whom could have links to Goebbels.'

'You put forward a valid and very persuasive argument, Captain Smith. Would you mind giving us a moment, please, to consider your proposal,' replied Blyth. The agent left the room and re-joined his fellow agents in the corridor.

*

After a few minutes' pause, Lady Julia and Mary had emerged from behind the table and escorted the dancers to the back stage area where Paul Whiteman was comforting Josephine Baker. He was still dressed in his tuxedo, with his trademark long conductor's baton sticking up high out of his breast pocket.

Harry's swift actions had ensured that Lucille Laporte was now awake and able to talk with her fellow dancers. She had lost a great deal of blood and would require additional medical help, but she was alive.

Jimmy V, having checked that his trombone hadn't sustained any damage, carefully packed it away and joined Lady Julia in the theatre. Harry had remained backstage in order to collect Jimmy V's other belongings and be on hand to receive news of the plan of action. The remaining musicians and dancers were safely back in their dressing rooms with the doors closed and out of earshot.

The meeting room door opened and General Blyth asked Smith to rejoin him. Within seconds, Smith reappeared and started to relay his instructions

'Gaston. Could you bring your vehicle into the alleyway, please? Perkins. If you would do likewise?'

'Mr. Pratt, may I have a word?'

A few moments later, Harry was following the two men out of the building. Smith walked into the theatre, where he knew Lady Julia would be comforting Fufu and Lucille.

'Lady Mortimer, would it be possible to speak to you, please?' requested the Captain.

Lady Julia stood and walked towards the agent, Jimmy V moved to go with her.

'James, would you mind ensuring that Fufu and Lucille are comfortable, whilst I speak to the gentleman from the embassy? Mary, would you kindly assist?' Jimmy V sat back down, obediently. He was still quite shaken by events. Whilst he had some experience of weapons being pointed at him, this had never been in a theatre, and they had never been fired in his direction.

'Lady Mortimer, I have asked Harry, Perkins and Fermeneau to bring vehicles to the rear of the theatre. Clermont and Stokes have agreed to provide two additional cars with drivers. We are to leave Germany tonight.'

'You intend to drive out of Germany, Captain?' asked Lady Julia in surprise.

'No Lady Julia. I intend to fly.'

Lady Julia nodded as realisation of the Captain's plan suddenly dawned.

Chapter 59

Lady Julia had drawn the conclusion from the reports she received at the embassy, that the two aircraft located in Rathenow would not be sufficient to transport the entire Paul Whiteman Band, the dancers, together with Jimmy V, Mary, Harry and herself. Captain Smith had also questioned the amount of power available; which he referred to as thrust from the engines.

She had therefore been required to make quick decisions as to who should be prioritised for seats on the planes. As the fleet of cars left the suburbs of Berlin and headed out into the German countryside, she hoped the decisions she had made would not be ones she lived to regret.

Smith and Perkins were in the front of the Mercedes, which acted as the lead car. The appearance of a black Mercedes, the most common car of the time being used by officials at the gates of the Rathenow site, would make the guards a little less wary. If, as the agents had discovered on their previous covert visit, some kind of testing had been planned, then it was most likely that the guards at the gate had been warned to expect a number of visitors over the coming days.

Although it was the early hours of the morning, they hoped that on seeing the large black car approaching, the guards would assume that it was arriving on legitimate business.

In the rear seat, Gaston Fermeneau crouched down and checked his Lebel revolver. He carefully screwed the custom made Maxim silencer on to the barrel, in readiness for their arrival.

Harry followed the Mercedes in the Adler Standard 6. The handling of this car was not as precise as that of the lead vehicle and he had to concentrate hard in order to keep the tail lights in view, as they wound their way through the narrow country roads. In the back were Lady Julia, Mary and Jimmy V. As they left the suburbs of Berlin and plunged into the darkness of the countryside, Jimmy V turned to Lady Julia.

'I wasn't aware there were airports outside of the city, Ladybee?'

'It's a very new airport James. I understand that much of it is actually still under construction. In view of the seriousness of the events at the

Europahaus, the embassy thought it best to charter the first available flights out of Germany.'

'I am sure they know best,' he said, as he took hold of her hand.

'I am sure everything will be fine, I am here to take care of you, so you have no need to look so worried Ladybee. I find the experience of flying to be quite exhilarating and really rather exciting. Harry has been learning, you know, he is quite passionate about it. I have even considered learning to fly myself. What do you think?'

Lady Julia looked at him and smiled as Harry glanced back through the rear view mirror.

She instinctively felt for her purse, where the familiar shape of her Webley revolver gave her far more reassurance than her companion's words, no matter how touching she found them.

She had the means to defend both herself and Jimmy V and Mary would have the considerable presence of Harry. Next to her Jimmy V, for some reason best known to himself, was happily humming a refrain from the popular tune Baby Face, whilst resting his arms on the case of his precious trombone nestled lovingly between his knees.

Josephine Baker and Paul Whiteman were in the third car driven by Lou Walters, the chauffeur and bodyguard for the military attaché, Colonel Stokes. Hidden beneath his coat in a shoulder sling was his pearl handled Colt 45, its weight a reassuring presence. In the final car were Fufu Lamore, Lucille Laporte, and Earl Hines, who had refused to leave Lucille's side since the shooting.

Their driver was Jean-Pierre Goutain, an official from the French embassy who, like his compatriot, was armed with a Lebel revolver.

The roads were deserted, as was to be expected in the early hours of the morning. The cars sped on past the eerie silhouettes of houses bathed in darkness, standing in silence like sentinels watching the parade, their sleeping occupants unaware of the drama being played out between them.

The headlights illuminated the eyes of rabbits grazing by the road side and the occasional deer, one of which, startled by the intrusion into its nocturnal world, shot across the road in alarm, causing Perkins to brake suddenly in order to avoid a collision. Two miles from Kotzen, he brought the Mercedes to a stop in order to allow Captain Smith to get out. Harry saw the Mercedes pull up and drew up a little distance behind it, where they could talk and be comfortably out of ear-shot.

'The gatehouse is located a number of miles into the forest. We will approach the gate and negotiate with the guards,' Smith began, as the other drivers joined them.

'Follow us into the forest, but when Perkins flicks the brake lights three times, it will be a signal for you to stop and wait for us to clear the way.' The men nodded.

'After five minutes have passed, you must proceed. If all goes to plan, the gate will be open and no guards will be in evidence. If you can still see the Mercedes, then there has been a problem and you know what to do.' The men acknowledged the instructions and returned to their vehicles. They had all been instructed before leaving Berlin that in the event of a problem at Rathenow, they were to drive to the Belgian border as quickly as possible and not attempt to assist the two British agents in any way.

Smith returned to the lead car.

'Show time, as I believe the Americans would call it, Perkins?'

'Yes, Sir.'

Perkins turned the ignition key and set off towards the familiar streets of Kotzen. On his right, the Taverne Willi was in complete darkness, its customers having long since retired to their beds. The Pension came into view and also showed no sign of life.

'I assume you didn't leave anything behind that you wished to stop and collect, Sir?' remarked Perkins, trying to lighten the mood. His companion made no comment and continued to stare straight ahead.

Fermeneau recognised the slight bend in the road that he and Limoux had used the previous evening and placed his hand on the shoulder of Perkins, who immediately tapped out the signal on the brake pedal. Through his rear view mirror, he could see the Adler slow down and Harry turn off the headlights.

'Have we arrived, Harry?' queried Jimmy V.

'Not quite, Sir. Captain Smith is going ahead to organise our tickets.'

'Splendid.'

Lady Julia tensed as she moved her hand inside her purse and gripped the handle of the

Webley. Behind her, she heard the sound of the two other cars pulling up.

Perkins slowed down as the gates of the compound came into view. Two guards were approaching the barrier, clearly dazzled by the Mercedes' headlights. They had rifles hanging from leather straps on their shoulders, but made no move to bring them into a firing position. Smith gripped the handle of his Luger, now equipped with a silencer.

'Gatehouse, Sir, right hand side,' said Perkins calmly, as he caught sight of a third guard appearing from a side door ahead. He appeared to be unarmed and was casually smoking a cigarette; the orange glow of the ignited tobacco shining in the darkness illuminated the lower half of his face. Fermeneau signalled that he would deal with him.

The Mercedes was almost at a crawl as it approached the barrier where the guards were now standing with their arms raised, requesting Perkins to stop. He did as instructed and moved his hand to grip the Luger nestling in his lap. The two guards split up and walked slowly to either side of the car. Fermeneau ignored them and concentrated on the man standing by the gatehouse, who was now conveniently bathed in light from the beam of the car's headlights.

As the men drew level with the front doors and bent down to question the occupants, there was a soft pop as Smith and Perkins both opened fire, sending them sprawling backwards. The guard in the doorway froze as he saw his colleagues falling lifelessly away from the car. The delay cost him his life, as a double pop saw him slump lifelessly forward, the result of two bullets thundering into his torso from Fermeneau's pistol. His eyes stared blankly towards the Mercedes, as if in surprise.

Smith and Perkins quickly alighted from the Mercedes and ran towards the gate, checking there were no other guards in the vicinity. Fermeneau stood by the car, his gun held in the firing position, watching for any movement from the buildings adjacent to the gatehouse. His ears were on full alert as he picked up a sound in the distance which he believed to be a wild boar, foraging in the undergrowth; was it their friend from the previous evening? Smith and Perkins returned, having satisfied themselves there were no other guards in the immediate vicinity.

'Perkins. Gate please.'

'Certainly, Sir'. Perkins took his bolt cutters and quickly split the chain securing the main gates, whilst Smith and Fermeneau dragged the bodies of the guards into the large ditch that ran alongside the fence. They covered the bodies in pine fronds, conveniently left behind from the felling of the trees surrounding the compound. Perkins in the meantime dealt with the body of the gatehouse guard, hiding it inside the wooden structure and closing the door behind him.

The three men returned to the Mercedes and slowly drove into the darkness of the compound, as quietly as the giant car could manage. There were no lights showing through the windows of the accommodation blocks or the large building they had visited the previous evening, as they made their way slowly along the unfinished road towards the area where the aircraft were housed.

Perkins parked at the side of the building and turned off the lights. There was a reassuring silence as they sat in the car and waited for a few minutes, listening for any sign that someone might have been alerted to their presence.

'Rear door, Perkins.'

The three men walked slowly to the door the agents had used the previous evening. Perkins turned the doorknob and was relieved to find it still unlocked.

The store room was now almost completely empty, with no sign of the packing boxes they had seen on their last visit. Smith looked through the window into the main building and breathed a heavy sigh of relief, as he saw all three aircraft still in position.

The engine had been fitted to the fighter and the flanking plates applied. The skeleton of the empty gurney stood by the side of what was now the unmistakeable shape of a single seat, mono-winged fighter plane. Next to it, balanced on a variety of stands, were six heavy machine guns waiting to be fitted. He nodded towards Perkins.

There was no detectable movement inside the hangar as Smith opened the connecting door and the three men moved swiftly into the building. Perkins had his bolt cutters ready to deal with the giant front doors, but as they reached them, the agents were surprised to see that the hangar was already unlocked.

As Fermeneau and Smith went to pull open the doors, a familiar voice spoke calmly from behind them out of the gloom.

'Stand still, Gentlemen.'

The three men froze before slowly turning around to see the figure of James Carrstairs, with a handgun pointing directly at them.

'Carrstairs?' said Smith, in surprise.

'Captain. Kindly remove your weapons, gentlemen. Slowly, left hand, two fingers only. You know the procedure.'

'Why?' asked Perkins, slowly walking to his left, trying to increase his field of vision whilst moving his left hand towards his gun. He was hoping the distraction might allow one of his colleagues the opportunity to draw their weapon.

'Stand still please, Sergeant, I have no desire to kill you all,' announced Carrstairs, calmly. Perkins stopped moving.

'Does it really matter why, Perkins? Let's just say that the NSDAP have exceptionally deep pockets. Now please kick your guns towards me, gentlemen.'

In the distance, they could hear the sounds of the other cars arriving at the compound. Carrstairs continued to look at the three men.

'Reinforcements,' said Carrstairs.

The familiar popping sound of a champagne cork broke the silence of the building. Carrstairs looked down at his shirt as a patch of crimson appeared just below his breast pocket. He dropped his gun noisily to the ground before falling forward on to his knees and then rolling onto his right side. His eyes remained wide open containing a mixture of shock and surprise as his life slowly ebbed away.

Behind them, the figure of Limoux limped into sight. He had been concealed behind the empty packing cases strewn around the side of the fighter plane.

'Good evening, Limoux,' said Fermeneau calmly, clearly relieved to see his colleague but trying his best not to show it. Smith and Perkins looked at each other and then at Fermeneau.

'We all have our secrets, gentlemen. I have found that taking out additional insurance is always my best course of action. Particularly when working with you British.' Fermeneau smiled at what he saw as a witty remark. Neither Smith nor Perkins rose to the comment.

'Perkins, deal with the body please.' requested Smith, as calmly as he could.

Perkins dragged the inert body of Carrstairs into the store room, where he left him slumped in a corner out of sight. He then returned to the hangar and climbed the metal steps into the first of the aircraft. He counted only eight seats securely attached to the floor pan and quickly assessed they would need both aircraft.

After examining the instrumentation on the flight deck, he was relieved to see that it had been fitted with relatively standard and very familiar controls. He quickly checked the fuel gauges before he rejoined Smith and Fermeneau.

'I can fly the aircraft, Sir, and I am pleased to say it appears to have been fully fuelled. I am afraid that we will need the second aircraft, as you suspected.'

Looking out over the compound, they could see the three cars still making their way slowly towards them, being careful to make as little noise as possible. Smith quickly gave out his orders.

'Be alert Perkins. Limoux, remain out of sight.'

'Reinforcements, but for whom?' wondered Smith, as his colleagues took up their posts as instructed.

Chapter 60

Harry parked behind the Mercedes at the side of the building and turned off the engine. As he opened the door to get out, he saw through the rear view mirror that only one of the other cars had followed him; the other had pulled across the entrance of the building and was now blocking the gates. Something was wrong.

From his current position, it was impossible for him to see what was happening at the front of the hangar. He motioned for Lady Julia to remain in the car, as he flattened himself against the side of the building and slowly moved forward, extracting the revolver from its holster under his arm.

As he edged round the side, he could hear voices. Lou Walters, the driver of the car containing Paul Whiteman and Josephine Baker, moved up behind him.

'What's going on?' he asked Harry.

'I have no idea,' Harry whispered back.

He crept forward until he could see through the hinge gap of the building doors. In front of him was the figure of the driver, Jean-Pierre Goutain, standing by the side of the car. He had his gun to the temple of the petrified figure of Fufu Lamore who was shaking uncontrollably as he used her body as a human shield. He had carefully positioned himself with the heavy open door of the Adler providing cover for his lower torso.

Smith and Perkins stood in the doorway of the building, Fermeneau was a little further forward and was talking to his compatriot in French. Both men had their weapons drawn, but Harry was too far away to be able to hear what was being said. He turned towards Walters, but the driver was no longer behind him.

Looking back towards the rear of the building he saw the Walters' back, as he disappeared around the corner. He turned to look again at the scene being played out at the front of the building.

Goutain is obviously playing for time, thought Harry. He can't hope to out-gun Smith and Fermeneau, he must also know that Walters and myself are here. He must be calculating that the longer he can delay our departure, the more likely it is that someone from within the compound will come looking.

Behind Goutain, still trapped in the car, Harry saw Earl Hines crouched down in the back trying to comfort Lucille Laporte, who was sobbing.

Harry pointed his gun, now equipped with its Maxim silencer through the gap in the door. He didn't have a clear shot - he would have to wait for his chance.

What was Lou Walters doing?

The time ticked by, every passing second threatening to jeopardise their successful escape. Goutain was clearly aware of this and was looking round nervously towards the gates of the compound, as if expecting someone to arrive from that direction.

From the opposite side of the building, Harry heard a low rumbling sound that gradually grew louder and louder. Goutain heard it and instinctively tightened his grip on Fufu. Harry saw him risk a quick look in the direction of the noise, before he quickly returned his focus to the men in front of him.

This could be his chance. Next time he looks, thought Harry.

He steadied the gun, as he had done many times in the past. Hands clasped together, left palm under the magazine to keep it steady. He gently moved the safety catch with his thumb. The words of the range master rang in his head, 'regulate your breathing... breathe slowly... keep your head still... focus... exclude all extraneous noise.'

There was a high pitched squeal, as a large wild boar suddenly emerged from the side of the building and bolted out of the gloom. It veered left and right as it charged across in front of building, splitting the gap between Goutain and the two agents. Harry continued to focus on his target, his breathing slow and easy.

Taken by surprise at the sudden noise Goutain, momentarily, and fatally, released his grip on Fufu who slumped forward. There were two pops as Harry and Limoux simultaneously opened fire. Goutain immediately dropped to the floor with a gaping wound in the side of his head.

Smith rushed forward and quickly caught Fufu, who had fainted, before she could hit the ground and injure herself. He took her up in his arms and carried her away from the car towards the waiting aircraft.

Fermeneau and Limoux dragged Goutain's body towards the opposite side of the building, where they were bundling it into a large waste bin as Lou Walters appeared out of the gloom.

'I assume that Porky created the necessary diversion?' he asked with a grin, as he walked towards them. The joke was sadly lost in translation for the two Frenchmen.

Perkins signalled to Earl Hines to get out of the car and help Lucille board the first of the aircraft. He saw Harry standing at the corner of the building, carefully unscrewing the silencer from his pistol before re-holstering his weapon.

Harry waited for Perkins.

'What's the situation?' he asked, as the British agent reached him.

'We need both aircraft. But we are one pilot short.'

'I can fly it,' said Harry, coolly.

Perkins nodded.

Harry turned and walked back to the car without further comment. He calmly opened the door for his passengers to get out.

'Is the aircraft ready, Harry?' asked Jimmy V

'There has been a slight hitch, Sir. The pilot has been taken ill, but in view of the urgency of our departure, the airline has agreed that I can fly the aircraft in his place.'

'That seems highly irregular,' said Jimmy V.

'I have every confidence in your abilities,

Harry.' said Lady Julia, quickly grasping the nature of the situation.

'Shall we board the aircraft, James? I am sure everything will be fine.' Taking his free arm, she walked him towards the front of the building before he could protest further. Under his other arm, as always, was his only luggage.

Lou Walters returned to his car and opened the door for Josephine Baker and Paul Whiteman to get out. They followed Jimmy V and Lady Julia into the building and got aboard the second aircraft.

As soon as all the passengers were safely on board, Perkins started the engines. His relief was clearly visible, as each of the four large engines fired up without a problem. He gently increased the power, released the brakes and carefully manoeuvred the 'plane out into the night air. Behind him, having completed the same procedure, Harry followed him out of the hangar.

The sound of the engines caused several lights to go on in the various structures around the compound. Looking out of the small porthole windows, Lady Julia saw a number of men emerging from what looked like a barracks close to the main gate they came through earlier. The men were in various stages of dressing.

Suddenly, flood lights sprang to life and their powerful beams illuminated the whole complex. For the first time, she could appreciate how large an area had been cleared by the woodsmen. A stream of men now started to appear from the barracks buildings and began to run towards the aircraft. Some of them were clearly armed.

The two aircraft continued to taxi towards the runway. Out of the corner of her eye, Lady Julia saw the boar which, having been frightened by the sudden bright lights, was now charging with its head down towards the armed guards, who were being scattered in all directions. The animal was causing mayhem as it ran around in panic, causing the men to take evasive action.

Perkins reached the end of the runway and immediately increased the power to the engines, which made the aircraft lurch forward viciously before it rapidly began to gain speed. Harry, following closely behind, lined up the second aircraft and followed Perkins down the runway. Within seconds both aircraft were safely airborne.

'Splendid take off, Ladybee, don't you think?'

Lady Julia smiled, releasing her grip on the Webley in her purse.

'Yes James, splendid.'

He smiled as he saw that his reassurance had clearly helped to relieve the tension in her face.

On the ground, a large black Maybach car had driven through the gates and a small man in a long dark coat climbed out and limped forward. He watched the planes as they left the ground and disappeared into the night sky beyond the tree line.

He strode back to the car and angrily barked out an order at the driver. With a screech of the engine, the vehicle spun around and drove back in the direction of Berlin.

Chapter 61

The Foreign Office, London

'Good morning, Lady Mortimer. Please take a seat.'

Lady Julia had been invited to a meeting with General Carruthers, to go through the events of the past few weeks in a final de-briefing.

After their escape from Rathenow, the two aircraft had flown to a small airfield on the outskirts of Brussels, where Major General Blyth had arranged for them to be refuelled, before continuing on to London.

They had landed at Penshurst Airfield near Croydon some hours later, where they were met by officials from the Foreign Office. A number of cars had been organised and were waiting to transport the passengers on to their respective destinations.

Smith and Perkins had remained behind at the airfield to secure the aircraft, until arrangements could be made for the machines to be transported to a secret location where they could be fully analysed.

'It would appear from the reports received from Mr Mitchell at Supermarine, that the German engineers have been developing a number of new technologies for use in their aircraft. He is particular interested in a system that increases the power output of the engine by introducing water into the system. All too technical for me I am afraid, Lady Mortimer.'

'I suspect that what we left behind at Rathenow may include far more than an improvement on the supercharger, General. It seems to me that the NSDAP and their leader, Herr Hitler have set about rebuilding the entire German war machine.'

'The Weimar government has denied such an implication, of course. The Ambassador has spoken at length to his contacts in the Reichstag and has received assurances that no military development is being carried out outside of the Versailles agreement,' continued General Carruthers.

'And what do you think, Sir?'

'History will no doubt answer that question, Lady Mortimer.'

*

Epilogue

'Good morning, Sir. How are you today?'

'Splendid, Harry. A splendid evening, don't you think?'

'Yes, Sir,' replied Harry, as he pulled back the curtains to reveal a perfect blue sky shining down on London. It was early in the day, but the streets were coming to life, as they always did.

'It was good to see everyone again.'

'Yes, Sir'

'Did you know that the embassy arranged for the chaps to return to London First Class the whole way?'

'Yes, Sir.'

'Splendid. I will shower before breakfast.'

Harry's eyebrows twitched as he contemplated the likely delay.

'Certainly, Sir,' replied Harry

The previous evening had certainly been a memorable event. The Paul Whiteman Band had performed at The Savoy, following their return from Berlin, in a concert billed as a tribute to Slide Williams. It had certainly been that, and London had rarely witnessed so many world renowned musicians in one place at the same time.

It was over a month since the trombone player had died and the official explanation remained a heart attack, most probably as a result of a congenital defect. Nobody had questioned the diagnosis, particularly after it had been officially confirmed by the American Embassy.

At Lady Julia's suggestion, and financed by Jimmy V of course, Coco Chanel had designed a number of new costumes for Josephine Baker and her dancers which would be more appropriate and acceptable to the conservatism of London Society.

Lucille Laporte had been able to join her fellow dancers after recovering fully from her injuries, which was in no small measure thanks to the excellent treatment she received from Dr Edward Bach at his Harley Street surgery, once again financed by Jimmy V.

Dr Bach had extensive experience of dealing with gunshot wounds, having been a surgeon during the war, and was retained as a private physician by both Jimmy V and Lady Julia.

There was a familiar yelp from the bathroom, as Jimmy V once again did battle, and lost, with the water temperature regulator on his newly installed shower unit. Harry smiled to himself. His thoughts were interrupted by a familiar knock at the door.

'Good morning, Harry. I assume James is awake?'

'He is in the bathroom, Ma'am.'

'Oh dear. Do you have coffee?'

'Of course, Ma'am. I believe I have time to prepare a fresh pot. I will bring it to you in the morning room.'

'Thank you, Harry.'

Lady Julia smiled, as another audible yelp from the bathroom confirmed her fears that Jimmy V was failing in his attempt to master the intricacies of the shower contraption.

Fifteen minutes later, Jimmy V appeared.

'Good morning, Ladybee. Hope I haven't kept you waiting too long.'

'Not at all, James. Harry has ensured I have been well supplied with coffee.'

'Splendid.'

'Mr Whiteman's train departs from Waterloo at 12.00 noon, Sir. I have arranged for a taxi to transport yourself and Lady Julia. It will arrive in 30 minutes' time.'

'Thank you, Harry.'

Harry turned and left the couple to enjoy their breakfast.

'I was so sorry to hear the news concerning your friend, Ladybee. Coming so soon after her husband's riding accident, I understand?'

'So I believe, James. According to the French newspaper reports I have read, it would appear that Simone was driving far too quickly in a desperate attempt to be by her husband's bedside. She lost control of the vehicle on a hairpin bend in the Alps and ran through a safety barrier, plunging into a deep ravine.'

'Tragic indeed, Ladybee. Particularly as her husband has since made a full recovery. He must be devastated by his loss.'

'Indeed so, James.'

*

Jimmy V and Lady Julia arrived at Waterloo station in good time to wish Paul Whiteman and the other members of the band bon voyage. The train to Southampton was making steam as they approached the party of musicians gathering on the platform.

'Jimmy, my boy. How good of you to come along to see us off.'

'The pleasure is most certainly mine, Mr. Whiteman.'

'Jimmy! After what we have shared together over the past few months I think you have earned the right to call me Paul.'

'Mr. Whiteman, I would like to thank you most sincerely for the opportunity to play in your band. The experience is one I will always treasure.'

Whiteman smiled and offered his hand.

'Next time you are stateside, Jimmy, look me up. It would be a pleasure to have you play with the band again.'

After wishing the rest of the musicians' farewell, Jimmy V and Lady Julia stood on the platform and watched the train pull away from the station.

'It has been an eventful few weeks, Ladybee'

'It has, James. Shall we have tea?'

'What a splendid idea.'